JEWEL
AND THE
MISSING KEY
TO THE
VAULT OF SOULS

JEWEL
AND THE
MISSING KEY
TO THE
VAULT OF SOULS

By
SHARON E. LOEFF

PUBLISHING

Jewel and the Missing Key to the Vault of Souls
Copyright © 2017 Sharon Loeff

Published by new72media
d/b/a new72publishing
www.new72media.com

Printed in the United States of America

ISBN-10: 978-1-946054-06-7 (paperback)

Library of Congress Number: 2017914773

Cover art: Photos by Janice Levy.
Used with permission from the artist.

Editor: Mary L. Holden

Cover Design & Layout:
property of new72media and new72publishing

DEDICATION

*This book is dedicated to my family: Thomas,
Hannah and Gabrielle, for they put up with
me on a daily basis. Special thanks to Hannah
for helping me with the start of the story.*

*Thank you to my sister, Janice Levy,
for the cover design.*

*Much appreciation goes to my sister Madelyn Saravalle
and my brother-in-law, Jim Lombardi, as well as Anita
Davis and Ruthe Levy, for reading drafts, assisting
with story development and for giving me praise.*

*I'm grateful for Mary L. Holden, the editor
who is also my friend, soul sister, and the
person who made this journey possible.*

Contents

Prologue

A t the very second the Universe came into existence, two Creators
also formed. These entities, whose true names still remain
unknown, have no shape or form. Their knowledge of the cosmos is
limitless, for they have the ability to change it with the energy of their
wills. These two Creators continue to grow and expand, as does the
Universe itself.

In the beginning time, the two Creators were bored with the
vastness of empty space so they combined their talents and knowledge to create planets, stars and other things found in the heavens.
They created the Earth with shared intention—to make it be a special
place—a laboratory.

They realized their power and they were glad for it.

Earth got its atmosphere, but the two Creators wanted more. No
other creatures existed to recognize, witness, and to worship their
omnipotence. They asked each other the same question: "How will
we put a bit of energy similar to ours inside other beings?"

Although the Creators were equal in strength and power, they
were not equal in wisdom and goodness. They could not agree as to
the kind of inhabitants who would exist on Earth and what the new
planet Earth's purpose would be. The Creators each desired Earth to
reflect his, and her, own individual consciousness. This took compromise, and resulted in contrasts that pleased them. They placed
Earth in line with a powerful, energetic, steady and life-giving sun,
a peaceful, ever-changing moon. They developed the cycles of night
and day, the seas and deserts, forests and tundra, mountains, valleys
and plains. Then they communicated back and forth about the kinds
of beings that would benefit from the light and dark, the landscapes
and spaces.

Disagreements raged between the two Creators for millennia upon millennia. Eventually they agreed to a compromise. The Earth would exist as one planet that contained two worlds. Each Creator took control over the design of one of the two worlds and the inhabitants of each. Windows—portals—allowed the two Creators to travel between the worlds, but these portals were to remain secret from a majority of the living organisms on Earth.

The first world was designed for human beings and animals of different species to take up space and time and to allow each to enjoy their five physical senses. Two genders, men and women, were designed to grow in intelligence and strength through books (like this one), plus innovation and technology, and would survive based on what one Creator named thoughts, emotions, feelings and instincts.

The other world was created for fairies, trolls and other shadow beings, whose purpose was to be outside of the kind of space and time of the other world, and to operate from a set of inner senses (matched by, but beyond the five senses possessed by human beings in the other world). The Creator of this second world blessed its inhabitants with magic, strength of character, second sight and unique physical abilities, such as flying under one's own power. This Creator made beings with wings on their backs—the Fae, or fairies—who lived in a synchronous way with nature. So beautiful were the images of the fairies that this Creator built a special Vault of Souls to hold the energies of their spirits after they died. This Creator could not bear to see the essences of Fae spirits disappear once their life force expanded beyond their physical forms and into the realm of death.

Although the Creators were above the man-made measure and meaning of time, they allowed it into each sphere on Earth so that all creatures could have a means of measurement. Once each world was fully developed and time had passed, the two Creators agreed to return to each of the worlds to assess the truth, goodness and beauty in each of the populations. This agreement was made because the Creators decided that truth, goodness and beauty were to be the standard basis of operations. They agreed to keep the Earth that upheld these standards, and to obliterate the Earth that failed to meet them.

Which Creator would be the one who's Earth survived: The Creator of the Fae, or the Creator of Humanity?

When that time came, neither world's inhabitants were to know, but the residents in each would be given messages through prophets, and signs through written words filled with meaning, to enforce the need to be kind and giving, generous of heart and spirit and to remain loving with each other. Those words were not of the Creators—they had no words—but their purpose was quite clearly from this intent and each world was made to know and understand the ideas and either implement or ignore them.

The fate of each world was in the hands of those who walked it as Fae or as Human. For purposes of this story, the Fae language has been translated to English.

And this is where Jewel's story begins.

Chapter 1

Wing Dream

On top of the dresser of a young fairy named Jewel was a painting of her grandmother, when she was just a girl. Her name was Rose. The painting—commissioned long ago on the day after Rose's sixteenth birthday—was of a person Jewel had never known. Every time she looked at it, Jewel remembered Rose as the older woman she'd grown to be.

Rose taught Jewel a night prayer to say after putting on her gown, before getting into her bed. Jewel said it every night after she'd visited with the portrait of young Rose.

"Good eve and good night. May my dreams be light. Good eve and good night. May the Fae world sleep tight. Good eve and good night. May my wings take flight. Good eve and good night. Let the morning be bright!"

There.

She'd said the prayer in her head. Now she could go to sleep in the canopied four-poster bed. Jewel's bedroom was inside a castle, a structure built of ancient stone, carved into solid and perfect shapes— like pieces of a puzzle.

The castle stood upon a tall hill. It allowed views of a landscape Jewel could see from a large window across the room from her bed. She loved the sight of the Great Oak tree on the edge of the grounds, its ancient branches always reaching high up into the sky. The townsfolk lived beyond the oak tree, in a village that spread out along the river.

Jewel, a fifteen-year-old member of the race of Fae, was a princess. She thought about her joyful life and her family as she drifted into sleep.

She lived with her mother, Queen Cordelia and father, King Rowland, her older sister Aspen and younger brother Tomwyn. After Jewel had called each one of them up in her imagination, surrounded them with love energy and wished them sweet dreams, she was ready for her own.

What people in the human world don't know about fairy bedtime rituals must be left unanswered because now, in her nightgown made of soft spun silk and weeping willow leaves, with her long, shiny amber colored hair, brushed and flowing, across the small pillow...

...Jewel was dreaming.

She saw herself as she floated down the River of New Beginnings and felt the raft's rough wood on her small legs. "Oh, those flowers are so pretty!" she thought as she drifted past blossoms of every variety, size and color. She picked some and adorned the vessel as the sun shone with brilliant light upon the rest of the land of the Fae. Her heart raced in her chest as the raft followed the river's winding path towards an enormous waterfall that cascaded into the chasm below. The wind blew through her hair, creating golden smoke-like spirals around her face.

She knew that her wings would burst through at any moment, marking her sixteenth year of age, and allowing her to soar above the falls before the raft crashed into the abyss below. The water on the river peaked in places and reflected like diamonds as the sun's rays hit them and created a shimmering rainbow around the raft.

Jewel's heart raced with excitement...and a bit of fear. "Something seems wrong," she said to the hummingbird hovering near a flower on the raft. "This is supposed to be the best day of my life. So why do I feel so scared?" When the falls came into clear view, her heart felt as if it was exploding through her chest. She struggled to lift herself from the raft, but her wings were not there!

"Ahhhhhhhhhhhhhhhhhhhhhh!" she screamed as the raft on which she sat went over the edge. As darkness engulfed her, she heard her name called by someone in the distance....

"Jewel! Jewel! Wake up!" Jewel opened her eyes and found her sister Aspen shaking her by the shoulders.

Her eyes snapped open and she propped her head up on the pillow. "I'm awake! What in the King's name is so important that you felt it necessary to wake me up in such a fashion?" Jewel rubbed her temples and winced at the sunlight streaming in through the window.

"Its been taken, Jewel! The unthinkable has happened!"

"Well if whatever's happened is so unthinkable then how do you expect me to have any clue what you're talking about?"

"This is no time for sarcasm," Aspen said while crossing her arms and letting out a dramatic sigh.

Although Aspen was only two years older, she always acted as though she was so much more responsible. What Aspen didn't know was that Jewel had discovered Aspen's diary and she'd been reading about how her sister had been sneaking away from the castle every night to visit the miller's son in the village. Jewel narrowed her eyes as she looked at Aspen but then her sister provided more important information.

"Jewel, it's the key! The key to the Vault of Souls! It's been taken!"

Jewel sat up and smacked her head against a low beam near the headboard of her canopied bed. All traces of her dream vanished as she realized Aspen was serious. "But that's impossible," she thought. "No one could steal the key to the Vault of Souls."

Aspen's and Jewel's father, Rowland, High King of the Fae, always wore the talisman key around his neck. Every royal leader in their line of ancestry had worn the key from the moment of their coronation until their death—and their move to the Vault of Souls. It was passed down from generation to generation, and when the King or Queen died, the key would reappear on the next royal worthy of ascending the throne. The key ultimately gave dominion to all fairy rulers, and it wielded great power. Its legend was that the Creator of the Fae, who'd shaped their world with magic, had forged the key.

"Get dressed and come down to breakfast," said Aspen as she turned on her heel. "I'll be back to get you in a minute…after I brush my hair."

As Jewel got out of bed and rubbed the growing lump on her forehead, she recalled her own visit to location of the Vault of Souls.

Chapter 2

Vault Visit

On a summer morning when Jewel was still fourteen years old, King Rowland, excused all others from the breakfast table. He brought Jewel's chair close to his. "Jewel, my dear," he said, "you are about to turn fifteen and it is time for me to remind you what happens when you become an adult. My father did for me what I am doing for you right now, so please listen close. On the day before your birthday, I will take you into the tunnels deep beneath our palace to visit our sacred reliquary, the Vault of Souls. There, below the earth, you will learn more about your brethren than I can explain. It is a very powerful experience."

Jewel enjoyed a wonderful relationship with her father, the King. "Thank you, father," she said. In her heart she was feeling the excitement of a new adventure—yet something told her that he had not given her the whole story.

So, on her last day of being fourteen, Jewel journeyed with the King into the place where the Fae kept their greatest treasures. Her father led her down the stairs made of black obsidian, polished by the feet of their ancestors who'd descended into the tunnels for years upon years. On the way down, the King lit with a torch a series of wall sconces. Each one cast an eerie glow on the shiny black walls. Jewel felt as if she were descending into the stomach of a dragon because the colors that surrounded her were like a balloon of orange fire. She followed the King as he walked through miles of twisting stone corridors. At last they reached a large cavern, glittering with enormous crystal formations.

At the other side of the cavern was a large golden door. The two of them walked side by side until they were both standing in front of the magnificent portal. When Jewel saw the door up close, its sacred energy overwhelmed her. The door was made of pure gold, silver and lead. It had beautiful reliefs, each one in a small square that depicted the history of the Fae. Jewel narrowed her focus to the relief at the top left, but when she did so, all of the other reliefs came into clear view. It was as if each relief was made like a hieroglyphic and they were telling Jewel their stories all at once.

"Jewel, now is the time to show you the magic of the key," said the King.

As he took it off his neck and held it in his outstretched palm, Jewel noticed its beauty. "Ahh," she said, "I've never seen it like this before!"

The key to the Vault was made from the purest gold and held a perfect diamond, the size of a hummingbird's egg right at the top. Gems of every color surrounded the diamond and when the firelight hit them, a circular rainbow glowed around the key.

The body of the key itself was very intricate and unusual. There was a series of circular tubes on the main shaft and each tube had a different bit. Each bit had a different series of cuts. Jewel knew that no one could duplicate this key even though many had tried. It was because none of the Fae truly understood how it worked in the lock at the door of the Vault.

The King closed his hand around the key and then held it out to open the door of the Vault of Souls. The three separate bits of the key rotated around the shaft and when the key was placed in the lock, each bit moved under an unseen power, rotating many times before the bolt actually opened.

Once the door opened, the King kissed Jewel's brow, turned quick on his heels and walked back through the warren of passageways. He did not utter a single farewell, nor did he turn around to look back at his daughter, who was looking at him, as he disappeared into the darkness.

Alone and bewildered, Jewel called out, "Father? Where did you...? Father?"

He did not reply.

As she turned to survey her surroundings, she noticed a glowing, pulsating light emanating from a crack around the open door. She made her way towards the source of the glow and was shocked when she discovered the entrance to the Vault of Souls was guarded by one of the most beautiful fairies she had ever encountered.

Jewel saw a figure clothed in the silky folds of a robe made of butterfly wings and a hood made of yarn spun from bird feather down. The figure was standing in front of a wide marble archway as she said, "I have waited a long time to meet you, young princess. My name is Islendelle. I am guardian of the Vault of Souls and sentinel to our Creator."

The sound of Islendelle's voice was like the melody of wind chimes.

Islendelle threw back the hood of her robe to reveal her glowing golden eyes, porcelain skin and blood-red lips. Her hair was adorned with diamonds and she carried a staff carved of white oak. She appeared to be ageless, but Jewel sensed she was as old as the Vault itself.

Jewel fell to her knees and looked up to see Islendelle's aura radiating wisdom and power. Islendelle smiled, reached down, took Jewel's arm and gestured for her to sit. Then she sat next to Jewel on a stone bench in front of the Vault and said, "Please listen to the true significance of the Vault of Souls. While every Fae child knows that this Vault is the resting place of the souls of all deceased fairies, you now know, Jewel, that it holds the physical embodiment of each Fae's life energy—living or dead. The Vault exists as a holding place for the essence of the entire Fae race. A special furnace, crafted by angels who work for the Creator, transforms each individual's essence into a dazzling vessel of glowing light that represents that fairy's soul. It is un-aging; every Fae's essence can exist forever. This is what keeps strength and prosperity in the race of the Fae."

Jewel smiled as Islendelle told the story of their race, and how the furnace came to be. She knew much of the story already, but to hear it told by Islendelle made it more remarkable.

Then, Islendelle stopped speaking.

Jewel did not know what to do, so she sat and waited.

After a long pause, Islendelle asked," Do you have any questions, dear?"

"Yes!" Jewel exclaimed. Curiosity was bubbling away inside her. "May I look around?"

"Of course!" Islendelle stepped aside.

Jewel stood and wandered among the vessels, transfixed by their hypnotic beauty. Surrounded by the entirety of her race, Jewel felt awed by the flow of magic coursing through her veins.

Several minutes passed, then Islendelle grasped Jewel by the shoulders and gazed into her eyes. "The power you feel right now signifies the strength of the history of our race. This place is the source of all Fae magic, and the one who wields the key is the one who wields the power of our entire people. If you are chosen as our next monarch you must understand the burden you shall carry, and the power you will have. If the key chooses you wear it as it chose your father, you must swear to use its magic for good, and to protect our land from evil. You must memorize this oath: 'If I am chosen by the key, I will shoulder both the burden and the joy of using its magic for good, to protect our land from evil.'"

Islendelle asked Jewel to repeat the oath.

"If I am chosen by the key," said Jewel, "I will shoulder both the burden and the joy of using its magic for good, to protect our land from evil." Jewel bowed her head as she finished saying the oath, feeling as though her destiny had finally been set into motion. Then she looked into Islendelle's eyes.

Islendelle smiled. "As a royal, my dear Jewel, you will have a special power gifted to you on your sixteenth birthday. Use it with great wisdom, for much has been written about you."

Being in so much awe of Islendelle, and so curious about what had been written about her, Jewel had lost the ability to speak and to even respond with a nod to the indication of her fate. Something pinged in her soul when she heard, "Much has been written about you," and, as she'd been about Aspen's diary, Jewel was curious. Her mind reeled with thoughts of special powers and how they'd shown up in her family members.

Each fairy in the royal lineage possessed a special power. Like other young Fae who sprouted wings at the moment of their sixteenth birthday, the royal Fae's wings burst from their back—but carried an additional power.

King Rowland had the power to control the winds—whether it was the air being moved by a hummingbird's wing or the wind as it swept through their village as a summer storm. The Queen possessed the skill of moving water. Spirits of the rivers could swirl themselves into the form of a maiden and speak with her. Jewel had seen the

Queen's power a few years ago when she snuck out of the castle late one night. She'd followed her mother to the river and when a maiden of the mist appeared, Jewel forgot her plan to stay invisible, rushed up to the watery image and tried to put her hand through the maiden's shape. That action had made Queen Cordelia livid with anger and Jewel cringed at the memory.

Aspen's power was one of beauty. Jewel watched as Aspen sprouted flowers around her head at the moment her wings were formed on the day of her sixteenth birthday. Aspen's power allowed her to hear the voices of the flowers and other plant life. These beings with roots in the earth spoke to her in gentle whisperings about their life cycles and gave her information about the coming harvest. She was able to smell the scent of each plant and flower. She could communicate with them on many levels.

Jewel wondered what power she would come into when she turned sixteen. She was so excited and nervous about the prospect that she'd spent hours going through the scrolls of the history of the other royals to see what the possibilities could be for her power. Some of royals could control weather, fire or even the minds of people around them. It didn't seem to make any sense as to why or whom, or what power—these gifts of power were part of their individual destiny chosen the moment they were conceived.

All these thoughts had taken place in mere seconds of time. Jewel brought her attention back to Islendelle.

———

"I know you are wondering about what power you'll gain on your sixteenth birthday," Islendelle said.

"I am. But I wonder if the key will choose me. My sister Aspen— well, she may not be a likely choice," Jewel said, "but my brother Tomwyn is twelve and…it's not just me, but everyone in the land of Fae thinks he will be the next King."

"Put away any thoughts of who is to be the future King or Queen after your father passes away. For now, it is your task to know of the individuality of each Fae soul and to always pay attention to the things that happen around you. You were paying some attention to the path you walked with your father, the one that led you to me, and now it is time to test others. All the paths you take will lead you back to the palace, but the amount of time it takes for you to get back is your test. I wish you well, dear. It was a pleasure to meet you."

With much to think about, including how to find her way back to the palace—alone through the tunnels—Jewel hugged Islendelle and asked, "Will I see you again?"

Islendelle smiled and kissed Jewel's forehead, turned her around towards one of the tunnels and gave her a gentle push.

Chapter 3

Serious Crime

_____

After getting news about the missing key Jewel got dressed for breakfast. She slipped a dress over her head and then saw Aspen standing in her bedroom again. She had a serious look on her face when she said, "Let's go, Jewel. Now."

"Wait…tell me again what happened? And when did father know the key was missing?"

"When father awoke this morning, the key was gone from his neck. All the staff is being assembled and the guards are protecting the exits so no one can leave. I had to wake you up to tell you what was happening."

"Thank you. Did you wake Tomwyn too? What are you going to do?"

"No, I just came for you. And I'm still waiting for you to get dressed so hurry it up!" Aspen tapped her foot on the wooden floor. Jewel put on a belt, dragged a brush through her hair and stepped into her slippers. The sisters rushed downstairs to the main hall to see what was happening.

Aspen was right. Jewel saw the royal guard being assembled. One of their members was speaking with the King. Shouts and screams were coming from the opposite side of the hall. King Rowland looked grave and spoke in a hushed tone. Angry Fae elders and more of the guards surrounded him. Across the hall, looking disheveled and forlorn, Queen Cordelia was sitting on her throne, staring at the floor, her hands in her lap, fingers knotted together so tight that her hands looked bloodless.

Jewel felt her stomach flip and a wave of anxiety hit her so hard that for a moment the room started to spin and she felt heat spread through her body. With a foggy consciousness, she felt Aspen grab her around her waist.

"Jewel! Are you OK?"

"I just felt dizzy," said Jewel. "I don't know what happened but thanks for catching me. Our mother wouldn't think that very elegant of me to faint right now."

Aspen stifled a giggle, but all levity disappeared as they walked together into the large room and approached their mother the Queen. When she looked up, Jewel saw that her eyes were red from crying.

"What will we do?" Queen Cordelia said to her daughters. "This is too awful to even comprehend." When she lowered her eyes again, Jewel thought of the question she should have asked Aspen when they were still in her bedroom. So she asked it now.

"Why does someone want to get into the Vault of Souls?"

Aspen looked at her sister like the answer was so obvious. She said, "They can open the vessels and steal all the souls and their powers."

"Oh…. Of course!" Jewel said.

Then the reality of the situation hit her as she looked again at her father and mother. Fear settled into her mind, but she kept it to herself as her thoughts went wild: "If someone got all the power from the souls in the Vault they could take over our village! No! Not just this village but the entire Kingdom of Dorawine, and all the surrounding Fairylands and my clan's folk. They would possess incredible powers." Jewel realized she should have figured that out right away.

The Queen raised her head again and said, "We'll not be having breakfast together this morning so please make sure you two get something from what the cook has left for us on the dining table."

Aspen leaned forward to touch the Queen's clenched hands. "Would you like me to get you something to eat, mother?"

"Oh no dear, I am much too upset to even drink a glass of nectar. But you two, please…go eat something. You must keep strong!" She put her hands to her eyes and shuddered.

The seriousness of the crime was quite apparent and Jewel was terrified at the prospect of the key allowing anyone access to the sacred cavern to steal any fairy's soul. And what of Islendelle? Would she be safe from harm?

Her father's loud voice interrupted her thoughts. "Guards!" he shouted, "take positions at the entrance to the Vault and along the passageway down the stairs until this thief is caught!"

The King approached his wife and daughters. His face was ashen and he was angry—angrier than Jewel had ever seen him. He looked at the Queen and said, "The guards determined that we were drugged. It was our new manservant who put some sort of elixir into our drinks and made us sleep like the dead. The guards told me they just found his body behind one of the oak trees. He was killed with a knife to the heart. Perhaps there's a group who wants to get into the Vault…or maybe it is just one person now."

It occurred to Jewel that her father seemed to be thinking and speaking out loud to himself, not to her or anyone else. It made her wonder how the murderer was able to convince another fairy to drug her parents and steal the key. Such a person had to be either brave or very stupid to perpetrate such a crime.

The King stopped speaking and turned to Jewel. "My daughter, I'm sorry about this turn of events. Your birthday is in two days and the preparations have begun for your celebration, but we will have to temper the festivities with some precautions. I don't want to ruin an important day for you, but I'm worried that someone in our midst has very evil intentions and we don't know when or how those intentions will manifest themselves and cause a serious disturbance. We'll have to be very vigilant, even when everyone is celebrating your big day."

Before Jewel could respond, he turned and walked out of the Great Hall.

Jewel looked at her mother and her sister. She was upset. She was worried about the key but even more anxious about her birthday. "I want to take a walk," she said. "I need some air." She turned and headed towards the center stairs that led out of the castle and into the meadow.

A guard stepped forward and said, "You may not leave the castle grounds."

What Jewel really wanted was to go to visit her best friend Ember who lived in town, but now it was going to be impossible. "May I go to the river?" she asked the guard, feeling that it would be a safe place to clear her thoughts and make sense of all this. She was upset about the pall that would be cast onto her birthday, yet she was upset with herself for feeling that way when so much was at risk.

"You may," said the guard, "but one of us must follow and watch you."

Jewel winced at him, then she ran down the stone steps and out the door to the meadow. "Follow behind me," she called out, "but leave me alone when I get there!"

Chapter 4

Beetle Mother

———————

At the river's side, the air smelled sweet and fresh and the sky was filled with white fluffy clouds. Some of Jewel's fear melted away as she looked at the beautiful scenery. She walked a ways down a path of stones alongside the river, then sat on an exposed tree root and looked towards the waterfall.

In two days she would sail off the edge of that very waterfall and fly for the first time. There was an eruption of a thousand butterflies in her stomach! She was excited, but also nervous about the moment of her first flight. What would her wings look like? What color? She had so many questions running through her head.

On her feet again, she approached a steep, rocky part of the riverbank and had a new thought. "Maybe I could figure out who did this and help father." Thoughts were racing through her head, as was the water in the river. Her power, whatever it was to be, would come to her soon and she would be an adult. Maybe she would gain some kind of sight, or power that would let her know who the culprit was in this horrific theft. Thoughts of her own situation mingled with visions of helping her father and the kingdom.

From where she stood at the bank, she could see the raft made of logs with its trellis made of vines that would carry her to the falls on her birthday. It was decorated with beautiful flowers of different colors arranged in patterns all around the rim and was tethered to a post at the sandy shore. Ribbons entwined in the vines and flowers fluttered in the breeze. She was drawn to it.

Scrambling down the embankment, Jewel looked ahead to where she could walk to the raft and admire the handiwork up close. When she got there she saw the logs were smooth, like polished stone. The silken ropes were braided in different patterns and they laced the logs together, forming an elegant crisscross design. The trellis was meant to provide shade from the sun as she'd drift down the River of New Beginnings to the waterfall. Again, her thoughts were wandering from thinking of her birthday to who would have stolen the key.

Jewel heard a familiar clicking noise and looked up to see her pet beetle, Bogart, saunter over and look up at her. She had forgotten all about him that morning with her dream and Aspen and all the excitement of the theft. Immediately she felt guilty and stroked his shiny deep purple, almost black, back. He made more clicking noises and rolled over to expose his soft stomach. Jewel laughed at the sight. His legs were moving like he was still walking and his yellow underbelly was waiting to be scratched.

"OK, I know I have been a horrible beetle mother to you today, but I promise to make it up to you now, Bogart! Just think—we will be able to fly together in two days." Bogart made another series of clicking sounds, flipped over on his legs and spread his wings while making a soft buzzing noise.

"I know! I'm excited too!" said Jewel.

Out of the corner of her eye, she caught some movement in the meadow above and heard a familiar male voice.

"Jewel? Jewel? Where are you, sister?"

Her brother Tomwyn was at the top of the hill. He was tall for his age with dark hair that was always in his eyes. Hidden under his big mop of curls were the most amazing eyes—they were the color of new grass in the springtime. His skin was bronzed and flawless over his muscles. All the little girl fairies liked to follow him around, all the while giggling and trying to get his attention. He was gifted in so many ways: witty and funny and always had an interesting tale to tell or a funny riddle that he would insist Jewel solve. While thinking of her brother, Jewel realized how much she loved her whole family and her home.

"Here I am, Tomwyn," she called back to him even as a creeping fear, or a premonition of doom, was descending around her like a shroud. She felt a wave of anxiety as she turned and jogged up the hill towards her brother. Bogart flew behind her making large circles around her head.

Something was truly amiss and she felt a great need to try and make it right no matter what it meant. Jewel felt like some unknown force was pushing her to her ultimate destiny, and she was moving as fast to it as she was to Tomwyn.

Chapter 5

Cordelia's Chamber

The day before Jewel's birthday was filled with a blur of activities. Just after breakfast, in the sewing room, Dahlia the dressmaker and her assistant Lila were busy fitting Jewel's dress for the ball. They were making extra room in the back for her wings to slide through. "When I turned sixteen, my dress was yellow," said Lila, "and there wasn't quite enough room for my left wing to come through. I think it's a little bigger than the one on my right."

"All will be well," the wise Dahlia replied. "I learned from making your dress to leave the threads loose at the top of each wing opening."

"Good idea," said Lila as she went back to her stitching. After a minute she said, "Oh, can you smell gardenias? And I think I hear Jewel and her mother in the hall. The decorators must be bringing in the flowers."

Gardeners were placing flowers in all the corridors leading to the Great Hall where the banquet and festivities would be held. As they placed containers and vases, Jewel and her mother supervised. "You know, I think these light pink geraniums are smaller than the ones we decorated with on Aspen's sixteenth birthday," said the Queen. "But they look nice with the green hydrangeas and the creamy white gardenias."

"I remember when Aspen got her crown," Jewel said.

"Yes, that is a good memory for me, too! It was so beautiful the way flowers wrapped around her crown to hold it in place. The petals picked up the glow that was coming from the jewels and reflected them out—all around her head! When Aspen's scent changed from that of my child to the scent of the meadows, I knew her power would be to communicate with plants."

"To me, Aspen suddenly smelled like perfume. Ever since, I like to guess what flower Aspen will smell like each day," Jewel said as she saw the smile on her mother's face. "Speaking of smaller flowers, mother, I'd better go now and see if Dahlia and Lila are ready for me to have the final fitting of my gown." After this final fitting, Jewel knew there would be other work she had to do.

"And remember, dear daughter," said the Queen, "you'll have to clean out your closet. Your old clothes will be given to others now that a new wardrobe has been fashioned for you. These clothes will accommodate your wings once they appear."

At midday, Queen Cordelia sent a note to Jewel: "Jewel, please come to my chamber so we may speak about the course of events for tomorrow morning."

Jewel read the note as soon as the guard handed it to her. As he turned to leave, Jewel said, "We'll go now. Come along, Bogart!"

Bogart trailed behind Jewel, stopping every now and then to spread his wings before moving ahead. Jewel thought this was his way of telling her he hated to walk anywhere and couldn't wait for her to start flying. He was so fast in the sky, but walking next to her was slow and Jewel had to wait for him each time he stopped.

"Hurry up!"

Just as they reached the door to the Queen's chamber, Bogart stopped, clicked, and looked at her, as if to say, "Hey, I am just walking around because you can't fly and I have to walk until you get your wings!"

Jewel tapped her foot on the floor. Bogart hopped on top of her moving foot and Jewel knocked on the door.

"Come in, Jewel."

Jewel opened the door and saw the most beautiful room in the entire castle. It was filled with colorful drapes woven by talented fairies in patterns of butterfly wings. Large, overstuffed chairs sat by a small hearth; fine rugs loomed with spun wool from Fae sheep were scattered over the stone floors. Jewel stood before her mother, but kept looking down at the rugs as if seeing them for the first time. The rugs showed scenes from their village. Jewel thought they looked like the weavers had frozen moments of time and energy into the cloth. The weave on each one was tight, precise and so clear that it looked like the figures could come to life, get up out of the wool and walk away.

The Queen's chamber was really just her mother's dressing room; the royal bedroom was between it and her father's dressing room. The room and its atmosphere was a snapshot of the Queen's personality, her passion and the things she loved. There were cut flowers everywhere in large vases. Her furniture was carved from the most amazing woods and inlaid with scenes from the fairy village. The closet door was open and Jewel saw her gowns of all colors hanging, shimmering. The large vanity, with intricate designs around the mirror (made of mica), was against the same wall as a full-length window. Paintings and drawings covered the walls, their frames placed by the elder fairy who'd created the town's museum. Some of the painting depicted family members long gone; others were recent portraits of the family.

There were glass vials of different colors on the Queen's vanity, reflecting themselves in the mirror. Each one was filled with a different and delicious smelling scent from the woodlands. A living colorful toadstool in a planter was set to the side of the mirror and a cricket sat nearby, rubbing his legs together, making a strange melodic tune.

The Queen thought she'd allowed her daughter enough time and said, "I want to go through the schedule with you, Jewel, so you can prepare yourself for tomorrow. You must be very excited about your birthday and I'm sorry that this other matter has cast a shadow upon the celebration."

Jewel knew her mother was upset and was trying her best to be cheerful. "It's fine," she replied. "I understand and I'm very upset about this whole mess, too. I want to help find the key, and maybe when I get my wings and my new power, I'll be able to use both to help father hunt down the thief."

Her mother paled. "Whoever did this is truly evil and only intends to hurt our people. Promise me you will not get involved and try to solve anything! Please, Jewel, I cannot bear the thought of something happening to you."

Jewel tucked her hand into her pocket. Her fingers found the magic stone that could be held to take the spell off an intentional lie. She didn't want to lie to her mother, but she also knew she was somehow going to be part of this mystery and part of the solution.

She didn't understand how she knew it, but she did. She gripped the small purple stone tight against her palm.

"I promise," she said after a few quiet seconds.

Bogart came to life at her words. He was clicking like crazy and vibrating his big shiny wings as if he was aware of Jewel's deception. Jewel tapped her foot on his right big claw as a sign to behave.

Bogart made a sharp sound. He was not a happy beetle.

The Queen let out a breath of relief and changed the subject to the schedule for her birthday festival. Jewel noticed that the cricket musician had stopped rubbing his legs, but as soon as her mother started to speak about her birthday, he started playing a tune again and Jewel let it put her into a slight hypnotic state.

As she spoke, Queen Cornelia drew her robe around herself, folding her wings together behind her back. Jewel thought her mother's wings were exceptionally beautiful just like the rest of her. Tall and lithe, Jewel thought every move Cordelia made was choreographed because she had such grace. Her hair was long and golden and hung past her waist. It was braided around her head with a circle of woven pieces that always seemed to keep her crown in place. Her hands were delicate and her voice held a softness that always made Jewel feel better at moments when she was upset. Her eyes were turquoise blue with flecks of gold around each iris.

The Queen was astonishing in her beauty, even in her robe, even at this moment while concentrating on the sheets of tree bark upon which the schedule was written. Flowing with the cricket's simple tunes, Jewel turned her attention to the images of her family members that were framed and sitting on the Queen's vanity.

Aspen looked just like her mother and Tomwyn resembled their father. Jewel didn't think she looked like either of her parents and was more of a combination of both. Her father was tall and muscular with dark hair the color of coal. His eyes were hazel, rimmed with bright green and contained the look of a wild animal, quick-minded, alert. It seemed to Jewel his eyes held a secret in their gaze that went back through the ages and connected to all nature.

Jewel looked into the mica mirror. She was tall and lanky, with long hair in colors of earth, browns and ruddy reds, with streaks of gold. Her eyes were neither green nor bright blue, but the color of deep water ringed in brown pigment. They were unusual; each eye had multiple rings around the iris, like the rings of a tree stump. She had never seen eyes like hers before, and each year as she grew, she thought another dark ring circled itself around her ever-darkening pupils. Her skin tone was a combination of both parents; not dark, not light but a medium brown with a warm glow that shone from the light of the sun she'd absorbed from being outdoors.

Jewel was neither vain nor concerned with her appearance but she knew people thought she was beautiful. She had many male fairies ask her parents for permission to court her but the King was strictly against any social interaction with boys until she was well past her sixteenth birthday. Plus, Jewel hadn't met a single one of them who held her interest.

Jewel came out of her reverie when she heard her name.

"Jewel? Are you listening?"

She nodded.

"Your father and I will come to your room just before sunrise. You will dress in your new gown and come with us to the riverbank. We will bless you by the shore and send you adrift with the sunrise. Your wings will come in just moments before you hit the rapids. Then, prepare yourself to launch off the raft and lift yourself with your new wings and fly over the falls. You will have some time to fly and test your wings, but you must be back at the Great Hall by noon when the festivities begin. You may or may not have figured out your specific power by then. It's a bit elusive at first. You will sense something different, perhaps experience voices or new noises. Eventually everything will make sense to you and you will know your power and learn how to use it."

"How long will it take to figure all that out?"

"For some, it is instantaneous; and for others it can take days or weeks. You, I'm sure, will take flight like you've known how to do it all your life. Do not be in fear, my love."

Jewel was relieved to hear this. She did not want to be in the group that took weeks to know what her power would be. That would be stressful, she thought, and probably just her luck.

"After the feast begins," her mother continued, "you will be anointed with special oils and given the crown of a princess, your birthright."

"I'm most excited about the crown," Jewel said. She knew it had been created when she was born. It was forged with the magic released from the energy of her first cry. A sorcerer who sensed Jewel's birth aura had matched her energy to the gemstone in the crown that contained the same force as her powers to be. The finished crown was delivered to the Queen from a pair of hummingbirds within the first day of Jewel's life.

Jewel hadn't seen it yet; it was always a surprise for the recipient on their sixteenth birthday. When worn, the stones and the crown had their very own magic apart from any new powers and in some way always complimented the new power quite well.

"I am excited for you, my dear. Your crown is like no crown I've ever seen. You will be as surprised as I was the moment it was delivered. Now go and rest for awhile and take your pet beetle with you!"

Jewel kissed her mother's forehead then retreated to her bedroom. Bogart trailed along again, clicking at her the whole way. After a few steps, Jewel spun around and stood her ground, hands on her hips, staring down at the shiny beetle. "That is quite enough clicking! I think I understand! You don't want me to do anything about the theft of the key, do you?"

Bogart vibrated his wings and clicked out several rapid bursts of sound.

"Fine!" she said, and stomped off ahead, but Jewel and Bogart both knew that "Fine!" was her way of saying just the opposite.

Chapter 6

Dinner Conversation

———————

The royal family sat at a great oaken table at the front of the common dining hall. Everyone there, including all the castle's staff, were sharing a simple meal: acorn soup, steamed peas with butter and mint, rice pilaf, a salad of field greens with goat cheese, raspberries and toasted almonds. Their glasses were filled with grape nectar.

Dinner conversation centered on theft of the key.

The King reported that he'd assembled a special army and sent them out to patrol the lands around their village. Another contingent of soldiers were guarding the castle. Tomwyn piped up and said, "I want to be a soldier someday! I wish I could go with the Special Forces!"

The King responded: "Tomwyn! You are still a boy, but I appreciate your enthusiasm. Eat your vegetables so you'll be strong and we'll discuss that wish of yours later."

Jewel saw Aspen reach over and tousle their brother's curls. "You brave boy," Aspen said. "We'll see what happens when you get your wings. You may not want to carry a sword and be a soldier after all!"

"Enough, please, Aspen," said Queen Cordelia. "Tomwyn, put down that knife and use your spoon to eat your peas. You know better, my son."

Jewel felt the tension and nervousness that enveloped all other fairies in the hall. When she wasn't listening to her parents and siblings, she tried to overhear some of the other conversations. The connection from the manservant to the culprit had not yet been discovered and the guards were anxious about the situation. The thief and murderer were still likely amongst them. She thought she'd heard a servant say the name "Malick."

She didn't feel like talking with her family. She wondered how to gather more information on her own. But then again, tomorrow was her birthday. Although her appetite had waned, she finished what was left of her salad and soup then waited for a lull in their conversation. When it was quiet, she stood and said, "Thank you for being my family now, and for all my fifteen years. I'll see you tomorrow when I turn sixteen. Love you all! Good night!"

"May I have her dessert?" Tomwyn asked.

"There will be no dessert for any of us tonight, my son," said Queen Cordelia.

Chapter 7

Ember's Note

Jewel was happy to get to her bedroom. It was earlier than usual because she knew that tomorrow would start before sunrise and run late into the night. She felt restless as she got undressed and tossed her gown into a woven basket containing all her old clothes that would no longer fit her body with its new wings.

Thinking about the situation, Jewel knew that in the history of their fairy kin there had been only a few evil fairies; too few to even remember. In general, the fairies of her clan were a very peaceful and loving group and violence was unusual. It just wasn't their way. It had been over 200 years since the last war.

Jewel's grandmother Rose had told her stories about one male fairy named Malick who was infamous for his crimes against her clan. Rose and this evil fairy attended school together, and were in the same class. The stories were horrible and fascinating and Jewel often asked Rose to tell them over and over. Jewel wondered where Malick was now, just as she wondered about the evil thief and who it might be. Was it her imagination…or had she really overheard his name spoken during dinner?

She yawned and stretched her arms out towards the ceiling. Soon that stretch would include brand new wings. Her stomach lurched with a funny nervous feeling. When she looked to blow out the candle in the lantern on her nightstand, she saw a card lying under the silver base. It was addressed to her, and it was in her friend Ember's handwriting.

"Ah…how sweet! Ember left me a note!" Jewel said to herself.

Jewel missed Ember. In the last few weeks, she'd been so busy planning, and then there was the army surrounding the castle. She wondered how in the world Ember had been able to deliver the note. Both girls knew the whole village would come to the shores of the river to watch her get her wings; Jewel wondered when they'd have some time alone together.

Jewel opened the note. Ember wrote to let Jewel know that tomorrow she would be by the old Willow tree's branch—the one that hung over the shore—and Jewel should look for her there. She asked if Jewel would meet her at their secret place before ten in the morning so she could tell Ember everything about the transformation experience.

The candle flame flickered in the lantern as Jewel blew it out. She sunk down into her bed and pulled the sheets up around her like a shield. Tomorrow was such a big day. Her sixteenth birthday. She had thought about this moment a thousand times and had talked to Ember about every possibility for her power. And now it was just a few hours away!

Ember's birthday was a few months later than Jewel's, but not being a royal, Ember would not gain powers. Sometimes Jewel felt that Ember was jealous of the ability Jewel would have, but Jewel would have felt the same way, so she understood her friend's potential discomfort. Jewel closed her eyes, but knowing sleep was a long way off she focused her thoughts on her best friend, and remembered the kind and funny things about Ember that filled her head with the wonder of their friendship.

————————

Ember was the daughter of the head of the Fairy Guard. Her father was Thor, a beefy fairy with a face that contained multiple scars and the look of a person who had seen hardship, chaos and mayhem. Jewel had never lived through any wars, but she knew that there had been skirmishes during their history with distant fairy clans, trolls and other foreign creatures that lived in their world. Since the average fairy life span was several hundred years, she knew that Thor had been in the last war. Thor never said a word about it, even though she knew Ember had asked him. Ember told Jewel that it was a subject her father would not speak about with anyone.

Ember was, in many ways, the opposite of Jewel. She was short and plump with curly red hair. Her face was filled with freckles and her eyes were the color of an evergreen tree's leaves. She was funny and self-effacing—since she lacked style and grace—and was constantly tripping or breaking something. She was the only child of Thor and Celaphina and she was indulged and spoiled by both her parents. But, Ember was as smart as she was clumsy.

When they were little, Ember and Jewel discovered a hideaway at the base of the Great Oak tree located in the center of their village. They had stumbled upon a secret entrance into the base that was either natural or had been created by another fairy at some point in the past. It was a natural knot that had formed in the largest root of the tree and there was a deep recess around the knot. When they pushed on its surface of this knot, tucked inside the indentation at just the right spot, the facade swung open to a small hollow.

Once they discovered it, they made it their own. They kept it a secret.

When they first entered the earthen room among the tree's large roots they found a miniature table and benches containing various small treasures: a tiny wooden box, a broken tea set painted with woodland flowers and small doll. Other small toys made of wood were scattered around the dirt floor. They were worn and old and it was obvious this hiding place had been untouched for a long time.

Ember and Jewel made it their special retreat. Even now, no one knew about it and they frequently met there to read and talk. They considered it their sacred refuge from their parents and the world.

Since Ember had no siblings and her parents were strict, most of her information about life events came from Jewel. Jewel had found out about "the cycle of life" from her sister, and then relayed it to Ember. Each felt that conversation had bonded their friendship for life.

Jewel read the note and put it aside. Bogart flew over and sat on her bed, his black eyes looking at her. "Oh...you want to go out and play, do you?"

Bogart was really a creature of the night. He would leave her room, usually after she fell asleep and hunt for his dinner or do whatever beetles did. He spread his wings and buzzed at her.

She got out of bed and opened the window. She turned around and chuckled since Bogart looked like he was in a hurry to leave. He spread his wings and flew out the portal and into the night.

Jewel looked out over the river through the window and saw the moon reflecting off the surface of the water. She stood there gazing out into the night for quite awhile, waiting for her eyes to adjust to the darkness.

Just before she was going close the window and curtain and climb back into bed, she thought she saw movement at the base of the hill near the Willow's hanging branch Ember had mentioned in her note. It seemed like a dark figure was standing there, watching the castle.

Chills ran up her body and the hairs on her arm stood straight up like hackles on a water rat. She tried to squint to see more, but in the next instant the shadow was gone. She thought maybe her eyes were playing tricks on her.

She closed the window, drew the curtain across it, and crawled back into bed. She wanted to read, but knew she needed sleep — tomorrow was going to be the biggest day of her life. "One...two... three...four...." she said while counting imaginary ladybugs, each one flying out of a single rose.

As she turned to her side and tucked the pillow under her cheek she whispered, "Good eve and good night. May my dreams be light. Good eve and good night. May the Fae world sleep tight. Good eve and good night. May my wings take flight. Good eve and good night. Let the morning be bright. And, wherever you are, I love you, grandma Rose...."

Jewel closed her eyes, but she couldn't close down her thoughts.

Chapter 8

Rose's Stories

Although her soul was in the Vault now, grandmother Rose was still one of Jewel's favorite fairies. Of all the stories she'd told— and she'd told many—the ones about evil Malick had stayed in Jewel's mind like blankets that had been folded and stored for winter. It was like winter now at the castle—not in the season, but in the sense of a freeze. Everyone was in fear. It was time to unfold those blankets to keep the cold from setting in and taking hold.

Grandma Rose said Malick was an ordinary young male in school but his face was rather pale and sullen. His parents died right after he was born. The accident that killed them involved a violent rain-storm that flooded the outskirts of their village. Several other fairies drowned during that night. Malick was just a baby, days old, when he was swept away in his basinet. He was rescued by a neighbor and given to an elderly couple who had never raised a child of their own. They adopted Malick and raised him.

Grandma Rose always thought the pair had been a poor choice to raise him since they were not in tuned to the needs of a child at that late stage of their lives.

About their years together in school, Rose said Malick became more and more removed and distant from the rest of the fairies. He was often ridiculed and bullied by others. Rose said she could sense his hostility grow with his impending adulthood. But, he was a very gifted student, especially in the sciences, and he had a sharp brilliant mind.

Early in his development, Malick got into trouble with his teachers for profound acts of cruelty to other living things. He was caught torturing a large butterfly by ripping its wings off, making it unable to fly.

Jewel remembered Rose saying that others could hear the high-pitched scream of the butterfly in the schoolyard just before a teacher apprehended the boy. The butterfly died and Malick was made to sit in a corner for the rest of that year. Even with such punishment, the frequency of Malick-inspired disturbing events accelerated.

On many occasions, Malick was found destroying precious objects or being cruel to small creatures. At one point in his teenaged years, the elders discussed banishing him from their village, but that did not happen. The Fae never think the worst of any fellow being; they believe everyone has goodness within. But, that was their first mistake.

As the years passed in her life, grandma Rose said the villagers saw him less and less until they thought he had moved away. But soon after his disappearance even more disturbing things happened. Jewel remembered how the story grew even more complicated and how she had to ask and ask grandma Rose to tell it many times.

Jewel was about eight years old when grandma Rose finally gave in and told her that a group of the elders found a morbid shrine built in front of the House of Law. Several insects had been eviscerated and tied to a series of tree branches. The scene at the shrine was horrid and went against everything the Fae held sacred.

Within days of that event, a young female fairy vanished after being sent on an errand for her father. The whole village searched for her for days, weeks and months. Jewel's grandfather, the King of Dorawine at the time, could sense a great darkness had settled over their clan and some evil force was behind the missing girl.

The girl fairy was never found.

During the next year, six more fairy girls vanished. The King was desperate to find out who was behind their disappearance so he plotted with the village's most revered sorcerer to create a trap. The sorcerer had the idea to make an image of a fairy who held no soul and who could walk in the night. He created a potion that was blended with earth and clay and the yolk of a raven's egg.

The ingredients were mixed and the sorcerer's magic was complete. A young fairy maiden was born from the mud. She was real, and not-real. It was a foggy evening the first time the sorcerer sent her out into the woodlands, as if on an errand. He waited and waited, but she returned to him by sunrise.

Many other evenings she was sent into the forest at night and she always returned…until late one evening when the moon was full.

On that night she didn't return.

The magic the sorcerer used to create the maiden had never done before. He programmed her so that once she was kidnapped, the magic would take energy out of the mud on which she stood and send a brilliant light into the sky marking her location like a giant beacon which only the King and the royal guards could see.

The guards were at the ready on that moonlit night, just as they were each time the soulless fairy was sent to the forest. It wasn't long before they saw a brilliant light shinning through the moonlight at a location deep in the woods. When they made a path to the beam it led them to a hole in the roots of a Willow tree. There they found Malick, and the remains of some of the missing fairies.

Jewel's grandmother never said exactly what they found but Jewel knew it must have been ghastly. Malick was taken away to the dungeon and was sent from there to a trial. At some point during the trial, as he was being led to the Great Hall, Malick overpowered the guards, escaped, and ran to a far end of the castle towers, away from the royal living quarters. As he ran, an arrow struck and wounded Malick. The guards followed his trail of blood to a pool of it near an open window, but he was never seen again.

The King sent guards out to search for him for months and months after this incident.

After the great escape by evil Malick, life eventually returned to normal and nothing happened until a year's worth of full moons had passed. Then, one of grandma Rose's royal cousins (at that time, a young female fairy) disappeared or was taken when she was sitting by the river.

Four days after she disappeared, the guards discovered someone had broken into the crematorium and a beautiful vessel lay shattered inside the furnace. It was never confirmed, but most villagers believed it was the missing royal and somehow it involved Malick.

Rose's husband, Jewel's grandfather, then the King, assumed Malick was dead. After all, an arrow had wounded him before he'd vanished through a window in the tower. That window was above a place in the river where there were white rapids. It was presumed that Malick flew out the window but because of his wound, he must have fallen into the river and drowned. Not a drop of his blood was seen on the river's banks.

Malick had vanished. Since no disturbances occurred after this disappearance, concern for Malick and his whereabouts faded—just as the memory of grandma Rose telling these stories to Jewel had receded and were nearly forgotten—like blankets lying in a deep drawer during summer.

Chapter 9

Birth Day

Scritch, scritch. Tap. Scritch. Tap, tap.

Jewel heard Bogart's wings hitting the windowpane. She woke up thinking it was the middle of the night but when she got out of bed and looked at her clock, she discovered it was an hour before sunrise.

While she washed her face and brushed her hair, she thought it was odd that no one but Bogart had come to wake her. She found the new gown Dahlia had hung in her closet. As she slipped it over her head, she felt the long slits opening on her back and knew they'd soon hold her wings. After a quick glance in the mica mirror, Jewel rushed downstairs.

The Great Hall was awash in light. The King and Queen were dressed in their formal robes. A group of guards surrounded them and their leader, Thor, was saying something that Jewel couldn't hear. No one seemed to notice she'd entered the room and as she watched the group from a distance, she worried that something was terribly wrong. The moment she had that thought, Queen Cordelia turned and looked straight at Jewel. Her face broke into a tight but gentle smile and she nudged the King. He looked up and over at Jewel.

"Ah, come in! Come in my beautiful birthday girl, my Jewel!" he said as he opened his arms to give her a hug. "Soon I will hug around your wings, my dear! Where are your siblings? We must make sure they too are up and ready and we should walk to the river as soon as possible."

"We would have wakened you, but we had a bit of a distraction," said Queen Cordelia.

Jewel noticed her father now had a grim expression on his face. "What's amiss?" she asked him.

"Someone tried to enter the stairway to the Vault last night," he said. "The intruder killed two guards; one at the entrance to the tunnels, and the other at the top landing. Before the criminal could get any further, an alarm was sounded and the perpetrator got away."

A flutter of butterflies took off in Jewel's stomach. She felt a tingle along her spine and a wave of darkness crossed her vision. Her mother caught her in her arms as Jewel slumped right into them.

Jewel's eyes filled with stars as her mother asked, "Have you not taken breakfast yet?"

Breakfast? The smoky fog in Jewel's head cleared as she heard her mother say, "As I have told you, when you get your wings it draws a lot of energy from your body. So you have to put something in your stomach. Was there no food delivered to your room when you woke?"

Before Jewel could answer that if there had been she hadn't seen any, two servants arrived with platters holding cups of fruit juice, plates of scrambled eggs, bread and cheese. She straightened herself and accepted the food. "Thank you," she said to a server who stood in front of her holding the platter as a table, "the eggs are good." As her hunger went away, Jewel grew aware that all the attention in the room was centered on her. A glow of golden light was emanating from her skin.

Her mother smiled and said, "We'd best get to the river so those wings can come in! Dawn must be approaching based on the glow coming off your skin."

Jewel took her mother's hand and they hurried out of the room and down the stairs to the door leading to the meadow. The village's entire population was already on the banks of the river. Horns were hooting, colorful flags were rustling in the breeze—but Jewel noticed something different from the celebration that took place when Aspen got her wings. The dark events of the past few days were still fresh in everyone's mind, and the crowd's reserve was apparent. Jewel decided she was too nervous to care.

Queen Cordelia and Jewel lined up in the procession led by town elders. The King, along with Jewel's sister and brother followed the elders. Jewel dropped her mother's hand, fell a few steps behind, walked by herself and focused only on the road ahead of her.

When the procession reached the raft, Jewel was seated on a special cushion woven from birch twigs and moss. Jewel felt like she was going to lose everything in her stomach and she was chanting under her breath and pressing a meridian point on her right wrist in order to calm down. How embarrassing it would be to throw up in front of the entire village! It would be quite an unladylike moment and her mother had been so strict in teaching her how to avoid one. If her wings coming in were going to take up even more of her energy, she wondered what amount, if any, she'd have left after all this was over.

So…she stopped focusing on the nausea and tried to grasp what was happening in the moment because now that the cord had been untied, she felt even more adrift! Jewel was in the middle of the river. The current was moving her and the raft ever closer to the falls. Townsfolk were cheering from the shore and the edge of the sun was coming up over the horizon. Her back was tingling. The sensation felt like rubbing fingers over a woolen rug in dry weather and feeling a tiny spark of energy. That was what she was feeling in her back; only it was a million tiny pricks of energy. Her skin was glowing so much that it looked like a light switch had been turned on inside her body. She was a glowing beacon, a beam of light, on a raft in the middle of a rushing river.

It felt to Jewel as if the falls were probably two minutes away. The sun had almost cleared the horizon. Jewel was so excited she couldn't focus on anything or anyone. Then, all of a sudden, she felt and heard a crackling of noise and a vibrating sensation. She thought it would be painful to feel her wings come in, but it wasn't. It was almost a pleasant—albeit a bit uncomfortable. The latter feeling only lasted a couple of seconds then she felt an interesting new weight open up on her back.

Her wings had come in!

They were wet but uncurling as Jewel looked back to see them opening up to their full span. She could only see the very tips since she couldn't swivel her head all the way around. The tips were emerald green with a brown tint. Then Jewel noticed the sound of rushing water. She turned just in time to see the edge of the falls a few feet away. She felt her wings flutter, then they flapped with incredible intensity before she even thought to move them.

She was lifting herself off the raft!

The sensation was incredible! Unbelievable! She was aloft! Free!

Flying! Flying under her own power!

Bogart buzzed in front of her at that moment, seeing her eye-to-eye, in air, for the first time. They were both hovering over the falls. Jewel looked down as the raft slipped over the top of the falls and crashed onto the rocks below. She was hovering above the edge of the falls as Bogart was doing airborne somersaults around her. "I'm hanging in mid air but not actually flying! Thanks, Bogie!" Jewel said as she pointed her body outwards to fly in a different direction.

It was beyond her greatest imagination. Flying. Maybe it was like eating a favorite treat for the first time and savoring every taste sensation. It for sure was a new way of movement. It felt so wonderful that Jewel decided she never wanted to walk again. Bogart was now flying next to her, and Jewel thought, "If beetles could smile, Bogart would be grinning from horn to horn!"

Most of Jewel's hair was trailing behind her, but some of it was whipping at her arms and face, making it hard to see. She made a mental note: "Tie back your hair when you fly." She grasped her hair with her hands, letting the new wings do all the work, and tied it over itself into a long knot. "That was easy, and it will do the job of keeping it out of my eyes for now," she thought.

She circled over the falls again. The townspeople were still there cheering her on. Some fairies were already starting to disperse and move towards the Great Hall. She had promised Ember to meet her at their hiding place in a couple of hours. That meant she had some time to fly around the village and see her world from up above. She circled around again and headed towards the village and the forest beyond. Jewel realized as she flew past the furthest point she had ever been that the Kingdom of Dorawine was much larger than she'd guessed.

The landscape was bigger than she'd imagined. It was huge! The land around the castle spread out so far it seemed to have no edges. She flew for a long time, circling around the fields and smaller towns until she realized she was tired. She heard the quarter-hour chimes of a distant clock tower and remembered Ember's request to meet at their hideaway spot.

Jewel headed back to the village and flew to the Great Oak. She landed feet first in front of the secret door at the base of the tree.

Ember was nowhere in sight. "Maybe she's here already," Jewel thought as she remembered their rule to always knock on the knot to see if the other had gotten there first. She knocked on the knot. No response. Jewel didn't want to go in first so she stood outside the giant root to wait and while she did, she got lost in thinking about how natural and fun it was to fly.

The sound of running feet came first, then Jewel saw Ember smiling as she ran and laughing so loud that Jewel wondered if others would hear her and attract attention to their secret spot. As soon as she was closer to Jewel, she started shouting: "What's your power? Do you know yet? How does it feel to get your wings? Did it hurt? Oh by nature! They're beautiful wings! What's it like to fly? Were you scared going near the falls? Do you love your wings? They're so big!"

"Ember's words are rushing out of her like the river going over the falls!" Jewel thought, but she smiled with joy.

"I've never seen wings that color!" exclaimed Ember as they hugged.

Jewel said, "Thank you, Em! I'll need two pieces of mica to see them. There is some inside. Let me go see! I can't wait to look at them! Do you really think they look nice?" Jewel was feeling such a rush of emotions; she didn't know what to do first. "Is anyone looking this way?" she asked, "Are we alone?"

"Yes, Jewel, it's just us."

Jewel pushed on the secret spot on the knot in the tree and door swung open. They both jumped inside and closed the portal.

For the next two hours they giggled and talked nonstop, admiring Jewel's new wings. Then Ember asked Jewel again, "Do you feel your power yet?"

Jewel stopped in her tracks and thought about it. She felt a strange warmth in her limbs, smelled her skin and thought of pine needles.

Ember gasped. Jewel turned to look at her. Ember was pointing to Jewel's ankles, where, like tattoos, around each ankle was a design of beautiful leaves.

Jewel lifted her gown above her knees, then higher. Green and brown designs encircled her legs and ran up her thighs to her hips. The pattern of leaves changed as it danced its way up her legs. It started with what looked like small buds. Then the buds bloomed into progressive colors; flowers and green leaves followed. It was as if time was showing how it could go from spring to summer in just one moment.

As the vine continued to her thighs, Jewel saw the leaves grow bigger. At a certain point they turned into brilliant oranges and reds. Then the leaves on the branch ended. They completely disappeared and only the end of what appeared to be a branch was left at each hip. The leaves seemed to undulate as if a gentle breeze was moving them on her skin.

Then they both noticed that a circle of leaves was now wrapped around her wrists and traveled up her arms in a similar pattern.

"My stars, that's so amazing!" Ember said.

Jewel was too busy looking at them to think about anything.

"Leaves?" Jewel asked in a whisper. "What do they mean? Leaves? Uh, leaves. Leaves?" She kept saying "leaves" over and over in her mind until she heard a quiet voice inside her head. At first she couldn't make out what kind of voice or where it was coming from, but the voice grew stronger and she realized it was not human. She was listening to the voice of the tree. It was talking to her.

She looked at her friend and asked, "Do you hear anything, Ember? Because I think I am hearing a voice from this very tree! It feels as though it is a different language, but I can understand it! Why can I now hear the tree? Am I bonded to the trees? I hear the tree speaking to me so that must mean that my power comes from the trees!"

Ember seemed as astonished as Jewel. "No one has ever been bonded to the trees before, that I know of," she said.

"I've never heard of it either," said Jewel.

As if on cue, trumpets sounded in the distance.

"Oh goodness" said Jewel, I am supposed to be at the Great Hall now. My parents are going to be so mad if I'm late! Do you mind if I fly right up there without you?" she asked. "I will be really late if I walk with you."

Ember laughed. "Go ahead. I don't mind. I'll see you as soon as my little legs will get me there."

Jewel gave Ember a hug. They squeezed each other and did a little jump up and down like they did when they were little and really excited about something.

"I love you, Em!"

"I know you do…and I love you too!"

Jewel looked out the peephole to see if anyone was around. No one was in sight, so she pushed on the door to open it. She climbed out to find Bogart sitting in front of the knot drumming his claws on the dirt.

She blew him a kiss and flew off, letting him know it was game on, a race she was going to win! It was one second before Jewel realized Bogart was not going to be beaten on his own turf. He glanced back at her just once then disappeared in a black blur of beetle wings.

Bogart was already at the castle, sitting on the floor next to the royal table by the time Jewel flew in the great window. His beetle back was rod straight, and he had a smirk on his face.

Chapter 10

Timber Truth

When she arrived, Jewel saw her parents and siblings already seated at the large oaken table. The King and Queen rose to their feet. They opened their arms toward Jewel. She half-flew and half-walked over to meet their embraces.

"Your wings are beautiful, my dear daughter!" said the Queen.

"Beautiful and strong...and...what are those? Leaves and branches? They are!" said the King, beaming a wide smile at Jewel. "A clue to your new powers!"

Her mother ran her fingers up the vines on Jewel's arm and they both watched as the leaves swirled like an invisible breeze was making them dance on her skin.

Now the King said in a quiet voice, "I have never seen a special power like this. You must have received a unique ability to have marks like these."

Jewel looked directly at her father and said, "The trees are speaking to me. The great tree in the middle of the village wanted to tell me its history before I had to come here, right before the trumpets sounded. I had to leave so I didn't get to hear his whole story. But I wanted to!"

"That is fascinating," said the King "I will wait to hear more from you...after this day and the troubles we have here are ended."

With those words of his, a loud explosion of music erupted at the opposite end of the hall. The great doors opened and a procession of elders came into the room. The last person to enter was the sorcerer and he was carrying Jewel's new crown. It was exquisite, and as it passed before the eyes of people in the crowd, many said, "Ahhhhhh!"

The crown was fashioned into a ring of leaves made of gold. Each leaf was encrusted with different colored gemstones, green, orange, brown and pink. It was as if someone had copied the leaves tattooed on her skin and then made a crown.

Jewel was thunderstruck as the sorcerer held it in front of her eyes. She remembered that the crown was created after her first cry. Even back then, as a baby, her essence was set, just like this crown. Her destiny was foretold. But now, on the arrival of her wings, she had obtained the gift of personal power. Even when she had taken her first breath and made her first sounds, the angels knew her life's path. She wondered about the difference between her spirit's essence and her personal power.

She looked at the crown and admired the complexity of the design. The center of the crown was a beautiful flower made with delicate pink stones. Flowing out in many directions was a branch with leaves from small to large. The leaves wrapped around to form a circular shape. The ends of the crown were fashioned like branches.

When the sorcerer handed the crown to her, Jewel noticed that a butterfly and other woodland insects were cast into the design. It was remarkable! The Queen now touched Jewel's forehead with scented oil that the sorcerer provided. Jewel handed the crown to her mother, following the tradition, and the Queen placed it with great care and love on Jewel's head.

Each parent kissed Jewel's cheek and stood back to look at her.

Jewel felt a vibrant energy flowing through her body. She felt great! It was all so new, but she felt quite different than she did before. Aspen stood up and approached her. With a burst of excited energy, the older sister grabbed her little sister, picked her up, and spun Jewel around in a circle. "You have your wings!" she said, "and they're fresh!"

She kissed her sister and moved aside so Tomwyn could pay his birthday respects. Jewel saw that he had a funny expression on his face. "Whoa!" he said, "you look older, and so beautiful, my sister. Happy birthday!" Then he whispered in her ear, "Have you figured out how to use your power yet?"

"I am bonded to the trees," said Jewel. "I can hear them talking to me, but I haven't had time to listen."

Chapter 11

Miranda, Beecher

Tomwyn burst out laughing and took Jewel's hand. He brought her forward onto the dance floor to the cheers of the town's people. He did a low bow, the music started a soft melody and they began to dance. At first he wasn't sure where to put his hands because when they had taken the required dance classes, Jewel had no wings. There was an awkward moment when he looked at his sister, and she looked at him and they both laughed again. For a brief time during the brother-sister dance Jewel felt relaxed and everyone around her seemed happy.

When the music ended, Tomwyn and Jewel stood and watched other dancers take the floor as large platters of her favorite foods were brought out and placed on all the tables. Ember walked over and handed Jewel a copy of the menu she'd chosen: roasted tubers pulled from the river reeds, beautiful baked flowers stuffed with cheeses, tiny sea-salt coated fish that were pan seared with thyme, and mounds of roasted mushrooms dripping in butter. Bread rolls of varying kinds were set in large baskets and in the back of the room, one table displayed many kinds of colorful sweets. Her favorite cake, made with carrots, currants and whipped cream, stood in the center. It was decorated with sugarcoated violets and their green petals were dotted with dewdrops of clear, sweet icing.

Jewel's stomach rumbled. She put down the menu and looked at her brother who was pointing to the dance floor as if he wanted to dance again. Jewel said, "I can't wait until this music piece is over so we can start eating!"

Just as she said that, the music ended. Tomwyn gave Jewel a low bow and led her to the head table.

The meal was delicious! Over the next two hours the celebration continued until everyone in the village had eaten and was sated.

Now, the procession of gifts was about to begin.

As part of the tradition, both villagers and visiting royals from around the realm came to pay their respects and honor Jewel with gifts. It was the only single occasion besides marriage when other royal fairies paid homage with their presence. Distant cousins and old friends of King Rowland and Queen Cordelia had arrived to spend the day and night. All the guest suites at the palace were filled.

Jewel hadn't noticed how many out-of-kingdom visitors had arrived until she was seated for the meal and had time to observe. Some of the fairies she recognized after meeting them at Aspen's sixteenth birthday celebration, but many others she didn't know.

A special chair had been carved for Jewel to sit in when she was being presented with gifts. It was placed next to her parents' thrones. Jewel hadn't given much thought to this part of the festivities, but now seated next to her parents she was excited and ready to receive. The idea of sending thank you scrolls to the givers crossed her mind. She knew her mother would remind her to get them completed in a timely manner—just as she'd done with Aspen, who grumbled about that task only a little.

Jewel hated writing thank you notes! Now that her power involved trees—which provided the basis for notepaper—she wondered if her gratitude could be shown in some other way.

The first gift-bearers to approach Jewel were her many cousins from surrounding villages. They laid their gifts before her on a long, low table. Soon, Jewel was looking at silken shawls, carved hair combs encrusted with gems, jewelry of all kinds with diamonds, and, several small bracelets and rings with pink stones that symbolized the month and year of her birth.

The cousins cleared the way for their favorite uncle, whose name was Nestor. He placed a golden cage in the center of the table. It contained two small bird-like creatures. Jewel looked at them and realized that they weren't exactly birds. They were half-fairy and half-bird. She was so startled that she got up from her chair and went to have a close look at them. One was the color of Willow bark tea with pale brown feathers that became bright and glossy at the tail. The other was a pale yellow, with dull brownish-yellow tail feathers. Jewel thought, "The brighter colored one must be male."

Before Jewel was any more surprised by their appearance, she heard them say in a melodic voice, "It is our honor to serve you, young highness."

Jewel almost tripped when she stepped back in surprise. Her uncle extended his arms to catch her as she fell backwards. He swept Jewel up into a bear hug of an embrace, swirling her around as he did when she was much younger.

"Uncle Nestor!" she exclaimed, "I have never seen creatures like this! What are they and how do I care for them?"

Nestor bellowed a laugh out loud and with such force Jewel felt like a crystal of salt sprinkling out of a shaker as he released her from his grip. "They just need to be served the same fare as you and I, although they do prefer woodland flowers and nuts to eat; not flesh. They also need to be protected from other creatures that may prey upon them, but otherwise they are just like you and me in their own small way." Nestor chuckled again. "Please let me introduce you to Miranda and Beecher, wife and husband."

Both the little creatures bowed to Jewel.

"It is with great pleasure for Miranda and me to protect you and guard you for the rest of our lives," Beecher said. He preened a small feather from his chest.

Jewel guffawed at the notion this tiny thing or person or whatever could protect even a butterfly. She noticed as uncle Nestor's faced reddened in color.

He looked at her with disapproval and with a serious tone in his voice, said, "Jewel, Miranda and Beecher come from one of the fiercest clans of sky creatures known to our world. They have venom in certain feather tips that can kill a giant troll before he takes a second breath. They can fly faster than any other creature in our world! At times their wings beat so fast they actually seem to disappear from sight and become invisible. In addition to all of those special skills…" he paused and grimaced, "…they are of the highest intelligence and their minds are quite brilliant. They are also known to be rather mischievous, but I am sure Miranda and Beecher have outgrown this phase by now."

Hearing these words, both Miranda and Beecher bowed towards uncle Nestor and in unison said, "We thank thee, for such lavish praise. You honor our house. We will send a messenger with a note of thanks to our Lord praising your generosity and kindness to us and to let him know we are so pleased that we may live amongst you."

Jewel felt very embarrassed and said to the two caged creatures in a whisper: "I am so very sorry that I did not know of your kind and I apologize if I have offended you in any way for what I thought but did not say."

When Miranda and Beecher heard her words they giggled. "Your royal princess, our enemies make the same mistake when they see us, but they never get the chance to change their ways for another encounter! We do not take kindly to beings that prey on us for their next dinner—or for any reason."

After Jewel got over her initial shock of seeing two small birdlike fairies, she looked at Miranda and Beecher as if she were seeing them for the first time and saw that they were both beautiful and wise.

Beecher had a fairy head with a beak-like protrusion just under his nose. It looked like a shield that guarded the lower half of his face. Jewel was too embarrassed to ask if the beak was real, if it grew or receded around certain moon cycles, or if it was just...normal. The 'hair' on his head was made of tiny wisps of feathers in a glossy pale yellow. It looked like he was wearing a headband made of rainbow-colored thistles. His arms were tucked under his wings but Jewel could see they were heavily muscled. The upper portion of his body was similar to any male fairy but the lower half was bird. Beecher had powerful legs that had talons on the ends of his tiny legs. The bird half of his body displayed feathers that matched the ones on his head, except for his tail feathers. His ears seemed to be a bit oversized and his eyes were like looking into obsidian stones—they didn't appear to have a pupil or an iris. They were just black orbs. Jewel wasn't able to tell what he was looking at unless he was talking directly to her.

Miranda's head also had fuzzy wisps of hair feathers that flowed down her back and continued to the tips of her tail feathers. Her eyes were also black orbs, but she had no beak under her nose. Her upper torso was like a fairy, and she had a scarf of feathers draped around her neck that shielded her breast. Her lower body was bird-like and the talons on her feet were smaller than Beecher's. Miranda was beautiful in a strange sort of way that Jewel made an effort to describe to herself, but could not do. So she looked even closer.

Miranda stepped forward and said to Jewel, "We brought a gift for you, young princess, and I would like to install it now."

Jewel asked questions in her mind: "Install? What did she mean by that? Is this odd or normal?"

She said out loud, "Well, uh, ah...what do you mean by install?"

Miranda bent down and lifted up a large acorn that was in a corner of the cage. She motioned for Jewel to open the cage door, and when she did, Miranda put it into her hand. Jewel took it and studied it while Beecher and Miranda watched. The top of the acorn was hinged. Jewel flipped it open. Inside were two perfectly round, blood red stone earrings framed with gold. The stones sparkled and glittered like there was a small fire inside each one.

"Wow," said Jewel, "these are so interesting! What kind of stones are these?"

"They come from the lands of our people," said Miranda. "They are mined in the deepest part of the mountains where our village is located. Master stone carvers are given the task to cut the red crystals into beautiful shapes. They fashioned these earrings specifically for your sixteenth birthday."

"I don't have holes in my ears," said Jewel in a quiet voice as she noticed the ends of the earrings were straight pins with gold backs. Before she could say anything else, a quick breeze hit her face. Both of the small bird fairies were gone, and she felt a prick of pain in each of her ears. Then Miranda and Beecher were back in front of her, smiling. The earrings in the acorn were gone and her ear lobes were feverish. She knew before she felt her ears that each one contained an earring.

Jewel giggled and winced at the same time. She said, "Well I guess you solved that problem and now I know what you meant when you said install!" The fairy birds bowed again, identical grins were on their faces.

The Queen made her unique, not-quite-a-cough sound that Jewel knew was meant to get her attention. The attention and procession of the gift-bearing townsfolk had halted and they'd become restless while Jewel had been absorbed in her interaction with Miranda and Beecher. Jewel hurried back to her chair and seated herself to receive the rest of the gifts.

By the end of the procession, the table was stacked high with presents. Jewel was overwhelmed with the amount of gifts that had been given to her. She was grateful for such generosity, but she didn't know how she could possibly write thank you scrolls to everyone! It would take her months! She thought to ask Aspen and Ember for assistance and wondered if that was the right thing to do.

Chapter 12

Ember's Gift

After all the guests had dispersed from the room, Jewel saw Ember walking toward her special chair. Her hands were behind her back and an excited expression was on her face. Standing before Jewel, Ember held out her right hand. It contained a box wrapped in a lily leaf tied with blue twine. Jewel took the gift, stood and hugged her.

"You have to open your gift," said Ember, "it took me months to make it!"

Jewel undid the twine to let the lily leaf fall to the ground. Inside was a tiny woven basket, with an attached cover, made with the long stems of river reeds. It was round, woven tight and well crafted. Jewel looked at Ember to show her surprise as her friend said, "Oh, well... the basket did take me months to weave but it's only part of your gift. Open it."

As Jewel opened the lid, she took care not to damage her friend's delicate artwork. Inside of it Jewel found what she thought was a golden rope—but it was a bracelet made from the purest gold—gold that had been melted and cooled in the cracks of river rocks. It was a perfect gift, Jewel thought, and one she'd treasure forever.

Ember created the bracelet using the Faes' ancient art of spinning gold. Jewel knew the technique well because all Fae children learn the art in school. The students learned to take river mud and turn it into clay to practice the movement of rubbing gold between their hands. Jewel felt she'd had no talent for this craft and felt embarrassed to show her clay strands to the teacher. They usually were uneven, fat in some places and too skinny in others. Ember had been brilliant at it, even from the first moment she touched the clay.

She'd watched Ember and others practice the full art many times. First, the gold is heated in unique kettles and placed in special furnaces that melt the beautiful metal. The kettles are taken to the river where the content is poured into the carved cracks made on heavy stone blocks. The blocks are lowered into the river to cool the hot metal. Once cooled, the gold forms are removed from the rocks. The artisan takes a long gold spindle and rubs the piece between their hands. It takes a long time and is best done in a group, where the artisans sit in a circle for hours, telling stories of their clan or family, as they rub the gold. All this rubbing causes the gold to heat to a little more than the temperature of their hands and it's what turns the gold into even longer strands. These thin, hand crafted strands are braided into golden ropes to make jewelry.

Now, Ember took the bracelet out of Jewel's hand and put it around her wrist with a bit of impatience. "Geez," she said, "you're taking way too long!" Jewel then noticed the clasp. It was made from a rare and beautiful clear crystal. The opposite end of the bracelet held a stretchy round loop, which slipped over the crystal to hold the bracelet together. "If you look closer, the inside of the crystal has a small bubble. Inside the bubble is a seed."

Jewel scrutinized the crystal. She looked at Ember but had no words.

"That crystal is pretty wild, isn't it?" said Em. "I took it to the school's master teacher after I found it in a secret cavern near the other crystal caves. He's also the elder in charge of the harvest and he was shocked to tell me that it was the seed of an ancient apple tree. He said he had never, in all his life, seen this phenomenon: a seed being preserved in a rock crystal. Now that I know your power comes from the trees, I think it was meant that I found this crystal so I could then give it to you for this birthday. I believe the crystal and seed is part of your destiny."

Jewel hugged her again and said, "I'll never take it off. I'll wear it forever and ever until the day I die."

"I hope so," said Ember. "Want to meet at our place in a few hours, once you're done celebrating and opening gifts?"

"Thank you. Yes, of course. See you there, my friend, ah, before sunset. Thank you, again."

Chapter 13

Private Moments

———————

When the gifts had all been received, cake eaten and cleaned up, the guests dispersed, the King and Queen and Jewel's siblings had all retired to their chambers. They were probably napping, Jewel thought, but she was not sleepy at all.

Jewel wanted to change out of her gown, put on simple clothes and figure out what to do with Miranda and Beecher. Both the fairy bird creatures seemed to be watching her every move. She looked at them now, as she sat on the edge of her chair, patient and quiet. They sat perfectly still; the little couple was holding hands, both seemed to be deep in their own thoughts. She went close to their cage and said, "So what do you two want to do? Would you like to go to the balcony or is there somewhere else you would like to go...or something else you would like to see?"

It was an awkward experience talking to such beings, she thought.

As if reading her mind, Beecher said, "Jewel, please think of me and my wife as your winged advisors and friends. Unlike Bogart, we can talk with you, even through thoughts! We'll be with you all the time and if you don't mind we usually find a place somewhere on beings of your stature to sit: either on your shoulder or inside a pocket. We don't like to leave our Master, or Mistress in this case, to whom we have been bonded. And we are bonded to you, my dear."

"Bonded to?" thought Jewel, "what does that mean exactly? Will Beecher be around when I change my clothes? That would be kind of weird...and uncomfortable!"

Again, Beecher addressed Jewel as if reading her mind. "I am very respectful of your own personal boundaries and we've arranged to install shades in our new home so all of us have our privacy."

"How did he do that?" thought Jewel. "He must be reading my mind."

With that, Beecher hopped down and opened the door of their cage. He and Miranda flew to Jewel's shoulder and perched themselves just under the wave of her long hair.

Miranda whispered into Jewel's ear, "We are now an extension of you, so yes, both of us hear your thoughts."

Jewel felt a rush of blood arise on her face and knew it was bright red. "Ah, well, that can be a bit intrusive, don't you think?"

Beecher laughed and said, "Your highness, we only listen when it concerns us or if we sense you're in danger. It's not our intent to make you uncomfortable in any way and we'll respect your personal thoughts...always. In fact, your personal thoughts are blocked from us—because your natural intention is not to share them!"

Jewel let out a long breath and felt much better. As she did so, the creatures went back inside their cage.

With that important exchange over, Jewel went to her chambers to change clothes. Her new wardrobe would fit her wings, and she was excited to wear these custom-made dresses. She changed out of the formal gown and put on a simple frock made of copper brown cloth. Her new wings slipped into the slits without her even thinking about it as she looked at herself in the mica mirror. She noticed that Beecher and Miranda were inside their new home and had already draped a bolt of fabric along one side of their cage. Jewel could hear them speaking to each other but couldn't see either of them.

This was the first quiet moment she had since she'd gotten her wings and discovered her power. She positioned a second piece of mica as a mirror in her room so she could look at her back and her new wings. They were beautiful. Their rich browns on her wings looked like chiastolite crystals she'd seen after they'd been mined from the caves. They were not as transparent as some wings, but they were definitely an unusual color.

Next she took off her crown and set it on her dresser top to admire. Prior to her birthday, the sorcerer told her that she would be the only one who could remove it from her head. It held a special magic. The crown was a new addition to her body just like her wings. This elegant headdress was indeed a new part of her and her appearance. It would always be on her head, except of course when she was sleeping.

The crown, like her skin, gave off smells of different trees. The pine scent was the most obvious, but there were other subtle scents that wafted off the surface of her arms and off the crown. All of the smells made her feel good. They were like a fresh clean morning in the forest after a night of heavy rain.

She felt great. As soon as she'd settled into that feeling, the fairy birds flew out of their cage. Beecher landed on her dresser and Miranda perched on the crown.

Miranda, or Mir, as Jewel now thought of her, was examining the beautiful details of the crown. She gasped, and both Jewel and Beecher turned to look at her. She pointed to a nubby section of the crown where a branch had formed a knot along its length. In the knot was a tiny image of two half-bird fairy creatures: a man and woman holding hands. "Ah, then they are part of my destiny too," thought Jewel. "It is so strange how our Universe makes things happen for us!" She said it aloud, almost as a thought, but one that popped out of her mouth in sound.

"Yes," said Beecher. "We both believe these things happen for a reason."

Jewel heard the tower clock strike the hour of five. Jewel hadn't noticed the time and felt she was going to be late to meet Ember. "Blast" she said. "I'm probably late and Em is going to be so mad at me!" She glanced down at her wrist where the beautiful golden bangle lay on her arm.

Bogart flew in through the open window and made clicking noise. "Did Em tell you to find me?" she asked—not really expecting an answer, but Bogart was clicking and tapping his claw on the ground. "OK, my friend, I'm on my way!"

She opened the bedroom window, hopped up on the sill and took off. She circled the castle even though she was late, but the allure of her new wings was too heady to ignore. The breeze was cool along her face and weightlessness was a feeling that was beyond anything she ever imagined.

She set her sights on the Great Oak tree in the center of town. The tree was an ancient one and could be seen for many hundreds of lengths. It was so large at the base that it would take a long time to walk around it. Jewel pointed herself towards the village and the tree then flew straight at it to meet Ember.

Chapter 14

Tree Meeting

Ember was already waiting for her. She wasn't mad, because it was Jewel's special day, but she did seem to be slightly miffed. They both looked around and when no one was in sight, Ember pushed on the secret spot and they both jumped through the hole and into their secret room.

"Your party was so nice, Jewel. You got a lot of gifts."

"Thank you, Em. I have to write thank you scrolls now, and you know how I feel about writing. Oh well, the first one I write will be to you."

"No need! You thanked me in person."

"Your birthday will be here soon, Em. Are you looking forward to it?"

"Yes! My day won't be as special as this one, but I am so happy I get to share it with you!"

Both fairy girls were surprised the next moment when Beecher and Mir flew out from under Jewel's dress. Ember was so startled she fell backwards and landed on the soft earth under the stool. Jewel laughed a bit but then held back after looking at the expression on her friend's face. "You OK?"

"Well actually my bottom is a bit sore, but otherwise I'm fine. Who and what are these little...ah..." she hesitated, "...things?"

"This is Miranda and this is Beecher," said Jewel. They were a gift from uncle Nestor. They are actually independent little beings, and quite the warriors. My uncle says that they're feared by many." Ember looked at Jewel and even without saying a word, Jewel knew her friend was rather dubious about the last statement, so she went on, "They have access to poison in their wing tips when they need it, and do all sorts of other things to defend themselves...and me... and...uncle Nestor told me they are also very smart."

Jewel drew back her hair and said; "Look, they pierced my ears when they gave me these earrings as a gift."

Ember gasped. "The red color is so beautiful! And they look great with your crown!"

Jewel noticed both Mir and Beecher were taking in Ember's comments with a pleasure and pride.

Ember sat down on one of the small chairs after admiring the earrings and started a conversation with the little fairies. Jewel thought it was more of an interview, and couldn't believe she hadn't taken the time to ask some of those same questions. She sat and listened to the conversation between her new guardians and her best friend.

"What exactly do they call your kind?" Ember asked, nodding at Beecher.

"We have an ancient name, *Pulchra avium*, but most other creatures just call us the bird fairies," said Beecher as he laughed. Mir joined in to laugh too, as if they were having a private joke between them. He continued, "We are royal children in our clans. My great uncle is the Lord of our lands. I married Miranda, one of my very distant cousins, as is the tradition. Certain members of our clan are chosen by the shadow beings to be protectors of royal fairies. It is a great honor and a tradition of our people, and it dates back through eons of time. We were chosen for Jewel, as it was foretold before either of us were born."

"How is that possible?" asked Jewel.

Miranda answered, "We don't really understand how the shadow beings know the future. We were told of this arrangement when we were very young. Beecher and I were bonded to each other as well as to you."

"There have been many strange predictions," Beecher said. "In fact, when we left our village, we were given a warning from the old wizard to be vigilant. He said soon after we arrived a strange and frightening event would take place that could alter the destiny of our world."

Jewel felt a chill go up her spine. This was a strange turn of events. Did it have to do with the missing key, she wondered.

"Could it alter my destiny?" she asked.

"Getting your wings seals in your destiny," Miranda answered, "but you now have a special power, and that allows you to take charge and make your own destiny. It is a big responsibility, but once you understand it, it is what gives your life vast meaning."

Jewel didn't know what to say. She looked at Ember but she was preoccupied with something entirely different. Ember was staring at a spot in the floor across the room. There was something on the ground and part of it was buried in the earth. Ember looked at Jewel, pointed to the ground and said, "Do you see that? The shiny thing. What is that?"

Jewel followed her eyes to the object. "I don't know," said Jewel, "let me go see." Mir and Beecher flew into her pocket when she stood up. She walked to the wall and bent down to pick up the object. As she grasped the shiny item she felt a stabbing pain in her hand.

She screamed, dropped it, and tripped backwards over an unseen root toward the wall of the inside of the tree.

Jewel's eyes locked with Ember's and both of their perceptions seemed to merge. Both saw and felt the scene as if it were taking place in slow motion.

As Jewel fell backwards, a blinding light filled the room. It was accompanied by a pop. The moment passed as fast as lightning and thunder and in the next moment, Ember was trying to refocus her eyes. She stood up and shouted. "Are you OK Jewel? Did you see that light and hear the noise?"

No one answered.

"Jewel? Jewel? Jewel, where are you?"

Ember realized she was alone.

Jewel was gone.

So were Miranda and Beecher.

Chapter 15

Malick's World

Dressed in a fine business suit, the soul of Malick stood tall and erect, gazing out of a window in his high-rise office. A soft knock on the door disrupted his reverie. Jane, his assistant, opened the door before he gave permission. A diminutive woman with sharp features under her too-large glasses, Jane wore her mousy hair in a French knot. "It's time for your next meeting, sir. Also, your father is on line one," she said.

"Thank you. Please close the door." Malick walked to his desk and pressed the intercom button as Jane closed the door. His father's voice echoed through the loudspeaker: "I'll be waiting in the conference room," he said. "The rest of the board will be here within the hour, so be ready, Michael."

When he heard the sound of his human name, Malick cringed. He had tried to change it many times, however his adopted parents refused to endorse it. As much as it irked him to admit, he needed their support. But that time was coming to an end. He knew that he would soon have access to more power than any puny humans could ever dream of. Soon, they would all answer to him. He turned again to the window and smirked at his reflection in the glass.

At forty-five human years of age, Malick—or, Michael, as he was known in the human world—certainly looked the part of a king. Well over six feet tall, with coal black hair and creamy ivory skin, he had a well-toned physique that emphasized his strength and otherworldly beauty. His most prominent feature, eyes the color of pale lavender, belied his evil heart. Like frozen icicles and steel daggers, this man's eyes held cool confidence in all that was cruel, covert and evil.

Most humans feared and disliked Michael-Malick. He was an outcast in the true sense of the word. Of course, this bothered him little—he had also been reviled in the world of his origin. Why should the human world treat him any different?

In his lonely heart, he did miss his homeland. He couldn't stand the insignificant trappings of the human place known as Earth. He often mused about the strange circumstances that had lead to his predicament; but he had been lucky in some ways.

He'd been lucky that the rich and powerful, yet infertile, human husband and wife who'd found him when he was an infant, abandoned in the forest, had so desired a child. They assumed he was the product of some fated teenager's surprise pregnancy—and that Michael had been abandoned to avoid scandal—so they adopted him.

But Malick had always known the truth of his banishment to Earth, even when he was trapped in the physical form of a human infant, helpless and miserable.

Now, as he crossed his office and opened the sealed vault, hidden behind a priceless painting, a smile played at his lips. Gently caressing the contents of a lockbox, he thought, "Mine! All mine!"

The sound of his intercom buzzing with Jane's voice jolted him back to his present reality. "Your meeting, sir. They're waiting for you."

With a flash of annoyance, he calmed himself and resumed his staid demeanor.

"Soon," he thought, "so very soon."

Chapter 16

Jewel Through

When she came to, Jewel tried to sort out what happened. She focused on the events preceding the bright light. Yes, Ember had spotted something shiny buried in the ground. Jewel picked up the object. What was it? Oh, a piece of very fine glass. Wait. No, it wasn't glass but it was so sharp that the edge seemed to have cut her hand.

She looked down at her hand, but there was no wound.

"This is so odd. What happened?" she said to no one.

She recalled falling backwards when she tripped on a root and had hit the wall of the tree. Then there was a sensation of falling and a bright flash of light. Jewel shook her head to clear that memory. "Where am I?"

She was sitting outdoors, at base of the Great Oak tree. How did she get outside the secret retreat? Where was Ember? She looked around. Something wasn't quite right. The tree was the same, but the village, Jewel's village was gone! She was sitting in a place that was so familiar, yet she didn't recognize anything beyond the Great Oak.

Her head felt fuzzy and she was having problems thinking. "Come on Jewel," she said to herself, "snap out of it. Did I hit my head? Am I injured? Am I dreaming." She pinched her cheek hard to see if she was awake. "Wow, that hurt! I'm not dreaming; and I'm in some strange place."

Next, she realized she couldn't feel her wings. "What happened to my wings?" Jewel looked over her shoulder to see if she could see the tips but they were gone! She tried to move them but only felt a strange ripple on her back.

Fear gripped her thoughts. Nothing was right.

"Stay calm," she thought as she looked down at her body. "But how can I be calm when everything about me has changed?"

She wasn't wearing her brown frock anymore. She was dressed in a skirt that fell below her knees and a long sleeved shirt. The skirt looked like a cascade of green leaves, but it was a woven pattern in a fabric of fine silk. The shirt was also made of silk. It was white with a pattern of grey ridges like the bark of birch trees in her forest. How did she end up wearing these clothes?

Her left hand reached up to see if her crown was in place. Yes! She felt the beautiful leaves of metal wrapped around her hair. She looked down at her arms and pulled up the sleeves to see the leaf patterned tattoo on her skin. She then looked under her skirt to see that her legs still displayed the leaf and branch markings. They were there, but they didn't move any more.

Jewel stood up, and felt her head spin. Feeling quite dizzy, she plopped down on the soft moss around the tree.

"Wait just a minute!" she said out loud when she realized another strange phenomenon. She stood up again and realized she was tall, big, HUGE! She stood several full-body lengths taller than what was her fairy body's normal. She was standing next to the tree. Never before had she been at eye level with this part of the Great Oak; at least not while she was standing! She had seen it from a higher perspective when she got her wings and could fly around the giant trunk. Now when she looked down, she could barely make out the knot at the base of the tree by her feet.

How did she get so big?

This was so strange. She could not wrap her mind around any of this, not the tree, not this forest, not her new size. Jewel was totally confused. She pressed her palm onto the bark to stabilize her footing. As she did, she felt a surge of warmth flow through her hand and up her arm. She relaxed for that moment, feeling safer and calmer. In her head she heard a soft voice.

Yes! It was a voice—not any voice—the voice of the tree. The same voice she'd heard that very morning when she was standing with Ember inside the earthen room. The tree had spoken to her through her thoughts and it was speaking to her now in the very same manner. "Where am I?" she asked the tree with her thoughts.

She heard the tree's voice as a soft murmur in her head. "You have passed through to the other side. You fell against the portal in my base and now you are in the world of human creatures."

"Human?" thought Jewel. "Human? And what did the tree mean when it said I passed through to the other side? What is the other side?" Fear and anxiety worked its way up from her belly to her mind.

"Do not fear, Child of the Trees," said the tree's voice, soft and deep. "I will protect you, for you are a part of me. When you wish to, you may pass back into your world." Jewel exhaled and relaxed. As she took a deep breath, the tree whispered, "You are not the first to pass through my secret door."

Jewel stood very still. "How can that be?" she thought. Like Beecher and Miranda, the tree could read her thoughts as she could 'read' the trees.

"An evil creature has passed through this portal before. His heart was black," said the tree. "He had evil intentions for he killed a maiden child born of the tree and stole her from us."

The word "maiden" stuck in Jewel's mind. "What do you mean, 'maiden child born of the tree?'"

"It was a tragedy that happened long ago," said the tree. "A human would call this maiden a wood nymph, but she was also of royal blood."

Jewel didn't quite comprehend what the tree meant, but she could feel a prickle of anger ripple through her body. Something felt familiar about the story, but she was more concerned about her own situation. "Tell me tree, where am I and how are you here as well?"

"There are two worlds. They were formed as mirror images of each other," whispered the tree. "Your world, where I am the center of your village, and here where I am just a tree in one of the forests. The trees, and I myself, exist in both worlds, but each world is very different and you have passed into this place because you were bonded to our roots when you turned sixteen. You bonded to our bark, and to the very energy of our existence. When you passed through the portal, I dressed you so you would not be naked, and I protected you from changing into a human's form. I gave you my knowledge of human language and all that I know so you may understand this world."

The tree went silent, as if waiting for Jewel to respond.

But Jewel was silent too. Several quiet moments passed.

In time, the tree continued, "Only a Child of the Trees can pass between worlds. It does not bind you to this place and you can pass back to your lands when you wish. Close your eyes, Child of the

Trees, and I will share my memories with you. I am very old and have seen much in these lands. I can share those images with you, but you must open yourself to my visions. Take a deep breath. Close your eyes. Trust me to guide you."

Jewel closed her eyes. She felt a sudden rush of wind, then she felt her heart quicken. She smelled the heavy scent of the woodlands and heard the rustle of a million leaves. In her head she saw images of things she had never seen before.

She saw a young sapling pushing its way up through the earth.

She smelled the musky ground as the sapling spread its roots into the dirt.

She felt the young tree grow and reach up to the sky.

As the tree grew she saw images of the forest around it—and there were strange looking animals, flowers, grasses and...humans.

The images floated through her mind like the bark paper book of images she'd made a few years ago with Ember. They had drawn the same fairy fifty times, but each time they changed the position of its head or legs. Then they each took turns and fanned the stack of pages made of bark with their thumbs, watching the fairy dance in front of them as the book and paper flipped through each image.

That is how Jewel saw the tree's memories as it imparted them to her. It was like looking at their paper book or down into one of the rugs in her mother's chamber. These images from the tree were pictures of beings similar to her, but different. These creatures had no wings when they were grown. They were big, with bodies like the kind she had since she'd passed through the portal. She heard a different language being spoken as she watched the images play themselves out like a dream. She was surprised that she could understand it.

The breeze rustled through her mind again and the scene changed.

Now she saw images from other trees. She could smell different barks and leaves and knew she was seeing other images born from the trees surrounding her own Great Oak. Each tree took a turn at showing her images she didn't understand nor had she ever seen before.

She felt what it was like to have lichens and fungi growing on bark.

She felt the sting of a woodchopper's axe.

She stood strong through ice storms, and bowed to strong winds.

It was all so overwhelming that Jewel felt exhausted as she watched the images pass through her mind.

Then, new images were given to her.

She saw large yellow contraptions with wheels atop a box that held a human, who was holding another smaller wheel.

She saw glowing boxes with images of humans inside.

She saw bright lights that were not made of fire.

She saw machines in the sky that looked like birds without flapping wings.

Jewel opened her eyes and felt dizzy again. She sat down on the largest root of the tree and rested her head against the bark.

It was dusk and the sky was darkening. The air was cool and the night was alive with sounds. She looked around the tree and saw a large clearing. It was perfectly flat, with yellow lines painted on the ground. Next to this area were very tall poles that had bright lights at the top. Each light gave off a strange glow and illuminated the big empty area. There was a large sign with strange symbols on it and without even understanding what was happening, Jewel knew the word for this place: "parking lot."

When Jewel felt a flutter in her skirt she was surprised. "Now what's happening?" she wondered as she grabbed a fold of the cloth. Something was moving in a pocket of her skirt. She watched as Miranda popped her head out from the fabric. She looked dazed as she half flew, half stumbled out of the pocket into Jewel's lap. Jewel opened her palm and Miranda climbed into it. Beecher rolled out after Miranda into the folds of silk. He appeared as disheveled and confused as Mir.

The tree whispered to Jewel "These creatures are bonded to you and as such have passed into this land unscathed by the shift. They must be with you to pass back and cannot go alone for they would not survive the shift without you. Keep them close."

Miranda and Beecher looked at Jewel. She wondered if they'd heard the tree's voice. Beecher sat in Jewel's lap and said, "Yes we can hear the tree because we can hear your thoughts, too. These sounds are all one to us and we share in the knowledge you've gained from the trees."

Miranda felt a bit frightened—Jewel felt her tremble. Beecher hopped into Jewel's other hand and she felt happy they were along for her sake.

The fog in Jewel's brain cleared. "This is crazy!" she thought. "No, on second thought, this is amazing! Do my parents know of this other world? Am I the first to be given this knowledge? Why are there two worlds?"

"You already know some of the answers," said Miranda.

Jewel remembered reading the sacred scrolls that held stories of a parallel world. At the time, she thought they were just myths. And now, in the present moment, she sat on the tree root trying to absorb what was happening to her. Mir and Beecher were still in her hands. She noticed that they'd grown in size too, but in a way proportional to what they'd been compared to Jewel in the other world. She placed her hands on the ground and each bird fairy hopped onto the soft moss.

Jewel wondered, "Who was the other fairy to pass through the portal? If he was evil, was he some how connected to the theft of the key? Who was the other Child of the Trees? There are too many questions without answers."

"Shall we return to our world?" asked Beecher.

Jewel considered this for a moment, then turned to the tree and said. "This evil fairy…do you know if he had a beautiful golden key?"

"The key to the Vault of Souls?"

Jewel was shocked. "Why yes," said Jewel, "how do you know about the Vault of Souls?"

"The Vault of Souls was built under my roots long before I grew to such a mighty tree. When the stairs were carved so your kind could enter the Vault, my roots were long and as they'd been growing deep into the soil. The angels protected my roots so I could grow on top of it and watch over the land around it. I have been a witness to your traditions and your people for hundreds of years. The seed that I sprung from came from my kind that was here when the world was formed. I have gained knowledge from that seed as my saplings gain knowledge from me."

Jewel then asked, "Did this evil fairy have the key?"

A strong gust of wind hit her face at that moment the tree answered, "Yes."

Chapter 17

Ember Alone

———————

Meanwhile, back inside the Great Oak's secret meeting place, Ember was in a panic as she looked around the room. Her voice was shaking: "Where is Jewel? She's disappeared! Oh, Jewel, where did you go? Can you hear me? If you can hear me, please let me hear you!"

She opened the secret door just a bit to see if Jewel had gone outside. All she saw was Bogart, who was sitting on another exposed root. "Bogart, have you seen Jewel?"

The beetle looked back at her with his giant black eyes. The sounds he made were not helpful. Click, click. Ember could tell that her demeanor was scaring him and she knew he sensed her fear.

She opened the door all the way, hopped onto the ground and ran around the roots of the tree, screaming, "Jewel! Jewel! Where are you, Jewel? Please come back to me!"

Jewel was nowhere in sight. No trace. Ember was in a state where she wasn't thinking in a logical way—fear and surprise had overwhelmed her. She decided to stop in her tracks. Maybe Jewel flew back to the castle and was playing a trick? "Yeah, that's what she probably did," Ember said, answering out loud to that silent question.

Click. Bogart flew to her and landed at her foot. Click. Click.

Ember looked at him. "What does he know?" she thought. "Maybe he'll come with me back to the castle. I hope Jewel is there. And if she is playing a trick on me, I am going to let her know how angry I am about this!" She made sure the secret door in the knot of the root was closed and hurried towards the castle. "Come on, you beetle!"

Bogart flew behind her.

As she ran, she thought: "What if Jewel is not at the castle? Should I tell anyone about this ridiculous practical joke? Should I mention that Jewel is missing? If this is a joke why should I tell anyone and cause worry—especially since everyone is already concerned about the missing key. Maybe Jewel isn't really missing. She's just hiding. Well, I guess I need to make a plan before I get to the castle…."

Ember decided that she would check Jewel's bedroom to make sure she wasn't hiding there, then go to all the places in the castle where they used to hide. "We've been playing hide and seek all our lives," thought Ember, "but now Jewel can fly anywhere and be there in a tenth of the time it takes me to get there. Perhaps she staged the whole game to make it more exciting by putting the shiny object in the ground so I would ask her what it was. Then she probably placed some black explosion powder in one of the tiny alcoves of the root. Yes…then Jewel rushed to see the shiny thing. She must have put it there. She probably lit the black powder when she bent down. Then she vanished in all that bright light from the explosion. Jewel knew I wouldn't be able to clear my eyes so she must have opened the door and flown back to the castle. Yes. That's what happened."

Now close to the castle, Ember looked at the clock in the tower. She had about an hour to search for her friend before she had to be home for dinner. If she didn't find her friend by then, she knew Jewel would figure out that she had won the hiding game and that Ember had given up.

"Jewel! Here I come!" said Ember as she dashed up the hill toward the castle. Finding Jewel was the only idea in Ember's mind.

If only she could have known what was really going on elsewhere….

Chapter 18

Martin's Malick

Malick's human father, Martin, was sitting at the boardroom table waiting for his son to appear in time for the late afternoon board meeting. He still had mixed feelings about his adopted son as he thought back to how he and his wife Miriam had so desired a baby.

They had tried for many years but for all their money, doctors and years of trying to conceive, it just never happened. Miriam had grown depressed and morose because she was barren. When the baby boy was found in the forest and needed adoption, well, it was like a miracle. "It must have been fate," Martin thought. "So long ago."

Martin remembered being at the police station regarding a school board matter when the call came in about the baby. Buddy, the sheriff, had been Martin's friend from childhood, and now he was talking about an upcoming charitable event for the town's only grade school. "Buddy, can you give me some manpower to assist with traffic control for the school's annual fundraiser?" Martin asked. He was a trustee on the school's board and Buddy had given help in past years.

Before Buddy could answer, the phone rang. Buddy picked up the receiver and after listening for a few moments said, "I'll be right there."

"What now?" Martin asked.

"Unbelievable! The park rangers found a newborn baby lying under one of the trees at Linden Mountain Park. Abandoned. I have to get out there and meet the detective. Want to come with me?"

"Absolutely!" said Martin

They left the office and went around the back of the building to where Buddy parked his car. The drive to the entrance of the park was only 20 minutes and the two men talked about why anyone would abandon a baby. "This is a first for me—and you know how long I've been sheriff," Buddy said.

When they arrived, a group of rangers and hikers were grouped together around one of the largest trees in the park. A ranger was holding the baby, who was bundled up in a shirt made of very unusual fabric. "Boy or girl?" Buddy asked. The ranger didn't answer but held the infant out as the shirttail flopped open and exposed the baby's legs and stomach.

Martin saw it was a boy.

The ranger said, "Oops! Sorry! What a way to meet the world, little fella!" He pulled up a corner of the shirt and re-wrapped the child as it opened its eyes.

The ranger said, "We got a call from some campers who heard him crying, followed the sound and found him laying with his head inside this shirt. I was first on the scene and when they led me to him, I uncovered him. Very strange! Come here, I'll show you where I found him. He was nestled into some roots around that big tree."

When they got to the place where the baby was found, Martin and Buddy looked from the spot where he appeared and then they looked at the baby. He was quiet; eyes wide open, and not a single tear stained his face. The infant looked up at Martin.

Buddy noticed and said, "He likes you, Martin."

Martin was mesmerized. The baby's eyes were lavender, like a lavender flower against white snow. "Buddy, have you ever seen eyes this color?"

"Never. This is one unusual baby. We're going to have to find a family who'll take him. I don't have any reports of a missing baby. Do you want to take him in until we can get some answers? I'm sure Miriam would be thrilled."

"I'm sure she would be," Martin said. "Yes, I'll take him home with me."

And now, Michael was late to the meeting. All the other board members had arrived a bit early out of respect to Martin. Some were tapping their pencils. A few of them were standing behind their chairs. One of them looked at Martin and said, "He's late again."

"He's my son and I can no longer make any excuses for him," Martin said. "As always, Michael is just being Michael. You should be used to it by now."

Chapter 19

Samantha Saves

Back in the human world, Jewel was sitting at the base of the Great Oak tree wondering how she could find the evil fairy who'd passed through the portal as she had...the fairy who had stolen the key to the Vault of Souls. She was so deep in thought that she didn't hear Beecher asking her if they were going back through the portal to their world.

It was only when he projected his voice into her perception she heard him ask "Your young highness, Jewel, are you alright? Can you hear me?" Beecher was using his loudest voice, which even in his enhanced human size was still not very loud.

Jewel looked down at him.

Without her speaking a word out loud, Beecher knew they were not going back. Not quite yet, at least.

"So you read my mind, huh, Beecher?"

He nodded.

"I guess you disagree with my thinking then?" She looked into his black shiny eyes.

"Well," said Beecher, "I do agree with your thinking. It appears that you may be the only person from the Fae world who can retrieve the key. It is too important to allow anyone but our King to have it, so Miranda and I will be at your service, to assist you."

Just at that moment a pair of lights appeared in the parking lot. Jewel ducked behind the tree to hide. The fairy birds followed and hid in her skirt. Jewel peered around the rough strips of bark at a large metal box with wheels. It had stopped in the middle of the vacant lot. She heard: "Car," and knew the name for that box. Behind the car's big front window, at the inside wheel, Jewel saw a young girl who looked to be close to her in age. Strange music was coming from the car. The girl's face was ghost white as she sat under the poles with big lights on top of them. Tears were streaming down her face and her nose was red, in contrast to her pale face.

Jewel felt empathy for the young girl without even knowing why she was upset.

As Jewel stood there watching this girl and this car, Miranda flew up to Jewel's ear and whispered a plan she had devised to find the key. Then she flew back into Jewel's pocket and grabbed Beecher's hand.

"That idea was brilliant," thought Jewel. "OK!" she said out loud, "here we go!"

Jewel came out from behind the tree. She walked up to the car and the girl, but the girl was paying no attention. Jewel touched a soft 'tap-tap-tap' on the window. The girl's expression changed from sadness and tears to surprise. Jewel wasn't exactly sure what to do next.

The girl somehow made the window come down about an inch and it made Jewel feel more curious than afraid. "Yes?" she said. "Who are you, and what do you want?"

Jewel took a slow, even breath. She hadn't attempted to speak in this language before and she was nervous about how it would sound. A strange noise came out of Jewel's mouth: "Igg auh hoo at."

The girl's face twisted into an odd expression. "Hey, you're not from around here, are you?"

Jewel shook her head.

"Then what are you doing here, all alone, and at night?"

The words flew into Jewel's brain and mouth! She felt them come in—a strange but great sensation—as she replied, "I don't remember anything. I think I hit my head…or…I don't know, but I am really confused and I can't remember. And, I don't know how I got here. I just…don't…remember anything."

Although it felt great to be in communication with the girl, Jewel's words were stilted and her voice sounded strange. Maybe that's why the girl was being quiet?

Jewel said, "I am so sorry to bother you, but I don't know what to do."

The girl opened the car door and got out. She was about the same height as Jewel. Her hair was short and black. There were pink spikes on the tips, which stood up in various right angles. She had a hoop through her nose and several earrings hanging from her ear. Her clothes were different, too. She was wearing a short skirt that appeared to be made of smooth black animal skin, a black shirt with writing on it and a jacket made of faded blue cloth. Her legs were bare from the skirt to her ankles where pink and white striped socks peeked out over heavy black boots. Her face was pretty except for dark streaks of black on her cheeks.

Jewel wasn't sure about the blackness and wondered if humans cried black tears.

"Hey…," she said, "…I'm so sorry. Were you in an accident or something?"

There was an awkward silence. Jewel didn't know how to answer. An accident? Maybe.

The girl said, "My name is Sam…well actually, Samantha, but all my friends just call me Sam." She wiped the streaks of black off her face using the sleeve of her jacket.

"Ahhhh…ah…a…," said Jewel stuttering a bit, for effect, " I don't… know my…name."

Sam seemed to be thinking about what Jewel just said. Jewel did not know what to do! Then, Sam asked questions without waiting for answers: "Do you remember anything? Do you have a purse? Do you know how you ended up in the parking lot? Did you come from the forest? Who was with you? Do you live in another country? You don't talk like the other people from around here—why?"

Jewel kept shaking her head "no" to all the questions except the last one.

Sam said, "Well, I guess we could call the police and get you some help."

Jewel thought, "What is that awful word? Pul…l…ee…ce?" Then she said, "What's the pul…eee…?" This so sounded like a bad idea! Then the voice came to her and she knew: police, authorities, guards. "Oh! No…no," Jewel said while looking straight at Sam. "I think someone is after me, or…no, something bad will happen if you call the…the… um…guards." Jewel hesitated. She really didn't like the word "police."

Sam just stared right back into Jewel's eyes and didn't say a word because she was thinking Jewel was right.

Sam was no stranger to the local police because she'd been picked up for shoplifting, even though she was innocent. She remembered how the officer took her purse and dumped its contents on the counter. It was humiliating and embarrassing. All her personal stuff was there for all to see: various kinds of makeup, a wadded up Kleenex, a tampon, a picture of a boy she'd drawn a heart around. She cringed at the memory. Sometimes people thought she did bad things because she dressed in clothes that were outside the norm or because her hair was dyed pink. Sam was always getting into trouble even though she never did any of the things people said she did. It made her a bit of an outcast and loner. Her experience made her understand Jewel's discomfort.

———————————

Both Jewel and Sam stood there in the parking lot, not saying a word to one another. Then Sam smiled, and Jewel did too. "I have an idea," Sam said. "Come home with me. I'll tell my mother you're a foreign exchange student. I'll tell her the family you were supposed to stay with had a problem and couldn't take you after you arrived. Hmm. Where should I say you are from? Your accent sounds sort of Irish to me. Yeah, we'll tell my mother you're from Ireland. Does that sound right to you? Oh…oh, and your luggage got lost but we don't know how or why."

Jewel had no idea what Irish was, or Ireland, or luggage, but if Sam thought it was a good idea, she figured she'd go along with it. "Sure," said Jewel. "Now what?"

"Get in the car. I'll take you home and we can try and figure out the rest. It is kind of creepy out here. I just broke up with my loser boyfriend and thought I could cry him out of my system if I took a drive. I always end up out here because no one ever comes to the park after dark."

Jewel went around to the other side of the car and stood there for a moment. "How do I get in to this thing?" she thought.

Just then Sam leaned over and opened the door. "Sorry, she said, that door always sticks and I have to open it from the inside."

Jewel slid into the seat and looked over at the strange dials and knobs inside this box—wait, it was called a car. She'd never seeing anything quite like it.

"The seat belt doesn't work either, so just hold on tight!" Sam was giggling.

Jewel didn't understand the joke, but she smiled anyway.

"You sure are pretty," said Sam. "I bet you're popular back home…I mean with the boys."

Jewel shook her head. "I don't think so, I don't really remember any boys. I would hope that I would at least remember if there was a boy I liked."

Sam giggled again. "Well, we need to make up a story that my mother will believe. Do you remember what grade you are in...in school?"

"School?" thought Jewel. "They have school in this world too, that was interesting, but again Jewel shook her head to say no without saying no.

"Do you know how to drive?"

Jewel knew that answer and said, "No."

"Maybe they don't drive at age sixteen where you come from. I just got my license six months ago when I turned sixteen. You need a car out here in 'Hicksville.'"

"Hicksville? Is that the name of this village?"

Sam burst out laughing. "Wow, either you really hit your head or you are one funny girl!"

Chapter 20

From Transylvania?

—————————

Sam started the car engine and music blasted out…somewhere. It startled Jewel and she jumped in her seat as she heard the word "radio." Sam laughed again. "Don't you like AC/DC?" Sam switched a dial on the radio and the music stopped. "I guess we need a bit of time to talk, anyway," she said. "We need to come up with a name for you."

Jewel was staring out of the car window at this new and different world. In the distance she could see lights from a village. Everything looked different, yet, there was something familiar. Jewel couldn't quite figure out the similarities and it made her feel like she was living through a dream and was not really in this new world.

The car swerved around a corner. Sam looked over at Jewel and got a close-up look at the crown. "Sorry! Hey, what is that headband you're wearing? Wow! That is a crazy, beautiful headband! I've seen crystal ones like that at the mall. Those carts always have cool stuff. I tried on some of their hair clips, but they were way too expensive for me."

Jewel didn't understand anything Sam was talking about. "Mall? What was a mall? What was a cart? What was Sam saying?" Jewel felt a rush of anxiety as she thought, "Maybe this is a bad idea. How am I going to pull off this charade?" She wondered if Beecher and Miranda could hear her thoughts, but felt movement in her pocket and realized they were trying to reassure her that it would be fine. Jewel glanced at Sam who was concentrating on the road. In her head, Jewel said to Mir, "Don't move too much or you will be detected and I sure don't know how to explain you two!"

Sam was humming a melody. Jewel looked at her just as she said, "Name. We need a name and a good story about you so my mom doesn't ask too many questions. If you come from Ireland I guess you should have an Irish name, but to be honest I have no idea what that could be. Here's my phone. Google it while I'm driving." Sam pulled out a small black rectangle and handed it to Jewel who touched it and saw some circles and numbers.

"Oh, wait. You don't know my passcode, and I don't know you well enough yet," Sam said. "Give it back. When we get to a red light I'll do it."

Jewel's mind was working hard. She thought, "Well, what is a red light? I'm going to have to pay attention." They passed by buildings with lights on them, and lights were above the road, too, just like the ones in the place where she first saw the car. Jewel now felt the car slow down and come to a stop. She saw a red light hanging on a string over the road and made the association: a red light means stop. Sam picked up the rectangle and punched at symbols with her thumb; her other hand stayed on the wheel.

Jewel was transfixed by the little black object and thought, "What is it? I've never seen anything like it. What is Google?"

Sam handed the black thing to Jewel and said, "Look at the list Google came up with and pick a name."

Jewel was staring at the writing on the screen. She wasn't exactly sure what it said. The tree had given her knowledge of language but not symbols and Jewel was at a total loss at reading any of the text.

"Don't they have iPhones where you come from?"

"Uh no," said Jewel "I've never seen one before. Maybe my parents didn't let me have one of these things."

"Things? You mean a cell phone? You don't even have a cell phone?"

"I don't remember if I had one. I just feel really weird and I don't remember anything. I don't even know how to read the symbols!"

"Symbols? What symbols?"

Jewel pointed to a road sign as they drove by it.

"Oh my God! You can't read? Well that makes sense if you come from another country, but they read English in Ireland, don't they?"

"I don't know "said Jewel.

"Damn, we need to come up with a place that has a different language if we are going to pull this off! Let's see what ethnicity you most resemble. Hmmm. Your hair could be from anywhere. I can't see your eye color in the car, it's too dark, but you have pale skin...hmmm, I know, we will say you are from Transylvania." Sam laughed.

Jewel didn't laugh.

"Don't you think that's funny? No one will know what the language is or speak it, so we don't have to worry about someone chatting with you and have you be clueless. And it is sort of a cool place to say you are from."

"I guess so," said Jewel.

"Now for a name. What names do you like?"

"I like the name Jewel." Jewel looked at Sam to see how she'd react. Beecher and Mir gave a little bit of a rustle in the pocket. Jewel sent them a thought: "Shhhh!"

Sam tilted her head to one side. "Yeah, kind of unusual. I don't know what sort of names they have in Transylvania, but we can say it's your nickname. What should we say is your last name?" Sam talked about unusual last names of people she knew but Jewel wasn't listening.

Jewel was wondering, "Last name? They have two names here? A first one and a second one?"

Now Sam was talking about a character named Dracula.

"Dracula? Am I supposed to know who that is?" she thought. "This world is going to wear me out."

"Yeah," said Sam, "we could use part of that name like, Dragos. That sounds like it comes from Transylvania. Jewel Dragos. I think that works. What do you think?"

"I guess that works."

"Jewel Dragos, welcome to Winthrop," said Sam.

Jewel looked up to see the lights of the Winthrop village, but as Sam continued to drive she realized that nothing about this place resembled her home. "Home," thought Jewel. "And what about Ember? I hope she's not mad at me!"

Chapter 21

Ember's Interview

She didn't want to attract attention. Ember spent some time sneaking around the entire castle, searching for Jewel, avoiding adults who might ask what she was doing. When the frustration got to be too much, she went to Jewel's room and wrote this note:

> *Hey Jewel...you got me!*
> *I didn't like your joke and I couldn't find you anywhere, so you win. I've given up and am going back to my house before I get into more trouble. Let me know if you have any time to hang out tomorrow. Send Bogart with a note. He likes being your messenger.*
> *~ Ember*

She tucked the note between Jewel's bed sheet and pillow then crept down the stairs and out the back door. As she walked home, she felt lonely—but she was also mad at Jewel.

Ember was sound asleep when her mother came in to rouse her the next morning. She shook her left shoulder and said, "The King and Queen are here to see you, my love. You need to rise to speak with them."

"What? Why are they here to see me? Is something wrong? Did I do something wrong?"

Her mother took her hand. "No, dear, they just need to speak with you. So hurry up and put on your dressing gown. Come to greet them in our front room."

Ember jumped out of bed, threw her robe over her head, shook her arms through the silky sleeves, pulled her hair back into a tiny wooden clip and followed her mother.

The King was pacing. The Queen was standing by the hearth. In her hands was a twisted handkerchief. The Queen said, "Ember, have you seen Jewel? Do you know where she is? When was the last time you saw her?"

Ember saw her father standing in the corner. She looked at him and said, "Ah...uh... well...I saw her yesterday afternoon."

From a pocket in her robe, the Queen pulled the note that Ember had left on Jewel's pillow. "What did you mean by this note?"

"We were together...then she just...ah...disappeared. I assumed she was playing the hiding game with me. I looked for a long time but I never found her."

"Where were you when Jewel disappeared?" asked the King.

Ember hesitated. She didn't want to tell her parents about the secret room in the base of the Great Oak. Her father caught her eye. She could tell he sensed her discomfort. He probably knew she wanted to hold back information.

"Ember, my girl," the King said, "our Jewel did not come to dinner last night nor did she sleep in her chamber. My guards searched, and are still searching the castle but cannot find her. Her pet beetle has been clicking nonstop which has us doubly concerned since that little creature always knows where Jewel is and his distress adds to ours. So if you know something you must tell us now. Please."

Ember kept her eyes on her father as she said, "Yesterday Jewel came to our, well, our secret place so we could talk...."

The King interrupted. "Secret place? What secret place?"

Now she looked into the King's eyes and said, "Your highness, when we were still very young girls, we found a secret door in the base of the Great Oak. It opens to a little chamber. Jewel and I have been going there for years. We never told anyone about it. Anyway, yesterday we met there, and well...ah...I don't know if you are going to believe me or not, but I swear by all that is true that I am telling you exactly what happened!" The words tumbled out of her faster and faster. She was so nervous. She'd spent a lot of time around Jewel's parents with Jewel as a buffer. Talking with them directly, and without their daughter was so strange.

"Please, child, go on," said the Queen.

"Well, we were in our hideaway and I saw something shiny, like a coin, on the ground. I pointed it out to Jewel and she went to pick it up. When she did, she screamed. The next thing I saw was her falling backwards, and a big flash of bright light, and when I could see again…uh…after the smoke cleared, well…she was…ah…gone!"

"Why didn't you come tell me?" her father asked.

"I thought she was playing a joke on me. Then I figured she was playing the hiding game and I never thought she was actually missing. I went to the castle and looked and looked for her. Then I left her the note."

The King, Queen and Thor exchanged glances before they all looked at Ember.

The King said, "Take us to your hiding place right now! I want to see this place!"

Thor scooped his daughter up in his arms and said, "I will fly you to the tree since we are in a hurry!"

With that, all four of them were in the air, Ember clutching her father's neck, fear and worry playing different scenarios in her head about what happened to her friend.

As they neared the Great Oak, Thor said, "Ember, please point to the place where we should land."

"Down there, by the tree root," she said and then watched the group follow. As they landed by the entrance, Ember looked at their worried faces and pressed on the secret spot to allow the door to swing open.

Chapter 22

Sam's Home

―――――――――

Jewel stood on the wooden front porch of Sam's house, waiting while she unlocked the front door. Under the porch light, Jewel could see that it was painted a pretty red color that reminded her of the geraniums Aspen so loved. Jewel's memory of her sister was just a fleeting thought…she was too immersed in this new adventure to worry if her family had missed her.

As Sam fumbled with the lock, the door opened. A woman who looked like an older copy of Samantha said, "I thought that was you, sweetie. Who's your friend?"

"Her name's Jewel. Jewel Dragos."

"Hello, Jewel," said Sam's mother. "It's kind of late. Are you here to stay the night?"

Sam and Jewel stepped into the foyer as Sam explained the situation that Jewel found herself in: The lie regarding the other parents who were unable to host exchange student Jewel from Transylvania at their home. "So yeah, mom, the night…and several more nights. She's going to live with us."

"Sam? Samantha. Ah…excuse us, Jewel. Sam, please come with me into the kitchen. Jewel, if you wait over there, in the living room, Sam will bring you a glass of water, if you'd like."

"Yes, please," said Jewel, but she was worried about what might happen next. Sam's mother seemed nice, but would this lie work? From where she sat on an overstuffed chair, Jewel overheard a little of the conversation going on in the kitchen.

"Sam! You can't just bring home a person like a lost kitten. Who is she? Where'd you find her?"

"She's really nice. I like her. Since you divorced dad, I've been really lonely. Please let her stay here. She can be like my sister. She won't cause any trouble. Really!"

"I want to believe you, but where are her bags?"

"They got lost during her trip. Then the family that was going to take her in told her things had changed, that there was a problem.. She wandered away from the house when she felt she was causing trouble. She didn't know what else to do. I can loan her some of my clothes. Please, mom. Don't worry. It'll be fine. Please!"

Their voices got quieter, then Jewel heard nothing.

After awhile, Sam came around the corner with a glass of water, handed it to Jewel and said, "Come on, I'll show you our room! I told my mother your luggage was lost and that I'd let you borrow some of my clothes."

"Luggage?" tthought Jewel as she followed Sam, "what is luggage and how did it get lost?"

Since Sam was already chattering about something else, Jewel shifted her attention back to what Sam was saying. "...and since you don't have any of your transcripts I'll have to tell the administrator at school that all your luggage got lost, including your paperwork, and we'll have to get you registered without them. I'm a sophomore, so we'll say you are, too."

"What does that mean—sophomore?"

Sam looked at Jewel, bewildered.

"What is a sophomore?" Sam repeated. "Really? Well that means you are in tenth grade and you just have two more years of high school until you go to college, that is, if you want to go to college. I personally don't think you need college anymore, but I know my mother would not like it if I didn't go."

Again, Jewel was lost and didn't understand the majority of what Sam was talking about so she looked around Sam's bedroom. It was painted bright yellow and had pictures of people on the wall. The images of the people on the walls looked real. She didn't know it, but she was seeing photographs for the first time.

Sam noticed Jewel staring at the pictures and asked her if she liked "the band."

"Band?" Jewel started to feel very uncomfortable with this plan that she had agreed to with Mir and Beecher. Just then she felt and heard the voices of her little wards inside her head. They were reassuring her that it would all be fine and not to worry. Jewel was feeling exhausted from the events of the past several hours, and before Sam could talk about whatever band meant, Jewel asked, "Would it be OK if I went to sleep now?"

Sam looked at the clock and was surprised that her new friend wanted to go to sleep at nine thirty in the evening. Sam was a creature of the night, but at the same time she realized that whatever had happened to bring Jewel here, it was probably very traumatic and would tire anyone out. "Sure. My bed has a trundle, so I'll pull it out for you. I keep it made up all the time in case I have a friend stay over, but I haven't actually had anyone I wanted to spend time with recently."

At that moment, Jewel felt sadness overwhelm Sam. Jewel gave her a hug. "I just felt like you needed that," said Jewel.

"Thanks" said Sam. "I guess I did need a hug and I am so glad you lost your memory, got lost in the forest and happened to meet me!" Sam then burst out laughing, so Jewel matched it with laughter of her own.

Sam turned to her dresser and pulled out a big pink t-shirt with tiny green, brown and white stripes. "Here, you can use this as a nightgown."

Jewel took it, turned away from Sam and started to undress but stopped when she heard Sam suck in her breath.

"What?" Jewel asked.

"I have never seen so many tattoos on someone your age!" Sam said. "And they are all so incredibly beautiful! Who did the wing tattoo on your back and the leaves on your legs, and...oh, my...those leaves that wrap around your arm?"

Jewel felt her cheeks start to flush warm and didn't know what to say.

Sam's response was shock. "Are you kidding me? You don't remember *that* either? Wow, if I had those tattoos I would remember how I got them. Your parents must be super cool to have allowed you to get those."

Jewel then noticed her reflection in the mirror over the chest of drawers. She had never seen herself in a long mirror. She stared at her reflection and saw the leaves wrapped around her arms and up her legs and marveled at their beauty. Yes, indeed it looked like a very skilled artist had drawn these vines. Then she turned her back to see her wings, or rather, the tattoo of her wings. The images on her back were a perfect replica of her real wings, but in this world, they were drawn and in only two dimensions. They were brown and green and shaded in a way that made them appear to have depth. She remembered what the tree had told her about passing through to this world, that her fairy powers would shift and change and even her wings would not return until she was back in Dorawine.

"I just love your tattoos!" said Sam again. "They are totally and completely cool, awesome...wow...I am so jealous. I hope you remember where and who did these for you because as soon as I turn eighteen and become an adult I want to meet that tattoo artist!" She laughed again. "Damn, my mother would ground me for life if I got a tattoo!"

Jewel finished putting on the t-shirt to cover herself and then pulled back the sheets to get into bed. She felt Mir and Beecher abandon their hiding place in the pocket of her skirt that she'd left on the bed, and when Sam was looking away, they crawled under the covers to curl around Jewel's legs.

Before she could even say good night to Sam, Jewel fell fast asleep.

Chapter 23

Water Maiden

No one was going to get any sleep any time soon in Ember's world. She and her father were with the King and Queen, hunched over in the small secret room in the base of the Great Oak. After Ember acted out the events of the day before for them, the King said, "This is strange, very strange, Ember. Let's go outside and search the ground for some clues so we can figure out what happed to Jewel."

As they left the room, Ember felt that they hadn't believed her story. She was nervous and light headed. She was breathing fast. Her arms and legs felt numb. She leaned against the tree for support but the Queen rushed over at that moment and gave her a hug. She held her close for what seemed like a very long time. Ember's breathing slowed and she felt better.

"We must station a guard here," said the King. "I want to know if anything else happens in here. You, young lady," he was looking at Ember, "are forbidden to return to this Great Oak space!"

Ember knew that once Jewel did reappear she was going to be furious with her for telling her parents about the hidden room. Oh well; she didn't have a choice. Jewel would just have to forgive her.

Tears were falling down the Queen's face. Her worry was apparent and all were silent as they stood watching her. She looked out over the river and began a soft chant. Then her voice grew into a sound akin to a wolf's howl. The water got choppy and then it swirled and sprayed high into the air.

Ember had heard that the Queen's power involved water, but until that moment it was just a rumor. The water continued to swirl in an upward direction as the Queen's howling increased. Her eyes were closed. Her arms and hands were outstretched as if she was pleading with an unseen entity. The water formed into a large tube and then became the shape of a maiden, with huge wings on her back. The motion stopped, the water froze in midair and the shape of a maiden took on the look of a real fairy, but completely transparent.

There was a sound coming from her mouth that Ember tried to recognize. It was similar to the way water sounds as it ripples over a series of stones, only it seemed to be music, too. At first Ember wasn't even sure she could trust either her eyes or her hearing, because the whole scene seemed surreal.

The Queen stopped chanting as soon as the water maiden spoke. "My Queen you have summoned me from my slumber. To what circumstances do you call me forth?

The Queen's mouth was moving, but Ember didn't hear any words come from her lips. The water maiden on the other hand, seemed to be reacting to her and her story even though Ember heard just the noise of the music-water as well as the water sounds from the river itself.

Boom!

Everyone was startled. What? A clap of thunder in a cloudless sky? A tree falling?

The sound came from nowhere, but it opened up some kind of new energy because all those who were present heard the maiden say, "Your majesty, I will summon all the creatures in my keep to find word of your daughter!" Then, the body of the maiden fell back into the river with a splash and disappeared.

Ember and the others were speechless. Then she thought, "I wonder if Jewel's new power made her disappear?"

Just as Ember was about to mention that to Jewel's parents, the sound of a horn was heard coming from the direction of the castle. It sounded like a warning.

The King grabbed Ember and took off with her, flying in the sky. Ember looked back to see the surprise on her own father's face as all the others leaped up to follow and fly to the castle.

Chapter 24

School Day

_____

Another warning, one in the Earth world, was being sounded in Sam's bedroom—her alarm clock went off at six in the morning. It was one of those funny clocks that had an electronic voice that says, "Wake up!" with different speech accents. It doesn't shut off until a button on the back is pushed in. Sam's mother had gotten her the clock to lighten her morning mood because Sam was always sluggish when it was time to wake up and get out of bed. Sam was grouchy every morning—the clock didn't help.

The clock woke Jewel to another new thing. She sat straight up in bed as soon as she heard "Vake Upp!"

"What was that? Where am I?"

Samantha stirred. In a croaky voice she said, "That means it's morning."

In addition to the croak, Jewel heard a rough edge in Sam's voice. She rubbed her eyes and looked around. The events of the night before came flooding back to her. "Good morning then," said Jewel.

"Ah...ummmmm," Sam replied. Jewel watched while Sam bunched up her linens, crawled over the end of the trundle mattress, got out of bed and stumbled into the bathroom. As soon as Sam closed the door, Mir and Beecher appeared from under the covers.

"Good morning to you, your highness! We slept well last night and feel refreshed," said Beecher.

Mir was standing next to him. Her feathers were sticking straight up on her head, bent in strange angles. Beecher looked at her and laughed. Mir did not seem very pleased with his reaction as she smoothed her feathers back into place. As she did so, she said, "We'll hide in your clothes once you get dressed, Jewel, so make sure you wear something with large pockets. Otherwise we'll have to be under your skirt."

Jewel frowned and wondered if she could wear the same skirt as she'd worn the day before or if Sam would make her wear something else. She got out of bed to pick up the skirt with pockets that had fallen to the floor. The blouse she'd worn with it was nowhere in sight. Jewel looked around Sam's room for it while Mir and Beecher settled back under the covers.

The door to the bathroom opened. Sam came out with wet hair. She was wrapped in a towel. "Your turn" she said "You better get in there and enjoy the hot water while it lasts."

Again, Jewel was uncertain of the words Sam used. She went into the bathroom. The room was hot and humid. Jewel saw a curtain and looked inside the curtain to see what was behind it.

Sam came into the bathroom behind her and noticed Jewel's hesitation. "I'll show you how to run the hot water since it's probably also a new concept for you." She turned the knobs and pulled a lever. Warm water sprayed like a waterfall. "Here's a fresh towel. Soap, shampoo and conditioner are over there in the corner. I'll lay some clothes out for you to look at and decide what you want to wear. You best take off your headband or it may get ruined in the shower. The hair dryer is under my sink if you want to use it, but I wouldn't. Your hair is so long and thick it will take a lot of time to dry. We may be here all morning and miss the first half of our classes."

Sam smiled at Jewel then left the bathroom and closed the door.

Jewel noticed the mirror over the sink and was staring at her reflection. She looked different than in the mica mirrors at home; this kind of mirror gave her a bright, clear focus. Mica wasn't as clear as this mirror, so to see herself as others did was a surprise. Her pupils were ringed with a new brown circle and her face looked older to her than she'd imagined it did. She looked at her image until the mirror got cloudy.

Everything was so different, and Jewel was fascinated by it. Then she thought about Ember and heard a small voice in her head that said to not worry. When she realized that there was a waterfall behind the curtain, Jewel's attention shifted to it.

She'd only taken baths in her world.

Jewel took off the t-shirt she had slept in and looked at the vine of leaves wrapped around her body and longed to be back in her own room. She pushed the shower curtain aside and got into the warm spray of water and let it block out her thoughts as she washed her hair with a strange liquid called shampoo and washed her body with lavender scented soap. She didn't understand anything about the hair-drying machine Sam told her about, so she did her best to towel dry her hair. Then she put the t-shirt back on.

Sam was dressed, again all in black, when Jewel came out of the bathroom. On Jewel's bed was a stack of clothing, piled on top of her skirt. On top of the heap were two interesting stringed items that also had triangles made out of fabric. Jewel had never seen anything like them.

"I didn't know your bra size, so I figured you could try one of mine, even though I noticed you weren't wearing one when you put on the t-shirt last night. My mother said that if you don't wear a bra, by the time you get to be her age, your boobs get saggy. Since I've seen her boobs, I'm going to wear a bra for the rest of my life!"

Sam laughed while Jewel thought, "Boobs?" and figured out what "bra" meant.

Sam helped Jewel try on her clothes after she'd figured out how to put on the bra and put her legs through the little cloth thing with leg holes Sam called a "bikini." She settled on what Sam called "yoga pants," a "tank top" and a large hooded sweatshirt with big pockets.

"You are so beautiful," said Sam. "All the boys at school will be drooling when they see you. We better get down to breakfast before Attila the Hun starts screaming from below for us to get our fannies to the table."

"Attila the...?" Jewel asked.

"My mother," Sam said.

"Your mother's name is Attila?"

Sam laughed. "Are you from another planet or what? I'm amazed at how you don't seem to understand me! You're like one of those Amish girls I've read about."

Jewel stared at Sam as she talked.

"Whatever. Let's go down for breakfast." Sam walked out of the bedroom and Jewel followed several steps behind. She gathered Mir and Beecher and stuck them in the pockets of the sweatshirt.

Sam's mother had made waffles with strawberries and whipped cream. The girls sat at a small table in the sunny kitchen. As Sam watched Jewel eat breakfast, it struck her as odd to see her expression, as she tasted the food. It was as if she'd never had waffles before. Jewel ate two waffles and asked if she could have two more, for later. Her mother wrapped them up and Jewel stuck them in a pocket.

Then, Sam's mother said she'd drive them to school.

Sam explained one more thing that Jewel did not seem to understand: "Mom wont let me take my car because there isn't any parking on campus for sophomores. Next year I get to drive and I can't wait. It is so embarrassing to have your mother drop you off at school! I almost wish I could take the bus, but then again it would pick me up way too early and interrupt my beauty sleep."

Jewel was quiet. She thought it best to just listen to Sam, especially in the presence of the Attila the Hun mother.

"Come on, let's get our stuff and get in the car. I'll loan you a backpack. I have an old one, but it'll work for now."

After the car stopped and Sam's mother told them goodbye, Sam said, "Follow me and I'll take you to the administration office to get your schedule. Let's get them to put you in my classes since you don't know anyone and it would be better if I was with you to help you. Your command of English is limited. Remember, we said you'd be from Transylvania!"

Jewel followed her new friend into the building. It was a huge structure with red stones cut into rectangles and stacked on top of each other. Jewel had never seen a building built in such a fashion. The place was filled with young people of all sizes and colors. It was overwhelming and Jewel felt her heart quicken with anxiety. As always, Mir and Beecher touched her thoughts and calmed her down.

While Sam talked to a woman with white hair and kind blue eyes about Jewel being new to the school, Jewel studied the woman's face. Curly white hair framed her wrinkled face. Jewel guessed she must be over 200 years old. Only the oldest fairies had lines on their faces and white hair so she assumed the same in this world. It meant to Jewel that this woman commanded respect and consideration, so she remained quiet and shy even while Sam was making up the story about Jewel's identity.

The woman turned to Jewel and said, "My name is Mrs. Wilson. I'll fill out your temporary student paperwork, but you'll need to find your luggage and bring me the official papers as well as the permission forms from your parents. Here's your locker assignment and combination lock with the code. Sam, please show her the ropes. I don't want you to feel uncomfortable in our school and I am sure we won't have any problems from you, so I'm going to put you in all of Sam's classes. I am going to give you the rulebook and I expect you to read it and sign it and have it back to me in the next few days. If you have any questions, please come see me."

Mrs. Wilson handed Jewel a stack of papers with her schedule on top. "Sam, I wrote out a pass for both of you since you are now late for first period. You better run along before you miss it entirely. Good luck to you Jewel, and know you can always come to me with questions or concerns. Welcome to Bowmount High."

Sam took Jewel by the arm, walked her to the locker, opened it and said," We'll pick up your books and get you to your own locker later. For now you can share my books," she said.

The two girls entered another building and went into a classroom. Jewel noticed how the entire group of students went silent when they entered. The teacher said, "Hi Sam. You're late. Do you have a pass for me? And…who is this young lady with you?"

"Hi Mr. Schumacher. Sorry. Uh…here's a pass for both of us. This is Jewel. She is a foreign exchange student from Transylvania."

The students laughed.

Mr. Schumacher held up his hand as if to get them to settle down. "Welcome to Bowmount High, Jewel, and welcome to my class, American history. Please take your seats."

Jewel was so nervous, but as she followed Sam back to the chairs in the far end of the room, she saw lots of maps lining the walls. She also looked at the other students. They were very different looking than her friends back home, and even from Sam. She couldn't quite put her finger on what made them look so different, but she felt like a stranger in a very strange land.

As she sat down, she noticed a boy in the chair next to hers. They looked into one another's eyes at the same time and Jewel felt her heart skip a beat. He had the most handsome face she had ever seen. His hair was as black as coal and his eyes were the color of the sky after a storm. His nose was straight and his high cheekbones were chiseled like a stone sculpture. He flashed her a wide smile, showing brilliant white teeth. When he smiled, he looked a bit goofy to Jewel at that moment and he seemed to be almost oblivious to Jewel's reaction to him; like he had been hit by lightening.

He then coughed into his hand and turned his head away.

Jewel looked around and realized everyone in the classroom was looking at her.

Including Mr. Schumacher.

Mr. Schumacher cleared his throat, looked over the other students' heads and said, "Please settle down and show some respect for your teacher because, you know, I'm brilliant!" The students laughed and he continued, "Now, where were we?"

———————————

The time spent in American history class ended when a loud bell sound startled Jewel. As they got up to leave, Sam grabbed her arm and said, "Next is English class with Mrs. White. She's the strictest, craziest teacher in this place, so be careful what you say or do when we're in there. Just keep following me."

Jewel rushed to keep up with Sam as they shuffled their way through the throngs of students. Beecher and Mir stirred in the pockets of her sweatshirt. She knew they could tell that she was having problems keeping up with Sam...and everything.

The next classroom Sam took Jewel into was like being inside of a box. It was painted beige, had no windows and, other than a picture of an old man with a beard and a funny looking collar, there were no other pictures on the walls like there were in the history classroom.

A woman stood next to the one picture. "That's her, that's Mrs. White," said Sam.

Mrs. White was large and very tall. Jewel had never seen anyone quite so tall and round. Her head was round, her body was round and her arms looked like large winter squashes sticking out from her dark green short-sleeved blouse. Her legs looked like tree trunks because she was wearing brown pants. Her hair was an unnatural shade of red and she had water droplets on her face, sweat, even though the room was cool. Some of the droplets were gathering and running down the sides of her face. There were places where droplets had been absorbed on the collar of her shirt, making it wet and darker green. Jewel felt movement in her pocket and sensed Mir and Beecher also being uncomfortable.

Jewel saw Mrs. White sneer as she said, "So...Sam...who did you bring with you today?"

Sam simply said, "Jewel," as she walked to the back of the room.

Jewel stopped and stood looking at Mrs. White.

Mrs. White looked at Jewel. Then she said, "I understand you are from Transylvania and your ability to understand English is limited. Yes?"

"Yes."

The teacher looked at her for another moment. She raised her hand and gave it a shake that Jewel learned was a sign of dismissal. "Go sit down," she said.

Jewel hurried to the back of the room to sit near Sam. As she did, she passed that boy again. This time he was looking down at his shoes. Jewel wished he'd been looking at her because he was the most handsome boy she'd seen so far in this new world.

Now Mrs. White was speaking fast. Jewel was lost until the teacher wrote words on the big green board and asked the class to take notes. It was something about an assignment...a term project, due...and three weeks.

Jewel looked at Sam who gave her a thumbs-up sign, and mouthed the words

"Don't worry."

So, for the rest of the class, Jewel wondered about the boy. He spent most of the time looking at his shoes. She watched him look at his shoes when she herself wasn't looking at his shoes. Jewel was startled again when the bell rang and she looked at Sam before she got out of her seat at the desk.

"Math's next." When Jewel did not respond, Sam said, "You know...numbers!"

After the math class, Jewel followed Sam to a class called biology.

Each class to Jewel was the same. She couldn't understand all the words or the ideas and did her best to concentrate. She was so focused on attempting to understand everything that she was mentally exhausted.

After the bell rang in biology, Sam said it was the lunch period. "Come this way to the cafeteria. I always sit at the table in the back."

She gave Jewel money and said to follow her to the food line. As Jewel approached the stainless steel counter, Sam handed her a tray and the smell of strange food assaulted her nose.

Sam laughed when she saw Jewel's face. "I bring my own lunch," said Sam while holding up a brown paper bag. "The food is truly heinous but I figured I would let you try it first. We can make you lunch at home if you want."

Jewel looked at the oozing brown liquid and lumps of what? Vegetables? "Sam, do I have to eat this? Your mother let me wrap the extra waffles and I put them in the backpack you gave me. I'm going to eat those instead!"

"Oh, sure. I forgot. Give me back that money." Sam put out her hand. Jewel gave back the piece of paper and two coins. Then she followed Sam to a back corner of the room and spotted the boy. He was sharing a table with a bunch of other boys. Jewel slowed her steps then stopped in front of the table where he was sitting.

She had not seen the other boys in any of her classes. They stopped talking.

Jewel felt her cheeks burn and willed her feet to move. She could hear other students nearby making comments about her, but she was too embarrassed to try and understand the words.

She looked for Sam and found her waving her arms. Jewel's feet moved again and she went to sit with Sam.

"They think you are hot," said Sam, "I've been hearing it since you got here. Why did you stop at that table?"

"Hot?" Jewel said as she set her tray on the table and pushed up the sleeves of her sweatshirt.

"No! Not temperature hot, you funny girl! Hot as in beautiful!"

Jewel was thinking that she'd never had anyone tell her she was beautiful before now and it came as a surprise. "Thanks," she said. "Do you really think so?"

"Yes! You even got Ethan's attention."

"Who is Ethan?"

"The guy you stopped in front of! The one who is soooo good lookin'! Ha! Jewel, you are so funny!"

"Oh." Jewel was feeling the heat in her cheeks again. She thought it was an odd sensation. She removed the two waffles from the ragged backpack, peeled back the napkin and took several bites—as if eating a sandwich.

"We have swimming in P.E. after lunch so you may not want to eat all of those waffles. I would hate for you to lose your lunch in the pool." Sam was giggling again.

"Swimming? I don't exactly know how to swim. And...in my clothes?"

"I'll tell Ms. Jensen that you're new and you've lost your luggage. I'm sure she'll give you an extra bathing suit."

Jewel looked over at the table with the boys...and the one named Ethan. She'd never felt anything like the feelings she was having for this boy...nervous and jumpy. She wanted to look at him all afternoon, to find out if he had a smell, to know if he had a muscular body. Those thoughts made her cheeks burn red and she wondered, for a split second, if Mir and Beecher were listening. Why this boy? Why here in this parallel world? She hadn't met one boy in her whole village that made her heart race like Ethan did. And it was from the first moment she saw him...with those turquoise blue eyes. He looked amazing. No, hot...well, beautiful.

Chapter 25

School Pool

After lunch, Jewel followed Sam into a room past a sign that read: Girls' Locker Room. While she waited for Sam to ask the teacher for a bathing suit she could use, it seemed to Jewel that the entire sophomore class of girls were in this big room with an interesting, mossy smell. They were taking off their clothes and putting on small stretchy pieces of fabric—like skins—to go into the water. Some of the girls were already wearing the black piece of cloth with a small skirt attached. Jewel felt uncomfortable without Sam and in the midst of all these strangers.

Sam came back, handed Jewel a black skin, then undressed. "Hey, you might want to put on a t-shirt over your bathing suit. Lots of us do," Sam said. "Do you want me to find one for you?"

"Yes, please!"

Jewel was unaccustomed to changing in front of anyone and she wasn't quite sure what to do. Now Sam was already in her bathing suit and said she was looking for an extra t-shirt. Jewel was still dressed and standing fully clothed in the locker room with the black skin in her hand.

"Is there a problem with the suit?" Sam asked.

"Ah, no, I just feel odd changing clothes in front of all these people."

Sam nodded. "Just go into the bathroom stall. Change in there. Here's a t-shirt for you."

Jewel felt a bit silly about her sense of modesty, but she couldn't figure out what to do with Mir and Beecher. She went into the stall and locked the door.

Mir and Beecher popped their heads out of each side of her jacket. "A bit warm and stuffy in there," said Mir. Her feathers were bent in strange positions again. She licked her hand-like claw and smoothed them.

Jewel marveled at how amazing these little creatures were and their distinctly unusual personalities. She whispered, "I can't hide you anywhere when I am in my swimsuit!"

"No worries," said Beecher, "we can take care of ourselves and we will be here in your sweater waiting for you when you decide to change back into your other clothes."

So Jewel changed into her bathing suit and put the t-shirt over it to make sure her wing drawings were hidden. She left her clothes in the stall and headed out to the pool but stopped to look at herself in the mirror in the bathroom. The leaves, or what Sam called a "tattoo," ran up her legs and arms. They were beautiful and delicate. The green of the leaves matched the flecks of green in her eyes. Her body was that of an adult woman, well toned and curvy. She marveled at how much larger she was in this body, in this world.

When Jewel opened the door into the pool area, both the bright lights and sun from the big skylight blinded her. The deck was white and made the whole area glow so much that she had to close her eyes for several seconds. When she opened them, she saw a huge pool. It was larger than any of the swimming places at the river in Dorawine. Dozens of her classmates—both boys and girls—were staring at her from where they stood in the pool, with water up to their waists.

Even the boys were wearing full-length suits—but theirs were red—that covered their chests—and they had shorts attached, instead of a skirt. Some of the boys were also wearing t-shirts like the girls. It was a strange sight! No one was speaking. She looked around until she spotted Sam amongst the crowd. Jewel stepped down into the water, just to the third step.

Sam waded over and pulled Jewel's arm down so they could both sit on the steps. Sam turned in close to Jewel and whispered: "They want to know about your tattoos. They're amazed you were allowed to get them and wonder if your parents are cool." Before Jewel could answer, Sam said. "Don't mind the boys—they shouldn't have us swim together, but they do. All our other sports are separate. It's crazy."

Jewel was thoughtful and when she spoke to Sam, it was in a whisper. "I have a feeling my mother was OK with these tattoos. Just a feeling," she said, "but I think I would remember if my own mother hated these markings!" She stuck out her arms and the leaves were shimmering in the sunlight. "I don't know how to swim. At least I don't think I do. I think I hate the water, but I just don't remember. I'm sorry, Sam."

Sam looked at her for a few seconds as if she was wondering what to do for Jewel. "I'll go tell Ms. Jensen and see what she says. Maybe she'll let you just hang out here in the shallow end while we take our turns swimming laps. But I warn you…you'll have to do the water aerobics first. Just stay near the steps and follow along. You'll be fine."

Sam stood up and walked out of the pool then vanished from Jewel's sight. Jewel looked around at the students. They were looking at her. She was uncomfortable. Some of the girls were whispering but the boys were talking out loud about her and one of them was pointing to a spot over her head. She wished Sam would hurry.

When Sam got back she said, "Ms. Jensen says that you can sit on the side of the pool and she will have someone help you learn how to swim."

"But I don't want to swim!" She was conscious of another problem that going in the water would cause. Her back, covered by the t-shirt now, would be partially exposed in the pool. She knew if her leaf pattern tattoos were causing a stir with the girls, then her wing tattoos would be a bigger curiosity.

"Don't worry," said Sam, "I am sure Ms. Jensen will not make you do the exercises or swim right now. Come on and sit on the edge and keep your legs in the water. You can watch us all flounder around. Get it? Flounder? You know…the fish?"

Jewel looked at her with a blank expression.

"You don't know what a flounder is, do you?"

"No."

"Geez, I sure would like to know your story, Jewel. You are either from another world or…."

Jewel noticed that she was struggling to find words.

"…or really sheltered by your parents—even though they let you get awesome tattoos!"

Jewel rose from the steps, went over to the side of the pool and sat down on the edge of the deck while dangling her legs in the water. Her nose twitched as she noticed another strange odor. She wasn't quite sure what it was, but she didn't like it. Her nose kept twitching and she thought she might sneeze.

Sam swam over to her and said under her breath, "You OK? Ah, maybe it's the chlorine. They put a ton of it in the water in case one of these idiots pees in the pool."

Jewel was jolted by the way Sam seemed to read her mind like Mir and Beecher, but she was repulsed by what Sam said. "Eeh! People pee in the water?"

"Well, not me, but one never knows." Sam turned and kicked her legs in the water like a fishtail, causing a huge splash to hit Jewel in the face. Sam surfaced with a rather sheepish smile and then dove under the water and swam towards the opposite end.

"Jewel?" said a lady in a white tunic with a towel around her shoulders. "Jewel? Which one is Jewel?"

Jewel saw this teacher standing in front of the crowd calling her name. She was skinny as a beanstalk, but her muscles looked well toned and strong. She had a shock of white hair that ran down the center of her scalp, surrounded by black cropped hair. Her lips were large, and very red. She had deep set eyes and although her face looked sharp, her manner seemed gentle.

"Yes? I'm Jewel," she said while raising her arm.

Ms. Jensen looked at her for a moment, assessing her like she was a fat goose at the market. Then came the nerves again and Jewel felt shaky while she waited to hear what this teacher was going to say.

"Jewel, I understand that you are a new student and don't know how to swim. I'm going to pair you up with one of the boys—he's a good teacher. His name is Ethan and he can give you some basics. I'll give him extra credit for today since he'll miss doing laps." She turned and pointed to the group of boys. "Ethan! You're going to give this new student some basic swim lessons today. No laps. Come on over here."

There was movement and laughter among the boys while Jewel watched Ethan wading toward the edge of the pool. He grabbed the deck edge and hoisted himself out of the water. He was also wearing a t-shirt. Jewel's nervous energy put her heart into flutters and she was now staring into his eyes again. "Oh my!" she thought, "Ethan!"

Ethan allowed her a bit of a smile while Ms. Jensen said, "Ethan, this new girl, Jewel, needs you to meet her at her level and do your best to work with her. I'm going to give you extra credit for your assistance today. Let me know if problems arise."

"OK, Ms. Jensen. Sure," said Ethan before he turned to Jewel and said, "Hey."

"Hey" she said back.

Ethan looked at his feet.

There was an awkward silence until Jewel said, "So are you going to help me learn how to swim?"

Without missing a beat, Ethan grabbed her hand, slid off the deck and pulled her into the water. "Let's go," he said.

"I really don't want to swim," Jewel said, then asked, "Do we have to?"

Ethan looked at her for a second. "Nope."

"Whew…good!" said Jewel, "I really don't like the water much and I don't want to be here."

"I can discuss some of the basics with you today, but at some point you'll have to swim. Ms. Jensen will make sure of it. Let's go sit on the steps," he said as he turned and walked toward them.

He sat down on the first, shallowest step; Jewel followed his lead and sat next to him. "So where do you come from?" he asked.

"That has nothing to do with the basics of swimming," Jewel said. She didn't want to talk about who she was or where she came from — she just wanted to sit and stare at this handsome boy and pray she didn't embarrass herself.

"Oh, true. Well, you have some wicked cool tattoos."

"Thanks. I think," said Jewel.

"The gang will be talking about those for awhile." He smiled at Jewel and flashed his big white teeth. "So if you don't want to tell me who you are, at least make it look like I'm teaching you how to swim."

Jewel thought for a moment then said, "Oh, I'm not so interesting. Why don't you tell me something about you?"

Ethan looked at her with piercing blue eyes and smiled. "What do you want to know?"

"Everything!"

"Well…" said Ethan, "…I grew up in this small town. I live two streets away from school. I live with my mother. My parents never married. My mom works at the local library and my father, well lets just say he is a major douche bag and I don't really talk to him. I guess that sort of sums up me. Your turn."

Jewel didn't know what to say. She didn't know what a douche bag was, but it didn't sound good. She couldn't come up with any details of her pretend life that would be convincing, because she still was totally lost in this world. Nothing made sense to her and she barely understood the language. She decided to do her best, after too long a pause. "There's not much to tell. My parents thought it would be a good idea for me to experience a new country so they sent me here as an exchange student. I've been rather protected by my parents."

"Protected? Do you mean sheltered?"

"Yeah," said Jewel, "sheltered. So mostly everything is new for me. I feel stupid most of the time, because I don't understand everything that is said or even the sounds I hear around me. On the way here, I got lost and so did my...ah...luggage. Sam found me and I'm living with her."

"Don't worry," said Ethan, "most of the time the nonsense that comes out of people's mouths isn't worth listening to!" He pointed to a gaggle of girls sitting on the opposite side of the pool who were watching Ethan and Jewel while waiting their turn to swim laps.

"So...why did you pick the leaves for your tattoos? Do you have any others?"

Jewel looked down at her legs and arms and again admired the leaves that wrapped their way up and around her body.

"They match your hair thingy," Ethan said while pointing to her crown, which was still in place on her head.

"Yeah, they do. I found this 'thingy' at the mall. It totally matches, right? She remembered when Sam had said the word 'mall' and it seemed to fit into their discussion.

Ethan looked at her headband of leaves then at her arms and nodded. "Crazy! The leaves are beautiful. The artist was really skilled." As Ethan said this, he seemed to get lost in thought. There was a moment when the conversation stopped and Jewel only heard the noises of splashing water and murmuring students.

Then Ethan turned and looked down at her legs and arms. To Jewel's surprise he picked up her hand and turned her arm so he could admire the detail of the leaves.

When he touched her hand she felt a slight tingle of energy run up her arm. She thought Ethan felt the same thing because he looked up at her in surprise. Jewel's heart was beating so hard she thought he was going to see it moving under her bathing suit. She had never felt this way before and it was both wonderful and frightening at the same time. Jewel didn't want the pool class to end. She just wanted to stare into his eyes for the rest of the day.

From somewhere, a wind stirred and was felt by Jewel. She looked up and saw fans swirling overhead that brought her the smell of his skin. It was like inhaling the smell of laundered clothes after they had hung on the outside line drying in the sunshine.

Now Ethan let her hand go and smiled at her. "So, how long are you actually going to be here? I mean will you be here for the entire school year?"

Before Jewel could answer his question, the P.E. teacher blew her whistle. Some kids got out of the water, others got in and the teacher looked at both Ethan and Jewel.

"Uh, move your arms like this," Ethan said as he swung his arms in a wave-like way. "She has to think I'm helping you!"

"OK," Jewel replied while imitating his movements. The new set of swimmers were taking Ms. Jensen's attention now and Jewel took advantage of it to stop moving her hands. "What else do you think I need to know about swimming?"

"That class is going to end soon and we should get out and sit on the side until she blows that whistle again." Ethan got up and reached his out for Jewel to follow him out of the shallow water and up the steps. The odd tingling in her hand returned and she felt her cheeks grow warm from another blush.

"Hey, if you need any help with your homework, let me know. I mean, well, since we have a bunch of classes together, I could probably give you some help. Do you have a phone? I can text you my number."

"No. No phone, I mean. My parents never let me have one."

Ethan looked surprised. He asked if she knew Sam's phone number and then said, "If you know it, I can write down my number and you can ask Sam to text me so I have a way to text you."

Jewel told him she's get Sam's number after they'd changed.

He told her to meet him on the other side of the locker rooms.

They sat together for a few more minutes while Ethan pointed out what the other swimmers were doing. When Ms. Jensen blew her whistle, Ethan got up and vanished into a group of students going into the boys' locker room.

Jewel was giddy when Sam found her after the class, still sitting on the deck. "So, some swim lesson from Ethan, huh?"

Chapter 26

King's Library

At the castle, the King sat at his desk, high up in the tallest tower. He pushed his chair in and out…not knowing whether to get up and go or to stay seated. He was anxious.

The guards had discovered another dead watchman.

He'd retreated to the top of the tower to clear his head, but it wasn't working. This room was his quiet place to think, read, figure out problems, or, to relax. It was a large circular room surrounded by shelves filled with books of all sizes with different colored bindings and unusual titles. It was his personal library and it held all the most important books in the Kingdom of Dorawine. The walls were thirty feet high and attached to a rail above the shelves was a long ladder. The ladder moved along the bookshelves so any book could be retrieved. Of course the King didn't need the ladder; he could fly. The ladder was installed for children in the royal families so they could explore the books. The room was one of the most difficult places in the castle to get to—it required those without wings to go on a long walk up all the stairs. None of the kingdom's "enemies" could fly; the King and Kings before him figured that if they were ever attacked, at least it would take someone a long time to find him or his family members if they were this room.

The books represented hundreds of years of the clan's knowledge and storytelling; they held most of the Fae's treasured secrets. Because of the books, the room had a distinct smell; it was of clean, sea-washed sand, dust, old paper and bark from Cedar trees. The smell brought up old memories for the King, and these memories comforted him.

He remembered the first time his own father had taken him to the library when he was about ten years old. His father flew to the room but left him at the bottom of the stairs because he believed it was good for the boy to work to get up to the place where such great knowledge was stored. His father had laughed after giving him the instruction to climb the long stairway—a distinctive, gentle laugh with a deep vibration that still rang in his memory. Climbing the stairs was what the child king was meant to do, and the King's father was made to do the same thing when he'd been a child.

When the child king got to the top of the stairs he found a note pinned to the door:

"Hello Son! I got hungry and left for lunch. Will you meet me here again tomorrow?" Upset that he'd climbed all that way for nothing, yet curious about the room, the boy opened the door and found his father to be still there—they both laughed over the joke. Now the adult King chuckled to himself at the memory.

It was the first lighthearted thought the King had in days, but he put it aside as he went back to thinking about his woes. The key to the Vault of Souls was gone. His daughter Jewel was missing, two of his guards had been murdered, and his people were on edge and worried. He was also worried because they had not found any further clues to the disappearance of Jewel or the key. He knew the answers had to be there, whether or not he could figure out where the trail of clues was leading. He went over the facts of the guards' deaths and Jewel's disappearance again.

Nothing made sense.

How could both disappear without a trace? "Without a trace," he said out loud. "That idea is bothersome. I wonder if there are any answers in these books?" He looked at the books…and a thought came to him. "Sixth shelf? Hmmmm…I remember father talking about a book, a history book about this place. I wonder…."

Where was it? He flew up to the sixth shelf and scanned the books in that row. He had almost circled the entire room until he spotted it. Its cover was made of birch bark and it was held together with long strands of willow reeds. He reached for the book and opened it at random, knowing the answer was inside.

Chapter 27

Written Destiny?

After the first week of school that Jewel experienced, Sam's mother purchased a new, sturdy backpack for her—one with enough pouches and pockets so she could carry her books and Beecher and Mir with ease. Jewel had made it through her first week of school and it hadn't been easy. She figured she'd only absorbed about half of what was said by teachers and students. Each night Jewel and Sam talked about each class as they worked their way through the homework assignments. Jewel still couldn't spell many of the words that were new to her, so Sam was constantly helping. Jewel was relived that Sam didn't seem to mind. It actually seemed to give her a bigger purpose and she did it willingly and with great amount of understanding and patience. "Sam?" Jewel asked after she'd finished an essay, "do you think you'll be a teacher someday?"

"I don't know," Sam replied. "But this is fun...working with you. Maybe."

Jewel really liked Sam.

Sam really liked Jewel.

They had become very close in a short time, after unusual circumstances.

Every once in a while, Jewel thought about Ember and her family. She wondered about going back through the tree's portal to let them know she was still alive. Whenever she looked at the bracelet Ember had made for her, a pang of loneliness hit her and she felt her eyes sting. She wanted to tell Ember about what she'd learned about another person who had come through the tree. "But no," she said to herself, "if I go back, father would never let me return to this world. He would say it was way too dangerous." She knew she was meant to be here since she was the only fairy bonded to the trees. "As long as I know I'm fine, my family and Ember will be fine. I have to stay here and find the key."

Still, she was worried about Ember, and she missed her. Jewel knew that Ember would also like Sam, and they would all be the best of friends if they were together. Jewel hoped Ember wasn't going crazy with worry. Maybe she should try and get a message to her… but how?

_____

On the Friday of the second week of being at school, Jewel was pleased to see Sam's happiness because there would be no school on Saturday or Sunday. Sam's world of Earth was different than Jewel's world of Fae, but many of their patterns were the same. In the Fae world, Jewel went to school and also had time off every fifth day, but of course the days of the week in that world were called different names. So many other things were different too, but each world had a similar tempo and cycle: eat, sleep, chores, school.

Now after school on Friday evening, Jewel was sitting in Sam's room alone. Sam was helping her mother prepare dinner. Jewel opened her backpack to find Mir and Beecher curled up together, sleeping. "Mir…Beecher…please, will you wake up? I want to send a note to Ember so she's not worried about me."

Mir and Beecher stretched and looked at her like she was speaking gibberish.

"How in the world do you think you can do that?" asked Mir.

"Maybe I could just go through the tree and leave it for her in our secret place…then come back here. I could explain what was going on and that I'll return as soon as I find the key."

Beecher and Mir whispered to each other.

Jewel got annoyed and said, "Wait a minute you two! No secrets!" but they continued to speak in hushed tones until Beecher turned to face her. He stared at her for a few seconds.

"We don't know if that is a good idea right now," he said. "What if someone tries to find the portal, goes through and dies in the process? Remember? The tree told you that only you had the true ability to pass through and we would have died if we had not been in your clothes when you passed through the energy field of the portal."

Jewel stopped to think. "True," she said, "but I just know my parents and everyone must be sick with worry. They probably think I'm dead."

Mir and Beecher nodded in agreement. Mir said, "Jewel, we'll get through this together. You cannot get a message to Ember now, but we trust that everything we don't know now will soon be known. Just keep going on your way. You're doing a good job." Then they returned to the backpack.

———————

Only Jewel had discovered the parallel world that was written about in the ancient scrolls. Up until this very moment in time, those stories were just myths, kept in old books. Now myth had met reality. Two Universes existed and were connected by just a few things—namely the two creatures and Jewel.

Mir and Beecher had been discussing that fact together from the first moment they had landed in this new world in the pocket of Jewel's skirt. They didn't believe Jewel understood the significance to this adventure. Everything their world held sacred was about to be put upside down. Two worlds meant that the creators were in fact real and the stories of judgment day must also be real. Maybe this whole adventure was preordained for Jewel?

The couple believed that their own destinies were already written. They knew this journey would reshape both worlds and there was a purpose to the events that had transpired...and that would continue.

Chapter 28

Ember's Walk

———————

In her world of the Fae, Ember sat alone on the floor in her room one afternoon before dinner. She was supposed to be doing homework. But she wasn't. Her worry about Jewel had peaked. Of course, Ember knew that her parents were worried too, and, the royal family was beyond worried. For what felt like the millionth time, Ember replayed in her mind the events of the afternoon when Jewel disappeared.

What had happened?

It seemed surreal.

How could Jewel have vanished? What could have happened to her? One minute she was there and then the next gone! Amongst all the chaos, the one thing that never seemed to have been found was the shiny object Jewel had been bending down to get. Did Jewel actually pick something up? Or did she disappear before the object was recovered?

"Hmmm," Ember said to herself, "maybe I should go back to our secret place, which is obviously no longer secret, and look for the shiny object. Maybe it's the clue to Jewel's disappearance."

Ember got up from the floor and looked out of the window in her bedroom. Clouds were gathering on the horizon. "It's going to be a beautiful sunset," Ember thought, "and it would be nice to go for a walk...watch the sky change its colors when I'm on the way to our secret meeting place."

Then she remembered how her father, Thor, and the King had given her strict instructions not to return to the room in the tree. She put on her shoes anyway and left her bedroom and house.

The path was smooth and although Ember felt like running, she slowed her steps when she thought about how worried her father would be if she didn't return home on time. No one yet knew how Jewel had disappeared, and Ember felt he was also worried something would happen to her.

Other than that, Ember didn't stop to think about the consequences that might be in store for her when she got to the Great Oak. She felt that she'd be fine—and that Jewel was probably off on some adventure. Ember quickened her pace again. Now she could see the tree ahead and it made her think again about that shiny object. "What was it? I just have to find out," she said to herself.

A few feet from the tree, Ember was stopped in her tracks when a guard stepped out of some bushes. "Where are you going, young lady?"

"Just out for a walk, sir."

"You're outside the territory where you should be. Please turn and go back."

Em curtsied, turned on her heel and walked back.

In her mind she was devising yet another plan to make it back to the secret spot without being noticed.

Chapter 29

Friday Night

Yes, Jewel was indeed having an adventure at the school in the world on the other side of the Fae kingdom. Like Sam, she was thrilled that the school week had come to an end. All the work and concentration had been an exhausting experience and she wanted some time to be alone and rest. She was thinking this thought when Sam came into the bedroom, chattering about clothing.

"Jewel, you need to get some clothes of your own."

"I can tell you don't like my skirt! Thanks for letting me borrow your clothes. I'm grateful, and I don't mind wearing them again and again. Where would I get new clothes?"

Sam looked at Jewel in the way where her eyes went up and down. Then she walked into her closet. "School is one thing," she said, "but we've been invited to a party next week. You need different clothes for that. My mother gave me some money for you to go buy some clothes. She feels bad for you that your luggage got lost. She still believes our story!"

"My luggage got lost?"

Sam laughed and said, "No. Your luggage didn't get lost. We don't even know if you had luggage! Really? You can't remember? Anyway, my mother says I should take you shopping. We have to go to the mall and find you some clothes."

"That was really nice of your mother. I have no gold to give her in payment," Jewel said. She felt a bit guilty that she was hiding her true identity from Sam and wondered if she should confide in her and tell her the truth. She decided to talk to Mir and Beecher about the situation and ask them what they thought.

Sam stepped out of the closet holding several hangers with shirts on them and looked at Jewel. Her face showed that she was puzzled. "Gold? Is that how you pay for stuff in your country?"

"Yes."

"Don't worry about it now," said Sam, "we'll figure something out. Your memory will come back one day soon and then we can unwrap this whole mystery."

Jewel felt like Sam was holding something back. She wanted to ask but she let the question go. "So when can we go buy some clothes for me?"

"Let's go after breakfast tomorrow because the mall doesn't open until ten anyway." Sam took a big pile of clothes that were sitting on the floor, picked it up and shoved it back into her closet. She closed the door. Bits of arms and legs of clothing items were sticking out of the door. Sam turned around and smiled at Jewel.

Jewel pointed to the closet and laughed. "So, we'll go to the mall tomorrow?"

"Yep. Another new experience for you, right? I wish I knew more about your real story. Maybe I should listen to see if you talk in your sleep!"

"If I talk in my sleep and you hear it, will you tell me what I say?"

"You're funny, Jewel! Of course I will. Maybe it's a good thing we're staying in on Friday night. By next week, you'll have things to wear to a party."

Jewel yawned. She was exhausted. "I'm ready to go," she said.

"Not yet! The party is next weekend!"

"Oh. Not to a party," said Jewel, "to sleep. I'm feeling so tired."

"OK, then, I'll turn out the lamp and leave you be. I'm going to go watch TV for a while. Good night, Jewel. Sweet dreams!"

When Sam left the room and closed the door, Jewel felt the room was dark as a dense forest in the dead of winter at midnight...under a new moon.

Chapter 30

Michael's Dream

Michael awoke from a strange and frightening dream. His sheets were wet with sweat, his head felt fuzzy and he had a strange tingling sensation in his back, below the skin that held the tattoo of his wings. He knew that the feeling meant something was about to happen. It didn't happen often, but when it did, he paid attention.

He thought back to the morning of his human sixteenth birthday when the tattoo had appeared on his back. He'd been asleep under an open window and just before the sun crested over the horizon, he'd woken to feel as if a searing hot needle was drawing a picture on his back side, penetrating his skin and making it bleed. Somehow, he knew to keep the pain to himself.

When he saw the tattoo for the first time in his bathroom mirror, he knew he would need to hide it from his parents and other people in this world, even though it was a fascinating image. Michael tried to sort out what his connection was to this world, the one he'd come from, and how one affected the other. This was his first sign of his crossover, a sign that had come to him through intuition. And his intuition led him to believe there would be other episodes like this in his Earth life.

At that time, Michael was still trying to discover how he had gotten into this world but when the tattoo came in, it made more sense to him. The tattoo had awakened his intuition even more.

What had happened in the dream still wasn't exactly clear; it was like smoke dispersing from a room. He could make out the room but it wasn't in focus. He shook his head, trying to make the dream sharper in his mind. It didn't work.

Michael decided to lay still and let bits of the dream come back to him. There was a beautiful young girl. She was a fairy, but she existed in the human world. She didn't have wings, but he knew she was a fairy. She was standing at some distance, her long hair flowing around her body. He smelled the scent of pine all around her, like she was standing on a bed of fresh pine needles. He thought at that moment in the dream that she had been born from the tree.

In the dream, she'd reached out to him and he remembered that her arms became tree branches and her legs, roots. They grabbed him and wrapped around him until he was encased in the tree's limbs. Then each limb and branch squeezed him, and squeezed more, him until he couldn't breathe. He was begging her to let go of him but she looked into his eyes and blood dripped down her face, like tears. He screamed at her to let go, but the branches kept doubling and each breath became more difficult until he wakened, gasping and sweating.

He felt uneasy now. What did this dream mean and why did it affect him so much? His wing tattoo was tingling again and he knew something was in the wind. He wasn't sure what, and if it was a good thing.

Michael got out of bed and dressed himself in a black cotton t-shirt and some dark blue pants. Then he went to work.

Chapter 31

The Mall

—————————

As Sam parked the car, Jewel noticed a red banner with yellow letters hanging from the side of one of the buildings that were all strung together like the boxes Jewel and Tomwyn had used to create pretend villages with when they were at play in the Fae realm. She read out loud: "S. A. L. E. Five. O. Funny symbol. Off?" Jewel said. "What does that mean?"

"Looks like we'll find some bargains today. A 50 percent off sale is a good thing. Follow me," said Sam as she got out of the car.

As Jewel followed Sam into the mall, she realized that never before had she been in this kind of environment. It was so far out from any of her experiences in the Fae world. She felt like she was walking through a dream. Each store was jammed with clothes and shoes and all sorts of things she'd never seen before. "Sam, you know, they do not have places like this where I'm from. Can we go into each of these different rooms?"

"Rooms! Ha! That wasn't really my plan, but sure. Remember, we're here to buy you some clothes. Let's start with underwear. Let's go to my favorite store here. It's called Ohm's."

"Ohm's?"

"Yeah. They sell bras, thongs, panties, camisoles, slips, garters… do you even know what I mean?"

"No, but let's go there so I can see."

When they walked into Ohm's, Jewel saw symbols that looked like Ω and they were everywhere. Then she saw bins of small pieces of clothing, like the triangle shaped ones Sam owned. Sam guided her to pick out a selection of them and asked a saleswoman to fit Jewel for the right size bra. Jewel wondered about being fitted for a bra—she'd only been fitted for a gown with holes in the back for her wings before. As Sam told her to do, Jewel followed a woman to the fitting room, and then, the woman asked Jewel to remove her shirt.

Mir and Beecher rustled in the pocket of her skirt. Jewel felt trapped. She unbuttoned the top button of her shirt while looking into the mirror. She saw the reflection of the woman's face behind her.

"Just trust this," she heard Mir say—but the sound came from inside her head. She kept unbuttoning; slow…one button at a time. When she slipped out of her shirt, the woman gasped.

"My God! I've never seen tattoos like that on a girl as young as you!"

"Mmmm," said Jewel. "Do you like them?"

"Well…yes. I'm just shocked. Here, let me measure you." The woman reached around Jewel's chest with a yellow ribbon that had numbers on it. Then she did it again, in a different place.

Jewel felt as uncomfortable as she felt curious. In the Fae realm, all garments had built in seams to fit the curve of any fairy's body. How funny it was that humans needed separate items for this purpose. The woman held up a strip of cloth with two cup-shaped triangles and said, "Try this one. Put your arms through and I'll fasten it in the back."

It felt very strange. Jewel stared at her image.

"It seems to fit you well," said the woman. "Do you like it?"

"I guess so…."

"I'll leave you with a few others. These are the same size as that one, but these two won't fit you very well so I'll take them back. I see you have some matching bikinis—if you try those, put them on over your regular underwear, please. Let me know if you need any more help."

"Will you please tell my friend to come in here?"

"Sure," said the woman as she opened the door to leave.

By the time Sam entered the fitting room, Jewel had also put on a pair of bikini underwear that matched the bra. They felt as strange as the bra, and, she was wearing them over the ones Sam had given her, which also felt odd.

"Looking good," Sam said, "but how do they feel?"

"Strange. Very strange. But I'll get used to them, I'm sure," said Jewel.

———

By the time the two girls got to the center of the mall, Jewel and Sam were carrying four bags each. Sam said, "I can't shop any more! We've been here for over three hours and I can't take it anymore. Let's grab a bite and go home because I am so tired I may sleep through this entire weekend."

"Fine," said Jewel. By this time, she had managed to buy a basic wardrobe consisting of underwear, skirts, pants, tops and a jacket—in colors of green, brown, blue, white and black. Every outfit had at least one huge pocket for Mir and Beecher. She also bought a big leather purse with two separate pockets on the inside, one for each creature.

After they'd eaten salads and enjoyed cups of frozen yogurt for dessert at a place Sam called "the food court," again Sam said that she really, really wanted to go home. Jewel asked if they could please visit a few more stores. Her fascination with the mall was strange to Sam, but she agreed to spend a little more time.

Two shops later, and a new pair of shoes for Jewel, Sam said, "Now. We are going home now!"

Once they were home, Sam went straight into the bathroom. "I'm going to color my hair," she said. "It could take awhile."

Jewel unpacked her new clothes, admiring each item before she put them away. Then she stretched out on her bed and fell into a short nap.

She woke when Mir and Beecher popped out of Jewel's pocket and tugged on her earlobe. "We have been having some troubling dreams, Jewel," said Beecher. "This is not unusual for us because we are very empathic and many things come to us in dreams, but they are dreams that appear to be warnings of trouble ahead and we are concerned for your safety."

Jewel felt tingling in her body and all the hair on her arms went straight up. That feeling had happened to her only once before—it was during a school day on her way to a class with Sam. They'd just passed a group of students and Jewel felt they'd been talking about her—or Sam—and it felt very odd. Jewel showed Sam the bumps on her skin. Sam called them "goose bumps" which was a rather odd description in Jewel's estimation. In the Fae world there were geese-like creatures, but they never had bumps (at least not ones you could see) since they were covered with feathers.

"Jewel, dear," Mir said, "we know you have a strong attraction to that boy named Ethan, and we just have to tell you that we both feel that there is something very troubling about him." Mir looked at Beecher for support.

Beecher put his arm around Mir and added, "Well, we sense something different about this boy and now with the dreams that seem to be warning us of doom, we feel you need to be very cautious around him."

Jewel was upset to hear this since her infatuation with Ethan had been escalating and she'd been thinking about him nonstop. "I hope you're wrong."

"We do too!" Both Mir and Beecher said it aloud at the same time.

"I was thinking that maybe I should tell Sam the truth, you know about me, about us and where we came from. What do you think?"

Before either of them could answer the door to the bathroom opened and Sam walked out, wrapped in a robe and shaking out her glossy wet hair. "Hey Jewel, did you say something to me? I thought I heard your voice."

Mir and Beecher disappeared back into the cloth bag and Jewel shook her head. "Ah no, I was sort of singing to that song you made me listen to by Gag..gog, ah, uh. Lady."

"Ha! You mean Lady Gaga."

"Yes," said Jewel "that one. The one who sings, 'I was born this way. Hey, I was born this way.'"

"I like you, Jewel, but you are just so...strange," Sam said as she sat down on her bed, and picked up her phone. "Looks like there's a party tonight, too, but I don't want to go. We'll stay home and do homework." She reached down and grabbed the math book off the top of a stack of books at her feet, then threw it on top of the stack of Jewel's new undies.

Jewel looked puzzled.

"Or we could wash your new undies. Your choice. But we're not going out tonight."

Chapter 32

"The Vanishings"

———————

Still in his tower, the King opened a large book. He handled it with care because it was very old. He remembered when his father told him that many secrets, myths, spells and legends were kept in this book and that it was almost as old as their clan. Written by fairies that were the healers and truth speakers of their time, it was a rare volume that only came off the shelf when necessary. The King turned the pages one by one, looking for answers to the questions of Jewel's disappearance and the deaths of his guards.

He'd been sitting for hours and was almost through the book when he came across a chapter titled "The Vanishings." His eyes skimmed down the page, but he read the words with care since their meanings were not always clear.

Much of the writing in the book was presented like riddles; codes for issues that were meant to remain secrets. Yet some of the writing seemed pure whimsy. The chapter on vanishings was difficult to understand. There was one paragraph that puzzled the King and he knew it had some bearing on the current situation with Jewel.

That paragraph read:

> 'Tis a dark and dangerous thing to leave the holes in a place they cannot be seen. Nigh a comfort to us all to know whence they come and go or even watch us fly. Be wary of these portals because they will kill those who tarry close or fall to the place below. Many a fairy has talked of these doors, but none of us who remain here, save one, found the entrance to the place beyond. She was most ancient, blind of sight but not of sense

*and knew the magic spot, for the wind did pass through the
door and brush her face from time to time.*

The paragraph ended without much more information and the
King read it over several times. He didn't know anything about the
"most ancient" fairy who knew the secret, but he knew he was now
going to have to find out. Maybe Jewel fell through some sort of hole
or door, but where did the doors lead? They had searched the entire
earthen room of the tree and nothing was found.

He looked around at his library filled with books and knew the
answer was somewhere in this room...but where?

And where, oh where, was his Jewel?

Chapter 33

Jewel + Ethan

———————

On Sunday night after enjoying a barbeque dinner Sam's mom made—something called a hamburger—Jewel realized that the weekend had come to an end. She was excited to go back to school... and was looking forward to seeing Ethan again. After their time at the pool on her first day, he'd made an effort to see her at lunch each day that week. Sam kept telling her that he was interested in her. Since he was the hottest catch in school Sam said she should be flattered. And, as far as Sam knew, Ethan had never dated any other girl at school.

———————

Jewel's third week of school started much like the first two. The biggest difference was that Ethan became her constant companion. He waited for her to arrive with Samantha in the morning and walked with her to class. He always sat next to her and Jewel caught him looking at her at random times. The more time they spent together the more natural their interactions became.

In Jewel's eyes, Ethan was funny and engaging. He made her feel calm and safe. When he brushed against her or touched her in any way, the tingle she first felt when he touched her hand was still there. She wondered if it was like a current that passed between them, and if he felt it too.

In the few times that Ethan introduced Jewel and Sam to some of his friends, Jewel noticed that Sam seemed to be interested in a boy named Harry. He was a bit of a misfit, but he seemed to be a match for Sam in many ways—such as in dress and attitude. Jewel liked him but thought he was a bit odd because of Ethan's influence on her. Ethan said Harry was a nerd, super smart, and a bit awkward around the ladies.

Jewel thought he didn't look very awkward when he was with Sam.

———————————

Late in the week when they were all at lunch, Jewel noticed that Sam was sitting next to Harry and she seemed quite happy to be talking with him.

After lunch while on their way to class Jewel asked her, "What were you and Harry talking about? You seemed happy."

"Oh. Our favorite books. We share a passion for Tolkien's writing and especially *Lord of the Rings*." Then Sam lowered her voice to a whisper and continued, "I like him. A lot."

———————————

Late in the day on Friday when they were at their lockers, Ethan offered to drive Jewel home.

"I'll have to ask Sam," Jewel said, "I'll go get her. Wait here."

Her heart was behaving like a butterfly in a strong wind.

She found Sam, explained the situation and brought her over to where Ethan was waiting. "Ethan, Sam. Make a plan."

"Why don't you take Jewel, Ethan, and I'll drive Harry?" Sam said. "Let's meet at that new coffee shop—the one by the post office—what's it called? Oh yeah, Lux."

It was at Lux where Ethan introduced Jewel to coffee, his small, thin computer and YouTube. The first time Jewel had seen Sam's laptop computer, she was as mystified as Sam was that Jewel was not aware of personal computing. Sam had explained the basics about the contraption, but to Jewel it was like some miracle machine. Ethan's machine looked different than Sam's—it was thin and didn't have an alphabet board. Ethan said he loved to watch funny videos, so he showed Jewel some moving pictures of dogs and cats doing silly things. Jewel laughed more than anyone else. She wondered if that coffee drink she liked the taste of had something in it that made her giggle so much.

———————————

By Jewel's third week in school, Ethan was spending a lot of time with her. Mir and Beecher hadn't said anything more about him and she was glad. Ethan was kind to Jewel. He carried her books. He opened doors for her. He told her how beautiful she looked.

And Jewel was getting lost in the relationship with him. She remembered her mission to look for the key, but she didn't want to miss any time with Ethan. Her attraction to him was like a magic spell. She couldn't stop thinking about him.

At night, when she was alone with Sam in their bedroom, the girls talked about how relationships worked. Sam told Jewel everything she knew. She even showed her things on the internet from the human world that Jewel never expected to see in her lifetime.

In the world of the Fae, sexual intimacy and coupling only occurs after two fairies join in a bonding ritual as life mates. Jewel saw that sex in this Earth world happens all the time! Sam made a point of showing Jewel all the videos she needed to see to fully understand every aspect of sex: foreplay, kissing, flirting, contraception, and even…diseases!

Jewel was shocked. She told Sam that diseases are unheard of in the Fae realm.

Sam insisted it was important for a woman to know her way around having a close and intimate relationship. "My mom told me some of this stuff," Sam said, "but I learned more from the internet."

"Oh Sam. This is so unusual for me," Jewel said. She felt breathless. The difference between the worlds was too much to take in all at once.

"You'll have to relax, Jewel. Didn't your mother tell you any of this?"

"No, no! She did not." Jewel was thinking not about her mother but of Ember. How—and when?—could she tell Ember about what Sam had just told her? "I'm going to have to think about this, Sam. Really…where I've come from is a place quite different than here. I wish I could tell you more, but I can't. If Ethan wants to kiss me… what will I do?"

"Kiss him back," said Sam, "but only if you really want to."

———————

By the end of Jewel's third week in school, Ethan asked Jewel to go with him to the party at Jake's house on Saturday night.

Chapter 34

The Party

_____

The party at Jake's was an issue for Jewel. When Sam saw how nervous Jewel was, she'd decided that they'd go to the party together.

Jewel and Sam arrived at the party in Sam's car.

When they drove up to the house, Jewel noticed that Jake's house was much bigger than Sam's and the furnishings were very fine. Beautiful paintings were on the walls, rugs were woven with beautiful designs, furniture was carved from elegant woods and the house had a feeling of grandeur. Kids from school were all over the house with red cups in their hands, laughing and talking. Music was coming from the center of the house and smoke drifted from one room to the other. Jewel turned to Sam and asked, "What's that smell?"

"Cigarettes!"

"What's a cigarette?"

"Wait. Don't tell me there are no cigarettes in Transylvania!" She laughed. "Sorry, it is just so freaking weird that you don't know anything. It's like you come from a different planet. Cigarettes are paper tubes filled with tobacco or marijuana that people light and then inhale the smoke. Marijuana makes you high and hungry. Tobacco makes your lungs turn black and gross and eventually, cigarettes kill you."

"Really? Then why do people smoke?"

"I guess cause they are stupid or think it makes them look all grown up and stuff, but they cost a fortune and they stink. Never mind the smoke, just don't try it yourself. It'll make you crazy or be sick. Come on, Jewel, let's find the kitchen. Harry might be near the snacks."

They walked into the large kitchen. There was a table at the end of the room with a big bowl full of pale yellow liquid that people were using to fill their red cups. The table had other bowls filled with food: orange worm-like things that appeared to be dried, cooked slices of potatoes that Sam called chips, creamy green goop that people were dipping chips in, small colored discs of candy filled with chocolate, and finally food that Jewel recognized and liked: pizza.

Jewel looked out of a window in the kitchen and saw Ethan, dressed in a t-shirt and shorts, standing outside by what looked like a pond. It wasn't the same as the pool at school that was long and rectangular. This one had curves like a natural body of water; it had rocks along the side and a waterfall that cascaded into the main pool. Lights were on inside the pool, and they illuminated the ripples made by several people in the water. Jewel saw that Ethan had jumped into the pool so she walked outdoors and approached the pool. She felt a surge of nervous energy.

He saw her as soon as she spotted him. He was chatting with a group of kids Jewel had never met, but they all looked up at her when she walked out to the deck. Ethan excused himself from the crowd, got out of the water, grabbed a towel to put around his shoulders and walked over to her. "Hi Jewel. I've been waiting for you."

Jewel was pleased he'd said that and she mumbled some sort of reply. She could feel her stomach doing flips and her palms felt hot. She was sure her face was the color of a beet. With that thought, she felt Mir's words enter her head: "You are just nervous around him because you like him. Don't worry. Be yourself!" Jewel felt the awkward tension start to melt away as she stood next to Ethan. He was saying something about how she still didn't know how to swim as he picked up an unfolded towel from a stack on a small table. It was dry.

Before she could respond, Ethan took her hand and pulled her over to some furniture set around the pool. He chose a chaise lounge that was off to the side, mostly in shadows. They sat down and Jewel shivered when a cool breeze brushed her arms. Ethan noticed she was cold, opened the towel and wrapped it and his arms around her. His arms were strong and muscled. She smelled the scent of his skin and it made her head spin. The tingling current from his touch felt like a constant vibration now that enveloped her.

That sensation prevented her from paying too much attention to how Ethan was now telling her how much he loved science and wanted to study medicine although he also liked business. "My father is in business," he said. Then he stopped talking and turned away from Jewel.

She sensed that something wasn't quite right with his relationship with his father, but she also remembered that Sam said his parents in this world did not always mate for life. In the Fae world, Jewel was supposed to marry a royal from another clan and be with him for life, but her parents had not yet discussed it with her since they felt she was too young. Her mother used to say, "All in good time." Jewel wondered what her mother would say if she could see her sitting with Ethan by this pool, at this party, in this other world.

Jewel couldn't even imagine marriage, but now, looking into Ethan's eyes, all her ideas of everything changed. Ethan made her heart leap because he was so attentive to her. They sat and talked for most of the party.

Towards the end of the night Sam and Harry came over and joined them. It was almost midnight when Sam realized she was due home because of her curfew and she excused herself to give Jewel an opportunity to say good night to Ethan alone.

Ethan looked at Jewel and said, "I've had the most fun talking to you and I don't want the evening to be over yet. Can I stop over at Sam's tomorrow and see you?"

Jewel nodded her head. Then he leaned in and gave her a quick kiss on the lips. His lips were soft and warm and his breath smelled like fresh mint. She felt her stomach lurch and her heart keeping beat with some far off, imagined music.

Then he said to her, "I really like you Jewel. I mean I have never met such an unusual girl like you before and I think I could get lost in those beautiful brown and green eyes of yours. They look like they have rings around the pupils—I've never seen anything like them before. They enhance your amazing face."

Jewel didn't know what to say, but she felt amazing when she was with him. She was looking into his eyes when splashing and yelling sounds caught their attention. Boys and girls were pushing each other into the pool.

Ethan got up to escort Jewel into the house when a big guy came over and grabbed Ethan from behind in a bear hug and lifted him off the ground. Ethan shouted, his arms and legs were moving in all directions. "Buck! Put me down right now!" Ethan roared.

The boy behind him was laughing and said "OK, but I'm not letting you go until you cool down!" Then he threw Ethan and his towel in the pool. The splash he made hit Jewel. Ethan came up out of the water looking really upset until he spotted Jewel standing by the edge. The front of her clothes were wet, her hair had water dripping down her face and she was blushing. Ethan laughed and the entire group of students around the pool also laughed.

"Way to go, Buck!" someone shouted.

Sam came rushing to Jewel's aid with a towel. Ethan hoisted himself out of the pool, his shorts, t-shirt, towel and hair were dripping, but his well-defined body had Jewel transfixed. He was so handsome.

"You OK?" he asked.

"Yes….my hair…."

"Yeah, I get that," he said as he shook his head and droplets went flying. "Here's more!" He backed away from Jewel, took off his t-shirt and squeezed water out of it and the towel then put the wet towel back around his shoulders.

"We've got to go," said Sam, "or I'll be grounded for life and you probably will be too, Jewel!"

Jewel handed Ethan the dry towel before he walked the girls out through the house to Sam's car. Jewel didn't notice that as they passed, but everyone in the crowd got quiet.

Sam climbed into her car and started the engine. Ethan opened the door for Jewel and leaned over for another kiss on her lips. "See you tomorrow," he said and turned his back to walk away.

He was still carrying Jewel's towel, but he'd removed the wet one from his shoulders and held it in the other hand with his wet t-shirt. Jewel watched as he passed under the light from the porch. What she saw made her heart stop in her chest. She was looking at the skin on his back and saw the outline of a tattoo. But not any tattoo. No, this tattoo was of two large wings. The same type of wings she had on her back.

"Oh!" she whispered, "oh oh oh oh oh…!" as Sam gunned the car's engine. Jewel's thoughts went straight to Ember. She wondered what kind of conversation they'd have…poor Sam had no idea what was going on, and Ember would understand everything!

Chapter 35

Ember, Disguised

———————————

It had been several days since Ember made up her mind to go back to their secret place to find the shiny object, but it took awhile to figure out how to escape without being caught by a guard.

She'd decided to put on a cloak, powder her hair, put on a bonnet and make up her face like an old woman, then walk to the site. She grabbed a basket, a tea towel and a cane. Surely no guard would stop a grandmother figure. Ember practiced walking with a cane in order to act the part.

As she put on her costume, Ember kept thinking that the object Jewel went to pick up before she disappeared had to be a clue, and Ember planned to do anything she needed to do in order to find it. Walking slow could help with her powers of observation. Still, she knew the site was guarded by the King's men, and that they had been given instructions to not allow anyone to enter the earthen room, but that still didn't stop her. She believed that the costume gave her a unique power, and she started out on her way.

As Ember approached the door, she saw Phan—a young guard not much older than her. She recalled when she'd see him at school, before he joined the guard. He was always nice to her, but she figured it was because of her father.

As she approached him, he looked at her—and she looked at him. He was tall and well built for a young fairy. His wings were the color of the sunset, golden red with streaks of purple. His hair was also red and his eyes were the color of the grasslands, which made his glance appear more certain. He always looked rather serious to Ember, but she didn't really know him well.

Her father frowned on her interacting with any of the guards. In fact, she wasn't allowed to speak with any of the young men for worry that they only wanted to get close to her to be closer to the commander, her father. Phan straightened his stance as she approached him. He acknowledged her with the standard formal greeting of bowing just slightly and lightly hitting his chest with his fist. He said, "Where are you going, grandmother?"

"I need to go find my packet of needles..." she hesitated, whispered, "...I was sitting under this tree several weeks ago and lost my precious needles. You know I sew for the King and his family. I must be permitted to look around so I can find them." She didn't think he would give her a hard time about looking for the objects she claimed were lost.

Phan looked at her with a blank expression. "I can't let you pass," he said.

"Well, I know what your orders are, but I must find my tools. You are welcome to come with me, son."

He seemed to be thinking. Ember could see he was unsure of what to do.

"It's not really a problem," she said. "I will only be around here for a minute, and as I said, you can accompany me."

With that he stepped aside and allowed her to pass. Ember bent down and was opening the door as he touched her arm and said: "What? You're not supposed to know about the secret chamber! I am going in there with you and if I get into any trouble for letting you in here, I am going to tell my commander that you threatened me."

She was surprised by his comment and she cast her eyes on her feet. "Really? You would lie and get me, an innocent granny, in trouble if we get caught?" When she looked up at him, she could see his manner was a bit more relaxed and that he was smiling at her. Ember felt a tingle run through her entire body.

Phan was handsome, and she felt an attraction to him that was new and exciting. She felt herself blush just a bit. She pushed the door open and he scrambled in after her. The ground was all turned up from the dozens of guards who'd investigated after Jewel went missing. The room smelled of the earth and it was such a sweet smell that Ember felt a moment of hope.

"What are you looking for? Needles? A packet of needles?" Phan asked.

"Well...I sort of lied to you when I said I left something in here," said Ember as she took off her bonnet and cloak, threw down her cane and basket and shook out her hair.

"Ember? What? Ember!" Phan recognized her and he was shocked. "Oh no! Not you! Your father will kill me!"

"I guess I should apologize for that, but I want to find the shiny object Jewel bent down to pick up just before she disappeared. I think it may be a clue to her disappearance."

Phan was sweating. He looked so uncomfortable. "If they find me in here with you, I know I will be in for quite a lashing, so you better be quick! I cannot get caught," he said, "do you understand? I cannot get caught!"

His face was stern. He was very angry.

Then he winked at her, which surprised Ember and made her smile. She was getting lost looking in his beautiful green eyes and wishing they were in a totally different place and not looking for clues to Jewel's disappearance.

"Where do you think Jewel could be?" he asked. "I've thought a lot about her disappearance. It's been days now...."

Phan's comment about Jewel broke her reverie and Ember dropped to her knees and pushed around the earth with her hands, in the spot where she last saw the object.

Phan said, "There have been so many guards in here, I don't know if you'll find anything. Everyone has looked through this room a hundred times trying to find a clue to Jewel's disappearance."

She ignored his comment and kept pushing dirt into big piles. Phan watched for another minute, then he got down next to her and sifted through the earth. Ember looked at him and smiled.

She felt certain that something special had transpired between them.

Chapter 36

Blackout Revelation

As Sam drove onto the street from the driveway, she saw that something appeared to be wrong with Jewel. "Hey...what's... are you OK?" Sam was worried. Jewel was slumped over. "Did you faint? Jewel. JEWEL!" Sam pushed on Jewel with one hand.

Jewel sat up with a jolt and looked around. She felt a stir in her pocket and heard Mir's voice in her head. "You fainted Jewel! You saw the wing tattoo on Ethan. We saw it too and felt your blood rush to your head. You blacked out for a few seconds but we are still here in the human world, so compose yourself."

"Jewel? Jewel! Are you OK? You're scaring me!"

"I'm OK. I think," said Jewel looking into the face of her new friend. "I think I forgot to eat. I got dizzy. It happens to me sometimes when I forget to eat. Well, I've had it happen a few times....ah....well, I'm fine now."

"I'm just relived you're OK. You scared the crap out of me when you keeled over. Do you want to get some food before we go home? I'll just tell my mom we're late because you fainted," said Sam.

"No. We can just go home. I'm fine. Let's not be late."

Then Sam said, "Jewel? Did you see the tattoo of wings on Ethan's back? He always wears a t-shirt and tonight he took it off because he got wet. I've never seen him without a shirt. It looks like you guys went to the same tattoo artist but I know that is probably impossible. That's crazy that you'd have the same tattoo. Something is weird about that, you know. I mean...really...weird. Jewel, you have something to tell me, and you're not telling me. Why?"

Jewel wasn't sure what to do or say. A long silence enveloped them as a rush of images flew through Jewel's mind. Then Mir and Beecher whispered in her thoughts.

"It's time for you to tell Sam," said Mir. "We trust her and we both think it is important for you to divulge the truth."

Jewel was relived to hear this advice. She had wanted to tell Sam, but she was never sure how or when to do it. By now, she realized that she loved the friendship they shared and hoped it would last after she got a chance to tell Sam the whole truth.

"OK," said Jewel, out loud.

"OK? OK, then, what?"

"Sam, I just said OK to my companions. They are telling me it is now time I tell you the truth about who I am and where I'm from." Jewel looked over at Sam. Her face had gone blank. She slowed the car to a stop against a curb and looked at Jewel as her doubt surfaced.

"I'm driving this car, and now you are going to tell me that you know who you are? Wait a minute. We're almost home. I don't want to get in a crash." She stepped on the gas and drove the car back into the street.

"Yes, I do know who I am," said Jewel, "but it's a crazy tale and I wasn't so sure you would have believed me when we first met. Now after these past few weeks, I know I can trust you wholly and completely, and hopefully, after you know the truth you will not think of me as some crazy, insane person."

Jewel watched as Sam's fingers clenched the wheel as she turned onto a familiar street. Two blocks and they'd be in Sam's driveway where she could park the car.

"You know I've been suspicious, Jewel, but I do care about you and want to know why you are so...so...well, very, very different from anyone else I've ever met in my life. All right, hold on, I'm turning in. We're here," said Sam as another strange expression passed over her face. She parked, took the keys out of the ignition and smiled at Jewel.

"OK!" Sam shouted. I'm ready! Tell me everything!"

Before Jewel could say one word, the porch light went on and Sam's mom came out of the front door in her robe.

"We're home safe, mom!" Sam yelled out the car window. "You can go to bed now...we're going to stay out here and talk about the party for a few more minutes!"

Sam's mom walked to the driver's side window. "OK," she said, "but give me your keys. And when you come in, be sure and lock the door and turn off the lamp."

Chapter 37

The Find

Phan stood up and brushed off his pants with dirty hands, making his uniform look even worse. "I can't do this anymore, Ember," he said. "My uniform is a mess. How am I going to explain why my uniform is dirty?"

Ember was past her elbows in a hole she'd dug. "I don't know... it doesn't matter! I think I just found something!" Ember pulled the object out of the hole. It was encased in moist black earth but there was a shine of silver. She brushed it off with the hem of her skirt and they both looked at the item. Ember asked, "What is it?"

"I don't know. Let me hold it so I can examine it."

Ember brushed off more dirt and handed the object to Phan. It was a half circle on the bottom, but on top it came to a point, like it was a triangle that had merged with a circle. There were small markings, or maybe symbols, inscribed on the object. It wasn't very big, but it was heavy and made from some sort of shiny metal. "I don't think it's made of silver," he said. "And look! Here's a button. Should I push it?"

"Yes, for sure," said Ember.

Phan looked at her before he pushed the button. A sharp blade shot out of the tip of the object and startled him. Phan dropped it. "Look at that!" he said, picking up the object again. "It's a knife, but one I have never seen before. And what is this stuff on it?" The knife had reddish brown dirt crusted around it. Something had been mixed in with the dirt. He smelled it and said, "There's blood in this dirt, too. Maybe it is Jewel's blood from when she picked it up. It looks like a lot of blood, so maybe this was the knife that killed the King's manservant? I need to report this to your father, Ember, and right away."

"Wait! Then he'll know the truth that you let me in here and we'll both be in trouble!"

Phan hesitated for a minute; he looked lost in thought. "Ember. It doesn't matter if we get into trouble. What matters is that we found something that may help find Jewel. My punishment is of no concern when the safety of the King's daughter — and your best friend — is at stake."

Ember knew he was right…and she was pleased to think that he knew of her close friendship with Jewel. They had to go to Thor right away with this object. The strange symbols on the unusual knife made her think it came from a very different place than her village. She had never seen anything like it.

"You're right, Phan. Thanks for being the one to make me see that the truth is better in this situation. I want to find Jewel. She's my best friend and I'm so worried about her. That's why I came here in the first place. I got caught once, so this time I wore a disguise."

"Well, then…let's go." Phan walked to the secret door, pushed it open and left the small room. Ember followed him out the door and to the base of the giant tree's roots.

Phan turned back to look at Ember and realized she was still fifteen and did not have her wings. He hesitated for just a moment. "If you don't mind, I can carry you as I fly up to the castle. We can get there faster."

Ember shook her head the 'yes' way because she was blushing. He picked her up with strong arms and lifted her into the sky. Ember's heart was beating so fast she could hardly breathe. She wondered if he could feel the pounding and if he did then she didn't want to look into his green eyes again anytime soon. She was so embarrassed.

———————

When they reached the castle and the gate at the guards' tower, it seemed to Ember that only seconds had passed. Phan landed with such a soft touch Ember didn't even realize they'd landed on the parapet. She still clung to his arms as he said, "It's not what you think!"

The other guard said, "Why is she with you?"

They both looked at each other, realizing there was no reason for her to still be in his arms. Another warm blush of color swam up Ember's neck and colored her face as Phan put her down and stepped aside so Ember could enter the castle.

The guard had a look of shock on his face as he raised his hand to blow into a horn made of a snail's shell. It sent out a strange trumpeting noise that alerted the guard troops to come forth. This horn was used to alert the castle when problems arose.

Ember heard it and knew that there was more than one problem. Problem number one was Ember and what she'd done to escape the guards and coax Phan to let her into the secret place. Problem number two was Phan leaving his post at the base of the Great Oak. The guard knew Phan was on duty for the afternoon. Problem number three was Phan flying to the castle with the commander's daughter in his arms. No one was even allowed to speak with her…it was the commander's direct decree.

And then…who knew how many problems were ahead due to the object she'd found?

Ember heard the sounds of dozens of heavy boots hitting the stone tiles of the stairs as they ran up to the tower door. The sound was thunderous! The heavy door burst open and standing at the head of the horde of men was Thor.

"Father?" said Ember.

There was a brief silence and then Phan made a coughing noise, like he'd sucked in a flower petal with his breath.

Thor did not appear to be pleased at the sight of Phan and Ember. She sensed she was going to be sitting at home for a long, long time. All the privileges afforded a young fairy such as her would be stripped and she would be banished to her room for months. Her short life flashed in front of her eyes. Then she remembered why they had returned to the castle. Thank goodness Ember had the presence of mind to speak up about the shiny object they had found in the earthen floor of the secret room before her father started bellowing out their punishments.

"Father, we found something in our secret room…I think it's the shiny object Jewel was picking up when she disappeared. Here it is." Thor took the object from her hand and studied the piece, turning it over in his long thick fingers.

"How did you come by this object Emberlyn? My instructions were made clear to you to stay out of that room!"

Ember winced at hearing her formal court name; he only used it with her when he was holding in his anger over something she'd done. She'd only heard him use it a few times in her life.

Out of the corner of Ember's eye she could see Phan coming forward. She had a feeling that he'd confess his act of disobedience and try to protect her, but she went on: "I put on a disguise then went to the room to find this object. I knew it had to be there and it might be a clue to find Jewel. I tricked your guard by throwing a large rock on the other side of the root. It made a huge noise and while he went to investigate I slipped into the room. He found me when he heard me digging inside. He spotted this object in the dirt and then we flew here to find you."

Ember was breathing hard and felt flushed—it was difficult to lie. With her hands at her sides, she gripped the cloth of her grandmother costume. She'd left the cloak, hood, cane, bonnet and basket at the secret place. "Good one," Ember, she thought. For the second time in a day, she'd felt the shame of a lie.

Thor studied his daughter. "So you say Phan found you in the room digging and then spotted this...?" Thor looked down at the thing in his hand, "...this contraption?"

Ember nodded her head. She was afraid to say anything more.

He then looked at Phan, who was standing just behind her.

Ember wanted to figure out a way to tell him to go along with her lie, but she had a feeling that he would not.

"Phan? Is that what happened?" Thor was studying the young guard's face.

"No sir, that is not what happened. Em...uh...she...um...Emberlyn, I mean, your daughter...and...uh...I didn't know at first it was her... approached me and asked me to allow her to enter the room. I said I would not, but she persuaded me to give her access. She explained there was something in the room that might be able to help us find the King's daughter, and I made the decision to help her. She found it while we were both digging. I told her we'd best fly directly to you so you could evaluate what it is and see if it offered any clues to Jewel's disappearance. I carried your daughter because she doesn't have her wings. I wanted to get us here as fast as possible. I believe every moment is important in this troubling situation. I know I went against many of your orders and I am ready to accept punishment."

Thor turned away from everyone and faced a wall. He let a full two minutes pass without saying a word. Ember was so nervous she wanted to vaporize and never be seen again...or go to where Jewel was...yes, if she kept her thoughts on Jewel, all would be well. Maybe.

Finally, Thor turned around and spoke. "Phan, I find your reasoning sound and justified. I am pleased you took the initiative to follow up on this potentially crucial clue to the disappearance of the King's daughter. I am sorry my daughter felt it was necessary to protect you because of her poor judgment, but I commend you on your actions and for speaking what I sense is the truth."

Ember looked at Phan and saw that he was shocked.

"Thank you. Sir."

Thor turned to his daughter. "Emberlyn," he said in the deepest voice she'd ever heard, "please return home. I will deal with you later. Guard!" he said to the eldest guard in the troop—the one they all knew was hard of hearing. "Deliver this little grandmother to her own mother."

As the old guard took her arm, Ember saw what she thought was a slight smile on Phan's face.

Chapter 38

The Truth

————————

Sam's mom left the porch light on after she went back inside the house with the car keys. The two girls sat in the car surrounded by yellow light. "I don't think you'll believe any part of this story," Jewel said to Sam, "but I know you'll come to realize I've told you the truth. I'm so sorry I deceived you, but this world—your world—truly is totally new to me."

With that Sam jumped up and screamed, "I knew it! Oh my God you're an alien! Right? You are an alien?"

Jewel burst out laughing. She had been in this world long enough to know what Sam mean by 'alien.' She said, "No, but what I am about to tell you may be even more bizarre than any story you've ever heard about aliens landing from outer space."

Sam sat back in the driver's seat. Jewel took a steady breath and for a moment her friend just sat there staring ahead, waiting for the rest of the story to unfold.

"I fell...through a portal...from my land...into your world." Jewel said it slow, so the words sunk in. "My world is very different than yours and my people don't look like yours nor do they speak your language. I am a fairy. I live in the realm of the Fae race. It's another world, far away, yet near to this one. My formal name is Princess Jewelshwyn Lera Brodwyn of the First Fairy Clan. I am the second daughter of the King and Queen. I have a brother who is younger than me. I don't even know where to begin, so I may jump around a bit in my story. So, in my world, as a fairy and a royal, I get both my wings and my powers when I have the anniversary of my sixteenth birth year. I mean my birthday."

"Wait a minute…you have real wings?"

"Yes, and I'm much smaller when I'm in the realm of the Fae."

Jewel noticed that Sam's face seemed yellower than the porch light shining on it.

Chapter 39

Thor's Report

Thor's job just got busier. He planned to have a serious talk with Emberlyn later that night, but for now all his energy was focused on finding Jewel.

As soon as he'd completed the interrogation of Phan and his rebellious daughter, Thor flew to the King's quarters from the guards' tower. When he got inside, he flew up the long staircase, landed at the top, approached the King's door, grasped the large brass doorknocker and banged it hard.

The King's assistant opened the door to let him in.

Thor found the King in his study with his head bowed low, spectacles on his nose, totally absorbed in reading a large book.

"Yes Thor?" said the King, "I expected you when I heard the sound of the snail's horn. What is your news?"

"Your majesty, my daughter has found the object which so distracted Jewel before her disappearance."

The King arose and took it from Thor's outstretched hand.

"Careful sir, the button on the side releases a blade, which is very sharp. The metal is still unknown to me and I will take it to our smith to see if he knows of its origins. The runes on the blade and the handle are foreign to me, and I advise that we bring in the ancient ones for advice and consul."

The King looked at the blade and the runes as a shiver of fear ran through his very soul. In the *Book of Secrets* he had seen similar runes. "Please, leave it with me for now and go get the smith. Bring him here. I do not want this object to leave my presence."

Chapter 40

Power Bondings

———————

Bathed in the yellow lamplight, Jewel looked at Sam sitting in the driver's seat. There were signs of minor irritation on her face before she answered Sam's question about fairy wings. "I have wings when I'm in my world. As you can clearly see, I don't have wings right now. I believe they were replaced by the tattoo."

"Right." said Sam. "Please continue, the anticipation is killing me."

Jewel continued describing her world and her family. "It was the day of my sixteenth birthday when things got crazy. Remember, I told you that when a royal gets wings, they also get a special power. For example, my sister, Aspen, is bonded to the flowers. My father can control the wind; my mother communicates with water. You don't really know what your power will be bonded to until it happens. In our world though, royals have a preordained power, which the angels bless us with at the moment of our birth. I discovered on my birthday that I have a bond with the trees."

"How did you discover that?"

"I was with my best friend, Ember, but sometimes I call her Em, in our secret room in the root of the giant tree when I bent over to pick something up, stumbled and passed through the secret portal and into this world. My bond with the trees lets me pass through any portals they might contain...although my guess is that only this tree had a portal...and come into this...or maybe even another world. I don't really know, this is just what happened to me."

"So...trees...or maybe just this one tree...had a gateway..."

"Yes. The Great Oak tree in my village, looks exactly the same as the one in the parking lot where you found me. There is a legend about the race of our people and it speaks to the idea of two worlds that exist, but honestly I didn't really believe the writings in the ancient scrolls until I landed here and experienced these two worlds."

"How come as a human, I can't find a way into your world?"

"I don't know. All I know is that the scrolls proclaim that the Creators made two worlds because they could not agree on how one world would look, so they made two. The sacred scrolls say the two worlds will become one when the best world, determined by the inhabitants' actions, are known to the Creators. Of course it is all myth, again, until now. But it appears to all be true. I mean, why else would I be here?"

Jewel paused.

Sam said nothing this time. Then she turned to Jewel and made a 'go on' motion with her hand.

"So...," Jewel said, then took a deep breath, "I stumbled through the portal the Creators left in the tree and passed through it into your world. The tree gave me the knowledge of some of your language but not much more. I had to make up a story so you would help me. I think I can pass back through the tree whenever I want, but I decided I needed to stay here, because, well...there's more to the story."

Sam's mouth was open. She shut it, turned to face the windshield, then opened it again to ask: "More to the story?"

"Yes. When I left it, there was a big problem in my world." Jewel hesitated. She saw that Sam was sitting very still, looking straight ahead.

Then she turned and said, "Jewel. Honey. I think we should call a doctor. Maybe you hit your head really hard before I found you and that is what is making you believe your story. It is a fantastic story, but come on. It is really...like...crazy. I think you're a really sweet person, but I'm not sure what you expect me to do with this information because honestly it sounds like total fiction to me."

"Fiction?

"Yeah, made up. Not real. Fantasy." She turned to face Jewel again.

Jewel took another deep breath and said, "Miranda and Beecher, I think I need you to help me convince Sam I am not a crazy person."

"What...? Mir and Bee...?"

At that moment, the two little creatures popped out of her purse.

"Hi Sam," said Mir, "nice to meet you."

"Howdy," said Beecher.

Sam looked from one to the other. Her mouth dropped open, no words came out, but Jewel could tell she was getting ready to speak. And...she did.

"Holy shit! Holy crap! Holy everything! Are you kidding me? What the…hell? Who *are* these…things? I can't believe it! This is like totally bizarre. I mean weird. Impossible. I don't even know what to say. I mean come on. When does this really happen. This is so totally crazy!"

"Slow down!" said Jewel. "I know it is a lot to take in, but I promise you I am not crazy. I needed to stay in this world because there is someone else here who passed into the Fae realm and stole the key to the Vault of Souls."

"The Vault of Souls? What in the hell is *that*?"

Jewel explained the significance of the Vault and what it meant. She described her journey into the Vault and what her father had taught her. When Jewel finished her story, the two friends fell into a long silence.

Sam was fidgeting with her hair and staring at Mir and Beecher who had hopped up onto the dashboard. Then she breathed out and said, "Finally. I've been wondering about you and how strange this has been for me since we met," she said. "OK. I guess this needs to be our little secret, right? I can't tell anyone?"

"No," said Jewel, "I don't think it would be wise."

"And you need to find the key before you go back?"

"Yes."

"Can I go through the tree with you into your world?"

"I don't think so. The tree told me anyone who passed through it without my special bond would not make it. I wouldn't want you to be the experimental person who got zapped or burned up or whatever actually happens."

"Yeah, that would suck."

"What exactly are Mir and Beecher?" Sam reached out to pet Mir's head but she backed away.

"They're not pets."

Sam stopped her reach and seemed embarrassed.

"It's OK," said Beecher. "I know we have presented you with a rather strange situation."

Chapter 41

Project Ethan

For the next two hours, the girls and Beecher and Miranda talked about everything in both worlds and Jewel was finally able to ask the questions about Sam's world that she wanted to know and understand. And, Sam asked Jewel all sorts of questions about her life and her friends. They also spent time talking with Mir and Beecher. Sam was in awe of the little creatures.

Towards the end of the conversation Sam remembered Ethan's tattoo. "Wow. Hold on just one minute. Do you think Ethan is the guy who murdered your parents' servant and stole the key?"

Jewel got very quiet.

"Well I hope it's not the case, but...I may be wrong. My wings became this tattoo when I crossed over. His tattoo is the same as mine, so I don't think it is a coincidence. He must be one of the Fae."

"Maybe that's why you're so attracted to him...or why he's attracted to you?"

"Well, if he is a fairy, and I have to think that's a strong possibility, he has to be the one who is behind this. Maybe he is only pretending to be interested in me because he senses I am also a fairy. Maybe he knows I am looking for the key?"

Sam was thoughtful for another moment.

"This is just like something out of the movies!" she said. "Now I have to pinch myself to believe this is all real. This is the craziest thing to ever happen to me. I am so out of my league on this whole thing. I mean, just knowing there is a whole different world connected to ours, and I can't tell anyone about it. This is like the biggest news ever! Bigger than any other world event, and I am the only human to know about it and I can't tell another living soul, not even my mother! Hey! My mother used to read me stories about fairies when I was small. I *loved* those stories!"

"I think it would be too dangerous to share this information with anyone. You thought I was crazy. People will think you're crazy, Sam. And," Jewel said, "I am supposed to go out with Ethan tomorrow, but maybe I should cancel. I don't know what to do."

"Go," said Beecher. "The only way we will start to unravel this whole thing is for you to spend time with him and figure it out. If you are going to find the key, you will need to get closer to him and be able to search for it. Of course, we will be able to help you search."

Mir chimed in and said, "We fly so fast he won't even see us if he is distracted by you. We will also have a better chance at finding the key since we may be able to read his thoughts."

Sam looked at Mir who'd flown off the dashboard and into Jewel's lap. "You can read minds?" she asked.

"Normally not human brains, as we have discovered, but always fairy minds. It never occurred to us to try since we just assumed we were not amongst fairies." Mir and Beecher looked at each other in a very intimate way.

Sam felt a moment of discomfiture before resuming the conversation. "I think you should go to Ethan's house. Tell him you want to see where he lives and get to know him better. Then you can let Mir and The Beech snoop around."

Jewel could see that Sam was trying to work out a plan of attack so Jewel was able to locate the key.

"It's late, ladies," said Beecher. "I think we should all retire and get a good night's sleep. We can make a final plan in the morn. And Sam, you may call me Beecher. I do not identify as 'The Beech.' Thank you!"

Sam smiled and turned to Jewel. "OK, Beecher. Sorry. Hey Jewel," she said, "can you talk to all trees?"

"I think so but I just got this power so it is kind of new for me."

"Tomorrow can we go out in the woods and can you chat with some of the big oaks. I would love to hear what they have to say! All right. Let's all go in the house and go to bed."

Once inside the house and up in their beds, Sam went right to sleep. Jewel sat on the edge of her bed with a pillow propped up behind her head. She was thinking about Ethan. How could he be an evil person? She liked him so much, but if he had the key, she had to find it. How strange that her destiny took her on this path. She knew her life was going to change when she got her wings; she just didn't realize how much.

"I wish I had my wings now," she whispered to Mir and Beecher who were still resting on her shoulder.

"You will have them again, when we cross back over to our world," said Beecher. "They would be very difficult to hide in this world!"

Jewel giggled at the thought of her walking around with big fairy wings at the high school. "Hey you two...now that Sam knows about you, let's find you a better place to sleep."

Jewel opened one of the small drawers at the top of Sam's dresser. She outfitted it with a large flat sponge from the cabinet under the sink in their bathroom and made it into a bed. Jewel used two of Sam's bandannas for sheets and put cotton balls into a pair of athletic socks to make pillows. Mir and Beecher told her it wasn't necessary but Jewel was enjoying making a new private space for the special creatures. "And here's some water...you don't have to fend for yourself any more," Jewel said she brought them a small paper cup she'd gotten from Sam's bathroom.

"Good night, princess," said Mir.

"Thank you," said Beecher after he'd taken a drink.

Jewel gave them a smile and got in bed. She turned off the light and within minutes fell into a deep sleep.

But...her dreams that night were dark and troublesome. She tossed and turned all night, fighting the demons that kept interrupting a chance for much needed sleep.

Chapter 42

Sally's Son

Ethan left the party about half an hour after Jewel and Sam. He was not having fun now that Jewel was gone. "Wow…I like that girl," he thought as he drove home. "She's the first one who made me feel…uh…it's a new feeling…and weird."

He dated a lot of the girls during his three years at the high school, but he'd stopped after only a few dates with each one because none of them held his interest. They didn't mesh with him; they didn't understand him. Whatever it was, none of the other girls he dated could hold a candle to Jewel. She was special. She was also beautiful and every time he was around her he felt happy. She smelled like a fresh breeze from a meadow. Her scent made him heady. He also was at ease with her, like he had known her his whole life. How was it possible to feel this way?

Before he knew it, he was parking the car at his home. The porch light was on. His mother called out to him after he closed the front door with an extra push that made a sound louder than he'd intended.

"Is that you Ethan?"

"Who else are you expecting, mom?" he shouted back to her.

"Don't be such a smartass with your mother!"

He grinned. "Yeah, I'm home. Going to bed. See you in the morning."

"I thought I'd make pancakes so we'll have breakfast on the patio together. Don't sleep in tomorrow, son."

"Right, Sally. Sure. Me? Sleep in? When there's *pancakes*?"

Ethan removed his now-dry clothes, brushed his teeth, put on pajamas, then fell into bed, but felt restless. From memory, he replayed the events of the evening and when he recalled walking away from Jewel, he realized that he'd taken the towel off of his shoulders. Had she seen the wings? The thought troubled him…and it also kicked off a series of other memories about how he'd gotten those marks.

Ethan respected his mother—even though he sometimes called her Sally. She'd raised him on the salary she received as a librarian, and with help from his grandparents. Even though they lived simple lives, she gave him everything he needed, including love and time. Sally kept it all together, and she even had a sense of humor, but Ethan was puzzled about why his father had been absent, except for short visits when he was a very young child. Sally kept the details vague about how she met his father, but he knew only that they'd met in high school and had never married. Sally promised Ethan she'd tell him the entire story, but that day had not yet come.

When Ethan was young, his father stopped by the house every now and then to give Sally some money and that was because Sally had threatened to sue him. His father came from one of the richest families in town and he'd decided it was easier to pay child support than be taken to court. Ethan knew that most people in town didn't like his father and he probably would have lost the lawsuit anyway. Ethan was unsure about the terms of this money, but Sally managed it well.

Though Ethan had only been alone with his father on a few occasions, his grandparents were very involved in his life. He spent a lot of time with them at their home. They rarely brought up the topic of his father and preferred to dote on him and focus on positive aspects of his life.

He'd asked his grandparents to tell him about his father and found them to be much more open than his mother. They told Ethan how they'd found his father as a baby, in the park under a large tree, and that they'd adopted him. They knew nothing about his biological parents, or where he had come from, but they shared happy memories of the baby's early years. They did not talk much about him past his early childhood, and there was a sense of sadness they carried around with them.

Ethan wondered if it had to do with his father.

His grandfather had brought Ethan's father into his business, and every now and then Ethan learned that his father was causing his grandfather some concern. He also knew the little interaction he did have with his father was due to the encouragement of his grandparents, but even they had given up after Ethan started going to school.

Ethan had already faced the fact that his father was not interested in him.

There was one event they shared, and it was not a happy memory. That evening with his dad had been the last Ethan ever wanted to have. It was very strange. His father appeared at Ethan's house the night before his sixteenth birthday. He told Ethan he wanted to take him to dinner. When Ethan asked his mother for permission, Sally told him he should go...since his father was at least making an effort. So Ethan went...but only out of obligation.

Ethan didn't like his father. His manner was brusque and there was an edge, an aura of cruelty about the man. After they had gone to dinner, his father insisted he spend the night at his house—even though that was not part of the plan. Ethan didn't have a change of clothes or a toothbrush. Ethan balked at the idea, but his father insisted; Ethan had no choice. And that's when he learned that his father's house was a grand place on the edge of town, a very contemporary home, built like something Ethan had seen in a copy of *Architectural Digest* when he'd gone for a check up at his doctor's office. Ethan didn't understand why the home was so large since his father lived alone, except for a butler or houseman, or whatever it was that Michael called that man.

That night was one of the strangest nights Ethan had ever had, and it got stranger as the next day, his birthday, unfolded. He remembered waking up in an uncomfortable bed, in only his boxers. He felt a slight burning sensation on his back. His father called him to the kitchen table for breakfast and when he got there he saw that a place was set with toast, butter, jam and a glass of juice.

He sat down but before Ethan finished the meal his father said: "Ethan, I have something to show you. Come with me now!"

"I've not finished breakfast, and if it's possible, I'd like to get some eggs and fresh fruit, too."

"Breakfast is over! Come with me now!" his father demanded.

Ethan got up from the table and followed his father to a room lit by a domed skylight with lots of bookshelves and an oversized desk. In the corner was a full-length mirror. Ethan's father pulled a hand mirror from a desk drawer, walked Ethan to the long mirror, turned him around and gave him the small mirror. "You'll have to take a look at what's happened to you overnight," his father said.

Ethan took the hand mirror and positioned himself so he could see his back. What he saw made his stomach turn and his anger boiled to the surface.

"How the hell did that wing tattoo get on my back?" Once he saw it, he felt a bigger burning sensation—like hellfire—ripple along his spine. "What did you do to me? How did this happen?" Ethan was furious as he glared at his father. He was expecting an answer.

"Don't you remember, son? At dinner we spoke of the tattoo tradition upon your sixteenth birthday. You said you didn't want one. I had to follow through with the tradition, so I was forced to place a few drops of a very potent elixir in your water during dinner. You slept so hard that you didn't realize I brought in a tattoo artist to work on you."

"So that's why my shirt and pants are missing? And now I have a huge pair of wings on my back? They're hideous! I hated you before and now I hate you more for doing this to me! As soon as I have the money, I'm going to have this tattoo removed!"

When he got home and showed his mother, she was completely shocked and told him she was sorry to have suggested that he go out with that man. She was furious with Michael for marking their son without her permission, or even Ethan's knowledge. Michael had never told her about any sort of tradition involving a winged tattoo even though she remembered that he too had a strange wing tattoo on his back.

During the time she'd dated him, Sally remembered seeing Michael's back for the first time. He'd told her how he'd gotten drunk one night and ended up in a tattoo parlor. His wings were black with hints of color, but it had been so long since she had seen them, she didn't quite remember the details. She had no other way to explain it to her son.

Ethan pulled the sheets up around his chest. He kept working on his worry that Jewel had seen the art on his back. Finally, he settled into the memory of looking into the most beautiful face he had ever seen...Jewel's...and her eyes. That face, those eyes, were the images he saw as he drifted off to sleep.

Chapter 43

Queen's Tears

The Queen was awakened in the middle of the night...by a dragonfly. It landed on her face. The little creature whispered into her ear and she sat up in bed. The King was still sound asleep so she got out of her bed with very little disturbance and went into her private chambers to put on her dressing gown. The dragonfly darted around the room until she was ready and then together they flew out the window to the river where a water maiden awaited her arrival.

A rock sticking out of the river was where the Queen landed. The river's water swirled up around her in a mist. Illuminated only by starlight, the maiden of the river appeared and spoke to her in a way only the Queen could understand. The news she delivered was disconcerting and the Queen was unsure of what it meant.

The maiden told her there was a disturbance in the aura surrounding the great tree. "All the insects and animals that live in the Great Oak are distressed by a shift in the energy of the tree," she said. "It is still unknown what caused the shift, but all the creatures are uneasy. Some small creatures have disappeared in the same way as Jewel did, and only legend has spoken of similar occurrences in the past."

The Queen watched as the river maiden lost her energy and sank back into the flowing water. "Thank you, dear maiden, thank you," the Queen said as she took off to fly back to her chambers.

The King was still in slumber, albeit a restless one, when she walked back to their bed. She decided to let him sleep through the night because the news did not seem to hold any answers. It could wait until the sun was up—then she would share the news. Maybe he would understand it better than she did.

Jewel's very sad mother lay in bed, in the dark, for a long time. She pushed her mind out and into her world to see if she could feel the presence of her daughter, but she felt nothing. It was a scary and worrisome feeling. No matter what, she had always been able to sense the auras and energies of her children. She always assumed her power was rooted in the fact that they were mostly made up of water. Not feeling Jewel's aura or energy meant she was very far away...or dead.

A few tears slid down her face. She had to believe all was well or she would go mad. The Queen closed her eyes again and formed an image of Jewel in her head. She hoped Jewel would be able to feel her energy.

Chapter 44

Evil Michael

Michael sat at his desk. His dreams during the last week had been disturbing and he couldn't stop thinking about the scenes they presented.

Each night he'd dreamed of the same fairy girl, one who reached out to him with a sweet longing; but each time, the closer he got to her, the more anxious he felt. And then finally, he reached her…and her embrace turned to branches of the Great Oak tree. The branches laced around his body and squeezed him in a strong embrace he could not escape. He felt panic then forced himself to wake from the nightmare.

After each dream, as he lay in bed sweating, Michael tried to calm his breathing. Each time he had the dream, it was the same experience of anxiety—both inside the dream and upon waking.

It took a lot of deep breathing while Michael was seated there at his desk to allow the anxiety brought by his memory of the dream to slip away. Then he looked into an open drawer that contained another, deeper drawer. The inner drawer had a lock. He slipped a key into the lock and opened the small drawer.

What lay inside that drawer made him smile. It was a sliver lockbox that contained many things he treasured. He opened the box and removed a sheet of passwords for the secret bank accounts he maintained offshore. He had been skimming money out of the company for years. His father was sloppy about checking the books…in fact, he never checked them at all. "That fool trusts me," Michael whispered to himself as a sneer crossed his face.

He was thinking about his contempt of his father, Martin, who'd adopted him. Martin had been stern yet kind to Michael. What Michael didn't understand, or even question, was that passing through the tree's portal as Malick and ending up in the human world as a baby named Michael had permanently altered his brain and any shred of good that was left in him was long gone.

Malick was the evil persona inside the human Michael.

He picked up the golden key that had been locked in the silver box. He held it up to the light. The diamond at the top was beautiful. Perfect! The other stones set into the key were also perfect. Lifting the key, still on the chain, Malick placed it around his neck and caressed the exquisite, cold diamond at the top. "Soon," he thought, "I can get back into my original world, open the Vault, steal the precious fairy souls and become Lord of the Vault of Souls, King of my own empire!"

He'd performed evil in that realm before—when he'd killed the other fairy who possessed power to move back and forth through the tree's portal—and he knew the power of his evil. Thinking about all that power made his head spin, and it felt good. He would show them all who was in charge of their souls. Another crooked smile crossed his face as he shut the small vault and the drawer.

He sat back in his chair and reflected on the turn of events of late. He could only imagine the chaos back in the Fae world over the missing key to the Vault of Souls. The royal family members were probably beyond consolation. Again he smiled at the thought of what he had done and the depth of their misery.

Now he wanted to plan his next step for the procurement of those delicious royal souls—and the power he'd receive by doing so. Just as his mind was considering the next step to accomplish the task at hand, the image of his son showed up in his thoughts.

Ethan.

He was a complication for sure. Michael never intended to have a child, and certainly not a human child. "Or is he human?" Michael questioned. "The appearance of the wing tattoo on his sixteenth birthday indicates he's Fae, even though his mother is a human. Ethan is only half fairy at best, but why did he get the wing tattoo? Well it's of no matter. Ethan would never be able to pass through the tree."

Malick believed he was the only one who'd figured out how to use the portal as a passageway to the human world.

Again he smiled and then rose to his feet because he still had some business to do. It was the first of the month and he was required to get a check to Sally for Ethan. The truth was that he didn't care about money; he had plenty, and it was a small price to pay for his little indulgence.

Sally had been so sweet and kind to him when they were in high school. She'd told him how much she loved him. They dated for several months. His parents were friends with her parents. Dating Sally kept Michael's adoptive parents off his back and gave him a lot more freedom since they approved of the relationship. But he had no intentions of marrying her. He didn't want to get married.

The pregnancy was a surprise to both of them. Even when Sally told him she wasn't going to give up the baby, he told her then he would never marry her. It had been an ugly scene. Human emotions confounded him, but then again he didn't understand Fae emotions either. He had been a bit curious about his mixed-blood son and how it would affect him.

Ethan was born of two worlds and two species of beings...and he appeared to be a regular human kid...or, at least he was until he turned sixteen. Would there be more effects as he grew into manhood?

"Maybe," Malick thought, "I should spend more time him with him now so I can monitor his behavior and keep a close eye on how he turns out. The boy clearly despises me so attempting any contact will be difficult. Hmmm...." He looked down at his desk and picked up the envelope with the check in it. "I haven't seen the boy since that birthday—what was it? Oh, yes, almost two years ago."

He wrote the check, placed it in an envelope, put it in his pocket and strolled out of his office.

Chapter 45

Beecher's Thoughts

———————

Mir sat up suddenly in the makeshift bed. The drawer was so black she forgot where she was. Then her mind cleared and she stretched out her wing to find Beecher. He sat up by her side.

"What is it, Mir?"

"I had a vision. Well, maybe not an image, but not quite a dream, either. I felt the Queen's sorrow and felt her pain squeeze my heart. I think she was reaching out to Jewel in her mind, and I picked up on her call."

He pulled her into his arms and she rested her face against his chest. He rocked her back and forth to calm her. "It's going to be all right in time, my love. We will face all dangers together." As he rocked her he sang a song of their kind, a song from their childhood.

> "The low light of dusk unfolds.
> And we are safe in our holds.
> We are brave and true
> to our family, clan and crew.
> "Each day we renew
> Our pledge of loyalty
> To those foretold
> Be they brethren or royalty.
> "We are the warriors
> Our hearts are pure
> We trust our senses
> And know love does endure."

It always comforted her and brought back happy moments. She smiled up at him and closed her eyes. He continued to rock her until she was in a deep sleep.

———————————

Beecher stayed awake for some time thinking about the human world. He was keen on getting back to the Fae world as fast as possible but the quest to retrieve the key and protect Jewel was too important.

Beecher knew something was going on with Ethan when he first heard his thoughts. In the time they had been with Jewel in the human world, Beecher couldn't read the humans Jewel came in contact with—not Sam or her mother or the other students. But Ethan was not the same as the others. Beecher could hear his thoughts, although in bits and pieces. One moment it was very clear, the next—nothing.

He hadn't discussed it with Mir yet but he felt she was experiencing the same thing. They were so mated, so of one mind, it wasn't even necessary to speak out loud. He stroked the feathers on her neck. She made a soft humming noise and nuzzled her head against him.

"Yes," Beecher thought, "Ethan is an anomaly. I do not sense any malevolence but that boy makes me uneasy, especially because of the way he affects Jewel. We need to be cautious and vigilant while in his presence."

He yawned, closed his eyes and fell asleep next to the warmth of his Mir.

Chapter 46

Message Sent

———————

The Queen awoke early after a restless night. She found the King was already awake, standing by the window, looking out over the river.

"Good morning, my darling. Did you know I was called to the river last night?"

"Why, no. What happened?" The King turned to look at his Queen. Worry was etched into the lines on his face.

"The river maiden told me something was amiss with the Great Oak. All the insects and other neighbors of the tree felt a great shift from its core, but none know of the reason for the change. Some of them disappeared. Many of them are worried."

"A shift in the tree? Did the river maiden know of anything else?"

The Queen shook her head. "No, that is all I was told."

The King turned back to the window. "I have been reading the *Book of Secrets*," he said. "It talks about doors that cannot be seen. Portals. It also says there was one of our clan who was blind of sight but could feel the wind blow when he or she was around the secret doors. I have been thinking Jewel must have fallen through one of the portals. It is unclear what lies on the other side, nor does the book say when one passes through if they'll be able to come back. My fear is great, my dear Cordelia.

"I have sent word to the Ancient One in the mountain forest of Jura to give me guidance. The great wasp was sent as a messenger two days ago. I am awaiting his message. I have a feeling the lost key and the disappearance of Jewel may be connected somehow and I must tell you my love, for the first time in my life, powerful fear grips my heart."

Cordelia felt her stomach pitch as if her husband's fear was also part of hers. She stood up and walked to her husband. She embraced him as he wrapped his arms around her.

"The Ancient One will give us guidance," he said to her.

Cordelia wasn't so sure. She felt the knot in her stomach tighten even more as she looked out over the kingdom through the window they shared.

Chapter 47

Morning After

On the morning after the party—and the revelation of truth to Sam, Jewel woke up early and stared at the ceiling. She was thinking about Ethan. Her stomach was filled with knots and she was anxious from a restless night of little sleep.

Sam sat up in bed and stretched. She sat there for a minute then looked over at Jewel. "I wasn't dreaming last night when you told me your story, right?"

Jewel shook her head, no, and smiled at Sam.

"Can I see your wings tattoo again?"

Jewel got up and lifted her t-shirt to reveal the beautiful wings on her back.

"It is really beautiful," said Sam. "I mean, it doesn't look like any tattoo I have ever seen, which makes sense now that I know they are your...frozen wings. Or whatever they are now in this world." Sam blushed worrying she may have said something inappropriate. "But...what about the leaves? And your headband..uh, crown?"

Jewel explained that when she got her power, the leaves appeared. Sam listened with rapt attention while she told her the story of her crown.

"I thought your headband—I mean crown—was a bit too nice to have been purchased at the mall. Can I try it on?"

Jewel hesitated for a moment. She was unsure if the power from the crown would do something to change Sam.

Sam thought her hesitation meant she didn't want her to try it on so she said, "Hey, if you don't want me to wear it, it's OK."

"It's not that. Of course I want to share with you. It's just that I don't know if it will change or hurt you in some way. I know that my crown also contains some kind of power and honestly I haven't had it long enough to know what that power is or how it is affected in your world. I would hate to see your head explode if you put it on." Jewel gave Sam a twisted smile.

"Oh. Yeah, blowing up and hair on fire are not good things! We couldn't explain *that* to my mom!"

After a few moments of silence, Sam picked up her iPhone and tapped on it with both fingers. "Ethan sent me a text for you. He wants to know if you still want to see him today. I said you did. Now I'm waiting for him to respond. What if I say that you'll walk over to his house later this morning? Do you want to do that? Then you can see where he lives, explore his room and look for the key. Mir and Beecher can also be looking around. Wow, wouldn't it be great if you found it?"

"I want to find the key. I just don't want Ethan to be the one who stole it."

Sam understood. Jewel was totally in the throes of love when it came to Ethan. "Well, maybe he's not the key stealer. Maybe he's just a nice guy with a big wing tattoo on his back—a coincidence."

"Doubtful," said Jewel.

Sam saw the light on her cell phone flash on and she looked down at the new text. "He says he has some chores to do for his mom today, but you could come over around four this afternoon. I'll tell him that works." Sam was tapping away on the device as she said, "Oh, and I told him I would walk you over to his house so you don't get lost."

Jewel watched her friend make plans for them. More tapping and then Sam said, "OK, it's all arranged. Let's go get some breakfast and talk about how we can find the key."

After breakfast, Sam and Jewel did some homework, did their laundry and helped Sam's mom with some chores around the house. Jewel did not like doing laundry, but loved sweeping the porches in the front and back of the house. Being outdoors was so much nicer. Sam liked staying indoors and using furniture polish spray and a dust rag. After the two friends finished their chores, each spent the afternoon hours in Sam's room. Sam experimented with some new makeup and sat before the mirror trying new shades while Jewel looked through some of Sam's books.

When the crazy alarm clock's hands showed it was three, Jewel said, "I'm going to take a shower and get ready to go to Ethan's now."

"OK, I'll go in after you're done. Want me to do a makeover on you when I'm out and dressed?"

"What's a makeover?"

"Oh Jewel. Just go take your shower and get dressed! We'll talk about it later."

––––––––––––––

When they were both showered and dressed, Sam offered to put some eye makeup on for her, but Jewel declined. Sam seemed to love putting colors on her eyes, lips and cheeks. The idea of makeup was new to Jewel and she wasn't comfortable with the idea of painting her face, although she did like the soothing feeling and the slight pink tint of the stuff Sam gave her for her lips. Other than the product Sam called "lip gloss," she figured she had enough painting, so to speak, already on her body.

From where Jewel stood before the bathroom mirror, she saw Sam's reflection as she sat in front of the vanity mirror in their bedroom. Jewel noticed that Sam had chosen to wear black clothing and shoes: skirt, tank top, leggings, socks and boots. To herself, she whispered: "Maybe that's why she likes all that color on her face?"

Faded jeans and a cotton-rich, button-down, white blouse were the clothes Jewel chose to wear. She looked at herself in the bathroom mirror and thought: "I look different in this world. All the clothes in the human realm are so different. The materials seem so exotic, not to mention very uncomfortable compared to my silky gowns back home. And jeans! What an odd item to wear." When Jewel first put them on she had to tug and tug and adjust on the crotch so they were more comfortable.

Shoes for human women were the strangest things she had ever seen. In the Fae world shoe uppers were made from butterfly skin and soles were of the bark of a tree that Jewel noticed was not growing in this world. Fae shoes resembled human slippers. The shoes she had seen at the mall with long spikey heels were just plain scary looking and she couldn't imagine walking in them. She had purchased a pair of pink shoes with strings that tied in bows, which Sam called "sneakers," and had approved as "cool." They were the most comfortable shoes she could find.

"It's getting late and we should go," Sam said. "Where's my sweatshirt—the one with the hood? Have you seen it? Get your stuff."

"I will. Oh and I think your black sweatshirt is folded and stacked with our clean laundry downstairs."

As Sam headed downstairs, Jewel grabbed a tube of lip gloss, picked up her purse, put the product in and kept the flap open. She gestured for Mir and Beecher to hop into the pockets inside. Beecher looked pale and Jewel worried he might be getting sick, but Mir assured her it was from lack of sleep and nothing more. "We are fierce warriors with a strong constitution and we never get sick," she said. "Our blood has a special chemistry that protects us."

Chapter 48

Visiting Ethan

———————

Sam and Jewel arrived at Ethan's house just after four. The house where he lived was a modest two-story home with a cedar shingle roof and wood siding. It was painted white and had a pretty flower garden surrounding the perimeter of the house. The walkway to the house was made of large slate tiles of irregular shape and it reminded Jewel of the path from the castle to the river in the Fae world. The shutters were painted brick red, as was the front door, which made the house seem even brighter and more welcoming. Sam rang the doorbell and a woman opened the inner door while leaving the screen door in place.

"Hello," she said. "May I help you girls with something?"

"Uh, we're here to see Ethan," Jewel said.

A smile spread across the woman's face. "Ah, one of you must be Jewel, the young woman my son was speaking of this morning over breakfast."

Jewel felt the red heat creep up her neck and burn her cheeks. "Yes, I'm Jewel, and this is my friend Sam."

"Please come in. You can call me Sally…like Ethan's other friends do."

Jewel liked Sally. She was a very pretty middle-aged woman with long dark hair the color of soot that she was wearing in a ponytail. Her eyes were a brilliant blue and Jewel recognized all the other features Ethan shared with his mother. She was tall and well built and she looked like a woman who enjoyed exercise. Her clothes fit close to her body.

Sally opened he screen door and let them in.

The interior of the house was charming. A large room, just to the left of the front door, was a sitting room. Wooden bookcases surrounded a beautiful stone fireplace. Two large overstuffed chairs were on one side of the room and a leather sofa on the other. The room was painted butter yellow and floral curtains hung on the small windows on either side of the fireplace. It felt like a very feminine space and Jewel felt the comfortable in the surroundings. Jewel could see the kitchen beyond the sitting room and she smelled fresh bread wafting on the air.

"It smells great in here," Sam said.

"Thanks...I love to bake," Sally said before she raised her voice. "Ethan! Your guests are here. Please make yourself at home. Ethan will be right down. Would you like a cup of tea and a slice of fresh brioche bread? It's Ethan's favorite."

Sam and Jewel accepted the offer and followed her into the kitchen. The space was filled with labeled canisters and spice racks, hanging plants and a window herb garden. It was small and cozy with a table in the back overlooking a beautiful garden. Jewel stood by the window admiring all the different colors of the flowers and the small stream that wound around the back yard of the home.

"It's lovely here," said Jewel. The way it was designed reminded her of the gardens in her own world and a sense of melancholy crept into her mind. Jewel missed her world and her family. She was still looking out the window when Ethan entered the room.

"Hey Sam. Hey Jewel," he said as he walked up to the counter and grabbed a thick piece of bread that Sally had covered with butter and jam.

"Hey, you, that's for your guests!" Sally tried to snatch the piece of bread from Ethan's hand, more out of play than anything else. As she did it, Jewel felt the strong and loving bond between this mother and son.

"Mom, this bread is so good you should sell it and we could be bread tycoons." Ethan picked up the plate with more slices of the buttered bread and signaled for the girls to follow him. He took them upstairs to his bedroom.

Jewel was surprised by what she saw when she entered his room. The walls were painted navy blue and there were plaid curtains hanging from his windows. His bed was larger than the one she slept in at Sam's house and the plaid bed cover was the same fabric as the drapes. Above the bed was an enormous painting of a large man playing what appeared to be some kind of instrument. Ethan saw Jewel look at the painting and said, "Yeah. Louis Armstrong. I love jazz."

Jewel wasn't sure what jazz was but she wanted to find out. There was a heavy wooden roll top desk in the corner of the room with a computer monitor glowing and stacks of papers and books. The floor was wood with a large, red and white striped carpet in the center of the room. He had a long dresser and it had trophies on top, plus framed pictures of his mother and him at different stages of his life.

Jewel noticed there were no images of a man who might be his father. She also saw photos of an elderly couple that Jewel assumed were his grandparents. The room was clean and orderly. It didn't look like the room of a murderer and a thief. Jewel felt Mir and Beecher stir in her pocket. Jewel felt that the two sensed the good feeling inside the house.

Ethan motioned for them to find a place to sit as he connected his phone by a cord to a small box with small holes all over it. "Would you like to hear some of my favorite jazz music?"

"Sure," said Sam," but I promised my mom I would be right back so I need to leave soon. I really just wanted to make sure I got Jewel here." Sam picked up a piece of bread and took a bite. Jam slipped off the edges and down her fingers and she licked the gooey red off her hands with a loud smacking noise. Both Ethan and Jewel laughed, but Sam was totally engrossed in consuming the delicious food.

Music was playing. Ethan turned to both the girls and said, "This is Charlie Parker. Love that saxophone."

The music was foreign to Jewel. She had never heard these types of melodies or instruments, even on the car's radio. It also seemed to be incongruent with her thoughts of a potentially dangerous man who murdered a manservant at the castle and stole the key. Nothing was making sense to her. She was expecting some dark lair with posters of zombies or worse on the walls and instead she got Mr. Neat-and-Normal and his pretty mother.

So who was this Ethan Peterson?

Sam got up, said goodbye and was gone before either of them could protest.

Sitting alone in Ethan's room with the jazz playing in the background seemed a bit surreal to Jewel. "Now what?" she thought.

Ethan came over to her and sat down. Within just a few minutes they were chatting together in their normal manner and it was hard for Jewel to think that anything had changed after she'd seen his wing tattoo. Jewel was so at ease around him she almost forgot her mission. She needed to search his room and look for the key, but even as much as she wanted to pull herself away from him she just couldn't do it. She was really enjoying the private moment with him and she didn't want it to end.

They talked together in Ethan's room for about two hours. He told her about all the musicians he loved and his passion for being out of doors and exploring. She marveled at the way he explained the notes and instruments played in the music and how passionate he felt about the jazz.

Jewel was so enamored with him that she totally forgot she was supposed to be looking for the key. Every now and then she would see him looking at her like he was looking into her soul, at those moments his face had a rather goofy smile on it. This time together was so easy for them, like they had known each other forever that neither of them wanted it to end.

"I have never met anyone like you," Ethan said to Jewel as the late afternoon sunlight shone through his window and illuminated her face. "You are so beautiful and so real. So many girls at school are just awful. Self absorbed and kind of bitchy, no offense to anyone…but you…you are so amazing!"

The statement, which came out quickly, held such a tone of honesty that both Ethan and Jewel were quiet in that moment. Then Ethan went on. "I feel like I have known you my entire life. It is the strangest feeling, and I have to tell you I don't want it end." He took her hand and held it for a moment then brought it to his lips and kissed it. "I could lose myself in your eyes," he said.

Jewel understood his feelings, because she too had never experienced this type of attraction.

Mir's voice interrupted Jewel's revelry. The whispering in her mind was hard to ignore. "Remember your mission, Jewel!" Mir said.

Jewel didn't want to remember anything but the way in which Ethan looked at her. His beautiful eyes were filled with kindness, respect and…passion. No, Jewel did not want this moment to end or be interrupted by a search for a key she hoped he didn't have.

Chapter 49

Further Investigation

─────────────

At the castle, efforts in the search for Jewel herself had hit another wall.

Thor waited for the King's assistant to bring him back into the private study. He had gotten a report from the smith regarding the metal knife Ember found when she was with Phan. The metal was a new substance to the smith; he'd never seen anything like it before. Nor did he have any knowledge about the symbols engraved into it. It just deepened the mystery of Jewel's disappearance.

Thor had been waiting for what seemed like an unusual length of time; usually the King saw him right away. Time seemed to slow down for Thor as he stood staring at the enormous ancient tapestries that hung upon dowels on the walls made of rough stone. They held images of town life. It was the first time he'd ever had a good look at them. He was engrossed in the images in one of the fine weavings—a village scene with the Great Oak, which was right in the center of the tapestry. The scene was a festival and the townspeople were in various stages of repose around the base of the tree.

As Thor's eyes drifted over the images, he caught sight of something odd. There was a door in the root of the Great Oak. "Perhaps that is the door Jewel went through," Thor thought. It was circled in yellow thread and made to appear as if light was coming out from around the door's frame and threshold. The complete root was showing. Thor studied the area of the tapestry where the root lay with the secret door above it. The weaving was precise and elegant, woven with much care to show several fairies seated below the door and on top of the root. Behind one of the seated fairies was an image of a beautiful female fairly with black holes where her eyes should be. Her hands were out in front of her and she looked as if she was pushing something away from her towards the root of the tree.

Thor looked even closer at the image and saw something so faint that he had to get right up close to the tapestry to study it. There, on the root was a very fine yellow thread, as fine as a fairy's hair, which outlined another small door.

Gusts of wind seemed to be swirling around the woman figure, the one with no eyes. Thor did not remember seeing another door on the outside of the root, one that was below the door he did know. He looked at the blind fairy again. She was radiant. Her gown, now yellowed with age, was probably white when it was created. Her wings were slightly feathered which was not normal for fairies of their clan. She had golden hair that wrapped around her waist and cascaded down to the ground. Thor backed away from the tapestry to get a better view of the whole scene. As soon as he did, the fairy's image, which so intrigued him, seemed to get lost in the shadows of the fold of the wall hanging.

At that moment, the King himself swung open the door to his chamber.

"Your majesty!" said Thor as he bowed with his fist over his heart," I have never had the time to study those tapestries outside your chamber, but today as I waited for you I became enthralled with them. Did you know the one directly outside your door shows the secret door in the root? And something even stranger is another door outlined very faintly on the root."

"Where? Please show me! I've been studying one of the ancient books when you knocked, but I wasn't finished with the section. I'm sorry to keep you waiting, but maybe that was meant to be!" The King removed a lantern sconce from the wall outside the door. He stood in front of the tapestry Thor was pointing to and held the lantern close to the fabric so the light illuminated it while he studied.

"Thor," he said, "These tapestries have been hanging in this castle for hundreds of years. They were made with the finest butterfly silk and each one took over fifty years to complete. I must admit that I've not paid much attention to them. As a child, I hid behind these tapestries, not re-alizing my body could be seen as a bulge under the fabric. And now you say that there might be a clue to Jewel's disappearance hidden here?"

"I'm not sure yet, sir," Thor replied as he studied the fabric's tales while standing further back than the King.

The King spent quite a while examining the scene Thor brought to his attention. The blind fairy was the one he was concerned with. He pointed to her and said, "I believe this might be the same fairy I've seen referenced in the *Book of Secrets*."

Thor did not respond. He'd never seen this book. After a few more silent moments the King turned to Thor and commanded: "We have to fly to the Great Oak and examine the root right away! Come along with me!"

Thor and the King flew out the portal in his chamber and headed to the Great Oak tree.

Chapter 50

Slip Shine

In Ethan's bedroom, the jazz music was playing low and slow. Jewel thought it matched the way their conversation seemed to be narrowing down—she was just about out of things she wanted to talk about with him. She heard his mom's footsteps and saw her shadow as Sally passed by the half-open door. Ethan and Jewel were both sitting on the floor, their backs against his bed, when Ethan turned to Jewel and leaned towards her.

Jewel wondered, "Is this the start of a kiss?"

Just as he was inches from her face, they heard the doorbell ring.

Sally called out: "Ethan…will you get that? I'm putting away the clean linens."

Ethan smiled at Jewel and stood up. He put his palm in front of her and wiggled his fingers as if he wanted to take her hand. "Come with me. Maybe it's Sam checking up on us!"

Jewel took his hand and they walked out of his room and down the stairs. Jewel let go of his hand as he rounded the corner into the foyer and opened the front door. Standing where she was around the corner, Jewel heard Ethan's voice take on a dark tone as she felt the energy shift.

"What do *you* want?" she heard Ethan say.

Jewel peeked around the corner and saw a tall, thin man standing on the other side of the screen. His jet-black hair was shiny and slicked back. He was wearing an open collared shirt and jeans. There was something menacing about him. She felt a flutter of movement in her pocket.

In the lead-up to the kiss, she had forgotten Mir and Beecher were tucked away.

But now she heard Beecher speaking to her in her head. "Jewel, we can hear this man's thoughts! He is like Ethan. His words come to us in bits and pieces. Our pinfeathers are up, which is very strange. They are our inner warning signs when danger approaches. Be careful, because we do not yet know what is amiss."

Ethan's body was rigid and Jewel could sense his mood had turned sour.

"I'm here with a check for your mother," the man said. "May I come in?"

"My mother is busy, so no, you can't come in. Give me the check and I will make sure she gets it."

Jewel shifted her stance to see better how this man was eyeing Ethan in an evil way. She noticed that Ethan wasn't shy about showing his disdain for his father. She didn't want to be shy anymore and moved closer to Ethan so the man could see her, too.

"Ah…," he said with a sneer. "And…who is this little friend of yours?"

"None of your business!"

Jewel stepped out in front of Ethan and looked at the man. "I'm Jewel."

The man's eyes widened when he saw her. There was a moment of silence as Jewel could see she was being examined with eyes the color of a lavender sky.

"My, my, my…" he said with an inhale "…such a beautiful young woman. I don't think I've seen you before. I'm sure I know all the families in this town." He exhaled. "Do tell me…who are your parents?"

Ethan looked at his father again with such hatred even Jewel was shocked by his expression. "I told you, Michael, it's none of your business!"

"Really, Ethan. Please address me as I am. Call me father. I find it very disrespectful when you treat me like you do your mother and call me by my first name. It's just wrong, son."

Jewel noticed Ethan was flexing his hand and then curling his fingers into a fist. "Why would I call you father?" he said with contempt. "You are a compete asshole to me and honestly I want nothing to do with you. So give me that check for Sally, then get off these front steps and leave!"

"Ah, my son, my son," said the man, "I have decided I want to get to know you better, Ethan. It's time. I understand I've been a distant father, but I never wanted children because I'm not the parental type. As you know, I myself was adopted. My father—your grandfather—has told me for years that I should invest in getting to know you because as he puts it, you are a charming and smart young man. I thought today would be a good one to start, but I see you're occupied with your guest...the lovely Jewel."

He looked at Jewel again. She had the sense he was stripping off her clothes in layers with his eyes and trying to see into her very soul. She was uncomfortable being around this man. No wonder Ethan didn't like his father and didn't speak of him. She felt Beecher and Mir shivering in her pocket.

"Please do invite me in, Ethan, even for just a few minutes. I know we have gotten off on the wrong foot, but I truly want to make amends."

The insincerity in his voice struck a chord with Ethan because he said, "You are so full of shit! I don't know what you are up to, but getting to know me is not on my to do list. Just go. Leave me alone like you've left me alone all these years, you bastard!" Ethan opened the screen door and put out his open hand. "Give me the check."

The man stood there looking at his son and at Jewel. He turned and said to Jewel, "You look like such a nice young lady. Maybe you can convince my son to give his dear old dad a shot?"

Jewel just looked at the man. Ice was in her heart. She said nothing.

"This is none of her business, Michael, this is between you and me. And I have no interest in spending time with you. I remember the last time you made me stay with you and it was very unpleasant for me. Give me the check...and leave. Please leave!"

The man now seemed frozen.

"The *check*!"

The man pulled an envelope out from his back pocket. He held it out for Ethan to take. Ethan reached for the envelope but just as he was about to take it, it dropped out of the man's hand and drifted to the ground. The man bent over in a swift motion to pick it up. As he did, an object on a gold chain slipped out of his shirt and hung forward in the light. It was a brief moment, but the sun struck the pendant and a million colors of fire shot off around it.

Jewel saw the charm dangling from Ethan's father's neck—there was a circle of gemstones at the top of a line of metal. At first she didn't believe what she saw was the key to the Vault of Souls because the size of it was much smaller than it was in her world. Thoughts were racing inside her head: "But, no! Wait! There it is! He has it! The key to The Vault of Souls! Ethan's father stole the key!"

JEWEL AND THE MISSING KEY

Jewel sucked in her breath at this realization. Beecher and Mir were shuddering in her pocket. She thought: "How did he steal the key? It doesn't matter, I know where it is now." She was relieved that it wasn't Ethan who stole the key.

But her relief turned to terror as she looked again into the face of his father.

As Michael straightened up his stance, the key remained on the outside of his shirt and Jewel's eyes were locked onto it. Michael noticed her attention to the key and tucked it back into his shirt.

Ethan grabbed the check from Michael, pulled the screen door shut and slammed the big wooden entry door. He looked at Jewel. He was leaning against the wall, mouth agape, his face was pale; he was shaken to his core by that interaction. "I'm so sorry!" he breathed, "Jewel, I see how that upset you. I had no idea he was going to stop by. I told you I don't get along with him. Well, I don't like him. He never comes over here so this visit was a surprise to me, too. Let's go back upstairs and find the place where we left off."

He grabbed her hand, pulled her up the stairs and led her back into his room.

Chapter 51

In Wait

Michael stood still outside the now closed front door. He felt the prickle of his wings behind the tattoo on his back. "She recognized the key," he thought. "At least I think she did. I heard her suck in her breath when it fell forward. Maybe she likes diamonds? Maybe it was just the sight of such a large diamond? No, something's different about her."

She was beautiful, and even had looked familiar to Michael, but he couldn't quite place where he had seen her before. He turned to go back to his car, thinking about what had just happened. He cared little about the anger that had rolled off Ethan. His son meant nothing to him. He was an annoyance at best. But there was something about the girl. "Where have I seen her before?" he said out loud as he opened the car door.

With that thought, the image of Jewel in his dream came to mind—her long arms reaching out to him, grabbing him with a suffocating embrace. His breathing quickened with the memory. A moment of fear rushed through his mind, making the hairs on the back of his neck stand up.

With everything he knew and understood about the two worlds, this was certainly not a coincidence. "I need to investigate this further," he said to himself as he got behind the wheel. "I need a quiet moment with Jewel, alone." Yes, he needed a plan to spend some time with her where he could interrogate her and persuade her to open up to him. He grinned at the thought. She seemed like a person with a few secrets to tell. Yet all of his internal warning signs were going off. He closed his eyes to visualize her in his mind. She was average height, her hair was very long, and her eyes…he noticed her eyes looked different to him and of course he noticed the leaf tattoo on her arms. Quite unusual for such a young person to bare such skin art.

Who was this Jewel?

Michael backed the car out of the driveway, all the time planning his next move. He couldn't go back to Sally's house. He couldn't invite Jewel to his house; he knew she would be an unwilling guest. "I guess a little abduction will have to be planned," he thought.

He drove down the street at five miles an hour, then parked under a large tree in the shade, within view of Ethan's house.

"No time like the present" he said out loud, and smiled to himself. "I have all afternoon to wait for her."

Chapter 52

Phan's Duty

Phan was waiting and watching. He was on guard duty again, at the Great Oak tree.

Once he'd been commanded back to this post, Ember had been sneaking out of her house to meet him during the times he was alone on guard. At first he was upset with her for trying to distract him from his duty, but standing by the tree all day with nothing happening was boring. Ember was like a sweet ray of light shining on his day and he looked forward to seeing her. He was waiting for her, watching, but he knew she wouldn't come again after what had happened just the day before.

He remembered their time together yesterday—when she'd been sitting next to him, telling him all about her life as the daughter of Thor, the commander. "He is really strict, but I know it is always for my benefit," she'd said.

It was at that moment when the King and Thor landed by the root to investigate it with newfound knowledge they'd gained from the tapestry.

Ember rose to her feet, her face flushed red and dread overcame her. Phan stood at attention.

Thor was angry. "What are you doing here, Emberlyn? You know you're not supposed to be here!"

She was at a loss for words.

Phan spoke up for her: "I am so sorry sir, she was just passing by and brought me some water to drink. I asked her to stay for a few minutes so I could inquire on the findings regarding the knife." He looked at Ember as if to see if she'd go along with the story, but she was staring at her feet.

"I see," said Thor. "You may go now, Ember. Please do not disturb this guard again when he is on duty." Ember scurried around to the other side of the tree and disappeared from sight.

Thor returned his attention to Phan. "If she comes around again, send her home. She knows better! Now, do you have anything to report?"

"No, all is quiet as before."

The King was walking the length of the root, examining the exterior of the bark. He was touching it with both hands, feeling around for something he wasn't sure of and trying to recall the door that was visible in the tapestry. Thor joined his search as Phan looked on.

"Can I help you with something, sir?" Phan inquired.

"Have you felt any wind or movement around this root?"

"No sir."

The two men spent the next hour walking the length of the root, touching it, examining the depressions in the bark but found nothing. The tapestry must have been an artistic impression, the King surmised, not really showing an actual door.

Thor agreed.

Phan overheard them talking, but he only understood every fourth word or so.

He wondered about this visit, the question about wind, and their mission in searching for a door on the outside of the tree.

"We're leaving now," the King said to Phan, "so keep your guard and do not let yourself be distracted by any young maidens, especially Thor's daughter!" The King turned to Thor, nodded toward the castle and both men took off in flight before Phan could even blush.

Chapter 53

Take Off

Jewel felt a sense of urgency to get back to Sam's house after Ethan's father left. As Ethan led her up the stairs she wondered, "Does he want to try again for a kiss? I'm not sure I want this...I need to think about what just happened and how Ethan's father had the key to the Vault of Souls! How is it possible? Who is Ethan's father?"

As they neared his bedroom, Jewel thought she could start by questioning Ethan. She already had an opening to do so after that exchange by the front door and she wanted to talk to him at some point about it, so this seemed like the perfect moment. Jewel wondered if Ethan would open up to her about such a personal story about his family — or if he'd just lean into her face as he'd done before the doorbell rang.

In a big way, Jewel was relived. She realized Ethan was not the one to have stolen the key; it was his father. But how did his father get through the tree? Was Ethan's father of the Fae? Many questions came flooding through her head, making harder to make sense of it all.

Just as Jewel and Ethan sat down on his bed, Mir whispered, "Yes Jewel, you must find out as much as you can from Ethan!"

Ethan took her hand. "Are you OK? You seem more upset than I am after interacting with my father. Although I don't even like saying he's my father, he is such a giant asshole."

"No, please...tell me about your father, Ethan, so I understand a bit more about what happened in your relationship to make you think about him and say what you do about him."

Ethan went quiet and looked down before he said, "He was really ugly to my mother and honestly he never, and I mean never, wanted anything to do with me. Growing up I knew he was my dad, and I really wanted him to be a dad, but he never stepped up to the plate."

Confused by this language, Jewel shifted her posture and he paused to look at her. She gave him a look of compassion that allowed him to continue.

"My mother dated him in high school. His parents were best friends with my mothers' parents. They must have encouraged the two of them to date. I think they had some kind of fantasy where my mother would marry their son and it would solidify their mutual love for each other; like one big happy extended family. My mother told me she dated him from the end of her junior year in high school until after she graduated. She got pregnant with me during that time. When she told him, he dropped her like a hot potato and that is all I know. My mother never really wanted to tell me the details; even now she doesn't like to discuss it. She obviously decided to go ahead and have me, but she did it alone. Well…my grandparents helped her too. They're nice people."

Ethan looked up at Jewel. "Can you imagine…?"

Now Jewel looked down. Thoughts of pregnancy were new to her…she'd never discussed the topic with Ember. Sam was the one who'd filled her head with information. She didn't know what to think. She could feel his eyes on her. Ethan seemed to be waiting for her to respond. She could only manage a thin smile. "Go on," she said.

"Michael's parents, my grandparents, were very supportive. They have always been there for me, which is great, but it didn't really make up for not having a father. They are the wealthiest family in town. Hell, they own half the town and the land around it. My mother told me they were always behind her and even supported the pregnancy. I think they knew Michael would never marry—not sure why—maybe they thought this was their only opportunity to have a grandchild? I guess it doesn't matter now; it is what it is! I know they have helped my mother financially, but she always refused to take more than we needed. I got the sense she wanted to make sure they knew she didn't get pregnant to hook him in, just because he came from a wealthy family. Sally is just not that kind of person. Anyway, I don't know too much about him. I really never spent any time with him at all, well except around my sixteenth birthday."

"What happened then?"

Ethan went quiet, and frowned.

Jewel sat and waited for him to continue.

"I've never told this to anyone except my mother, Jewel, but I didn't even tell Sally all the details of that night. It was the weirdest night of my life," he said. "Michael showed up at the door the night before my birthday and said it was time we got to know each other. Sixteen was a big birthday and I was becoming a man or some shit like that. My mother told me I should go with him, since he was making an effort to become involved. I really didn't want to go and I remember having an argument with Sally in the kitchen while he was waiting for me. She told me if someone was willing to change they should be given a chance. So I went. He took me to some restaurant and then my memory...well, it's fuzzy from that point on...he said he put some drug in my drink. Who does that to their own kid?"

Ethan looked at Jewel again. She put her hand on his shoulder. "Then what happened?" she asked.

"He took me back to his house after dinner. It was the first time I had actually seen where he lived. He had a guest room prepared, even though I hadn't brought a change of clothes or my toothbrush, and even gave me hot chocolate when it was time to go to bed. Like all of a sudden he was trying to be this loving father. Maybe I wanted it so badly I got sucked into it or maybe it was the drug he gave me. Anyway the next thing I remember was waking up, wearing only my boxers and I had a burning sensation on my back. After he gave me breakfast he took me into his office and showed me this hideous thing on my back. He told me the drug he gave me at dinner made me sleep really soundly. The asshole thought it would be a great rite of passage to have a tattoo artist come to his house and draw on my back. He claims it is some sort of familial rite of passage. Again, I have no memory of any of this since he drugged me."

"You have a...tattoo?" Her tone of voice went up. Jewel knew she had to act surprised.

"Yeah," he said, "but as I said it's hideous!"

"Can I see it?"

"I don't know...it's one of those things I am so embarrassed about I am really uncomfortable showing anyone."

"I promise I won't say anything. I just want to see it."

He laughed and said, "Oh, you'll say something when you see it. I promise you that. I would say something if someone showed me something hideous. Like, 'what were you thinking when you had it done?'"

He laughed again, but Jewel knew he was laughing out of discomfort, not amusement.

"I promise not to say anything at all. Please, just show me."

Ethan stood up and faced her, "I think you need to stand up to get the full effect."

Jewel got to her feet.

He was facing her with a look of dismay. "I don't know," he said, "you may think differently of me after you see it."

"I know I won't feel different about you, so don't be ridiculous."

He backed away and stripped off his shirt. He was still facing her. "You ready for this?" he asked.

Jewel nodded her head and Ethan turned around. Jewel knew what to expect and yes, on his back was a tattoo—two wings.

To Jewel they were beautiful. The color was an amazing shade of deep purple, black and indigo with red and gold highlights around their inner sections.

"They're beautiful," she whispered.

Then Jewel did something, which even later, after she thought about it, still surprised her. As Ethan turned back to face Jewel, she turned her back towards Ethan and stripped off her shirt. She heard him suck in his breath as he looked at her wing tattoo.

Then she put her shirt back on and turned around to face him.

Chapter 54

Ancient One

The King was sitting in his study, looking out of a small window, high up in the tower. In his imagination, he called up the image of Jewel on the morning of her sixteenth birthday. His mind's eye had opened to allow the image of her flying above the rushing river—a beautiful sight. A tear formed in his eye.

In his lap was an old book that contained spells and chants. He'd been reading it to find some clue as to how Jewel had vanished. Earlier that day, he received word from the distant winds that the Ancient One had received the King's message, knew of the trouble and was coming down to the village from the Great Forest of Hagar. This forest was located below the mountainous Kingdom of Jura, a long way from the Kingdom of Dorawine and it would take many hours of the day before the old wizard would arrive. The king was relieved to hear he was on his way to help with the search for Jewel.

It was rare for the Ancient One to leave his earthen home that was buried deep within the sacred forest. The trees in those woods were giants; reaching up to the clouds and beyond. No one knew their age, but his people believed they were born at the same time the Fae world was created. It would take a kinsman an hour to walk around the perimeter of one of these great trees. They were simply magnificent.

The King felt that the Ancient One would arrive at the castle by sundown. He'd only met this soothsayer once before, and many, many years ago when he was a boy and his father had a similar problem: a young female fairy had vanished from the village. The King had a vague recollection of the events surrounding the story, but many of the details had slipped through his memory. He was embarrassed by the idea of not even being able to recognize the wizard since it had been so many years since he was last at court.

The King had made great plans for the Ancient One's arrival, and all the guards were on alert; some were posted to watch for him along the expected route. Queen Cordelia's servants were preparing the best suite of rooms at the castle for him and a great welcome feast was being prepared.

A brilliant, large-winged dragonfly landed on the windowsill and caught the attention of the King. The insect half flew, half walked to the King and bowed his head in respect. The insect flapped his large wings in a slow rhythm; first with a continuous beat, then changed the pattern of his movements in a way that created a breeze.

The King, whose power was master of the winds, understood the message. The Ancient One was now close to the village—he'd arrived earlier than anyone expected. The King arose from his seat, thanked the insect, and then they both flew out of the portal: the King flew to the Queen, and the great dragonfly flew off to find his next meal.

Chapter 55

Hemson, Pip

The Ancient One did not like to leave his home in the Great Forest. It had been many years since he'd left those woods, but now he had no choice. After he'd gotten the message about Jewel's mysterious departure, he knew the King was faced with a serious problem.

He'd received word from the dragonfly that the young princess had disappeared on the day of her sixteenth birthday. That worried the old fairy, especially since it was Jewel—the royal he knew would have a special power with the trees. Every species of tree in his forest was whispering her name—and the whispers created a weather system. The Ancient One knew she was special and would grow to be a great noblewoman whose destiny was tied to his. His mission had been foretold almost three hundred years ago.

As he neared the castle, two small winged creatures flew out from the deep folds of his robe. The Ancient One had kept company with these *Pulchra avium* since his own sixteenth birthday. Hemson and Pip had been chosen at his birth to be his constant companions starting from the day his wings burst forth from his back.

The Ancient One was overcome with the sweet memories of a life shared with Hemson and Pip, his constant companions. The company they supplied eased his solitude over the centuries and he loved these little creatures as a parent loves a child. The two had protected the Ancient One on several occasions when his forest was under attack by a clan of night creatures. Hemson and Pip were crafty and funny. They could still cause mischief even at their ages—they were as old as the wizard. Because of the way his life and their lives were closely joined, he wondered if they would perish with him when his time came to go to the Vault of Souls. The moment he had that thought, they both looked up at their wizard. He was so accustomed to the fact that they were able to read his mind he no longer censored his thoughts with the worry they could be offended.

"We have a lot more things to do in this world, old man," said Hemson, "so don't get any ideas about joining the Vault anytime in the near future." With that, Hemson laughed and pulled Pip in for a quick rub of his beak along her neck. He had great affection for his wife, who he knew to be frank with her opinions.

Now Pip turned to the old fairy and spoke using her mind. "Our brethren are with Jewel. We were told a couple had been sent to the young princess as a birthday gift from our clan. They are equally as important to your people as to ours. We must assist in finding them as they are part of this plan—the disappearance of young Jewel."

The old fairy knew this was a truth; one he had expected would come at some point. It had all been written in the scrolls he found long ago, the ones buried in the Cave of Needles.

He had been given a special education, based on his lineage, and with the understanding he would take on the role of the truth-sayer, wizard, and Ancient One as he grew to adulthood. He had accepted his role with gratitude and a sense of contentment, but had always been a solitary type of person. This power to become a sage set him apart from those of his siblings, and all the non-noble fairies during his youth; played the role of a social outcast because of it. The powers he had been given rarely went to the common Fae; they only were given to those of noble blood: Upon his death, a fairy would be born to take his place in this world; just as he'd replaced the last Ancient One. It was all part of his destiny.

Over his life, the Ancient One had traveled far from his kingdom and met many a strange creature and experienced life in a way that was unusual for a fairy. His father had told him that his life would not necessarily be one he would have chosen, but it would be a great one and he should be thankful to the angels for bestowing such a great gift on to him. And, he was grateful.

Pip looked up at the sky. "We need to get to the castle soon for I sense a great storm coming our way and I really don't want to arrive all wet and bedraggled. I spent quite a bit of time on my feathers today and I want to look perfect."

Hemson rolled his eyes.

The Ancient One picked up the pace. He had cast a spell on his wings so they would move faster than normal and allow him to arrive into the Kingdom of Dorawine in half the time it took an average adult fairy. As he flew, the Ancient One thought about how he had not been to visit these lands for quite some time. He did not even venture to Dorawine when the old King had passed away along with his beloved wife, allowing the current King to be crowned. Court politics were not his business, nor did he wish to be involved with them. He had great affection for the King's father and he had gone to school with the King's mother, the former Queen Rose. She was a woman touched with everything good in the world and he wished she were alive so they could reminisce about the old days and the times in which they'd grown up.

The winds picked up, and flight got difficult. Pip and Hemson were safely in the pocket of the Ancient One's robes, which billowed behind the old fairy like thunderclouds. He felt hungry; he knew he would be hungry when he got to the castle. He'd spent a lot of energy to get there so quickly. "Ah," he thought, "a grand feast will most likely be waiting for me when I arrive."

Shortly after he'd had that thought, the castle came into his view. "Now…food and rest and then we must find the missing princess." He landed near the Great Oak as a gust of wind blew his robes over his head. Hemson and Pip flew out, grabbed a piece of the hem in their beaks and brought the garment right.

Chapter 56

After Shirt

———————

Jewel felt the heat of a blush crawl up her neck and make her cheeks burn. What had possessed her to take off her shirt and show Ethan the tattoo of wings on her back? Maybe because he thought his wings were so hideous, when all she saw was beauty in them. She was too nervous to turn around and face him as she clutched the shirt to her chest.

Ethan said, "I...Jewel...I don't understand...your wings...." He paused and then asked, "Did you go to the same tattoo parlor as me? Is that why you are showing me your tattoo? Wait, how is that possible? You're an exchange student. You've only been here for a month. Your tattoo is not a new one, so...what the hell is going on?"

Jewel was scared to turn and face him now. Mir and Beecher were talking to her in her head. "We didn't expect you to show him your wings so fast," said Beecher.

Mir let out a giggle. "Good for you Jewel. You need to gain his trust now that we know his father is the corrupt and evil person who is lurking in this world."

"You will have to tell him all now, or he will not trust you and may not help us," said Beecher.

Jewel knew this was the moment of truth, so she put her shirt back on then turned and looked at Ethan. He had the strangest look on his face, and he backed away from her. Again, he said with a lot more force: "What the hell is going on here? I think you need to come clean with me, Jewel. Who are you? Damn, I can't believe you have wings on your back like mine. That is so freaking crazy! I hate them, I can't wait to get them removed!"

"Ethan, I don't think you will ever be able to remove them. I have a story I need to tell you but I know it will be hard for you to believe me. I just told it to Sam last night, and…well, the good news is she believed me. The bad news was I told her she couldn't tell anyone. I think she will be happy to know someone else knows this secret and she can talk with you about it."

Ethan's eyes narrowed. He looked suspicious about what she'd said. "OK…you better go ahead with this story."

She took his hand into hers, even though he flinched when she reached for it. "I'm not from this world, Ethan. I stumbled into your world through an invisible portal between my world and the human one. It happened on my sixteenth birthday, just after I got my wings… my real wings. You see, in my world all our people have wings; they get them when they reach the age of sixteen. We are also a bit smaller in my world than you are here. A lot smaller.

"Since I have been in this world I have read some of the human books and I guess you could compare us to the tales of the Fae people or fairies your myths speak of. I am a princess, daughter of King Rowland and Queen Cordelia in the Kingdom of Dorawine. I have an older sister, Aspen and a younger brother Tomwyn. My best friend, Ember and I were in our secret place; which is located in a root at the base of the Great Oak tree in our village. We discovered this earthen room when we were very young. It appeared that no one knew of this room and so we claimed it as ours and spent a lot of time there."

Jewel looked at Ethan to read his expression. He looked blank, like he had mentally left the room but his body was till there. She went on. "I know you like history—and my world has its own history."

She then told him what she knew about the Creators, and how the two worlds were in competition with one another. Ethan still had a blank expression on his face, but it seemed to be softening a bit.

"Jewel. Jewel, I think you need help. I really, really like you, but what you are saying is really unbelievable and crazy."

"I know," she said. "Sam said the same thing to me."

"Does she really believe you?"

Jewel felt a flash of anger, but let it pass. "Yes of course she believed my story—it's the truth!"

"Really? 'Cause honestly this is the weirdest thing I have ever heard. It makes absolutely no sense to me."

"I get that," she said, "but let me finish my story and then I'll give you the proof you need which will validate all of what I am about to tell you."

She started the story again, from the time of the morning of her sixteenth birthday—how her wings came in right before she was about to travel over the falls. How it felt to fly and to also learn about her power.

"Power?" Ethan interrupted her. "Wow. This story is getting even more fantastic, Jewel. Do you really expect me to believe this? Hey are you taking any drugs you want to tell me about?"

Jewel felt insulted by his lack of faith in her, but Mir kept encouraging her to finish her story.

"So, I told you I am a royal, and, only the royals acquire a pre-ordained gift from the angels. The gift is a special power. My sister is bonded to the flowers of our land. She can hear them speak to her about the harvest or they tell her if they are sick. My father can control and hear the tales of the wind and my mother, the water. I was given something very unusual, which I had never even heard of—the ability to speak with the trees. You see, many of the same trees exist in both worlds. I fell through a portal in a tree, which still exists, in my world and in yours. The tree gave me knowledge of your world and a command of your language. Sam just happened to pull into the parking lot of the forest's edge, and I made up a story so she would help me. You see, I can return at any time but the tree told me about someone else who passed through the tree—someone very evil who had taken something very dear to my world and my people. So I had to stay and find it to bring back to my world because I may be the only person who can pass through the tree." Jewel now had Ethan's full attention.

"What was taken that was so dear?"

"This bad person took the key to the Vault of Souls. The Vault of Souls holds the magic and energy of thousands of generations of our people, including the royals. When a Fae dies they are cremated in a special furnace designed by the angels and their soul and energy is preserved in a glass vessel that, if broken by someone, can be absorbed by that person. My father was wearing the key, just as all the ruling kings or queens of our land did, when he was drugged and it was stolen. The key is passed down from generation to generation, and is always the choice of the angels, since they pick the new King or Queen who will rule our lands."

"Jewel, I am going to ask you again, how do you expect me to believe this? Honestly, put yourself in my place. This is like a child's fairy tale." Then he laughed. "Oh that's funny! A fairy tale!"

"Fine" said Jewel, "I know it's crazy, but the proof is in my pocket and on my back and all over my body. Mir, Beecher, I need your help here. Ethan thinks I'm crazy."

"What? Now you are talking to people who...what?...are invisible?" Ethan's voice took on a high pitch that sounded unnatural.

"Oh my goddess!" said Jewel. She reached down and opened her purse so that the *Pulchra avium* could climb out of their pockets. Mir was the first to pop out. Her feathers were askew, but her face was serious and fierce looking. Beecher followed her. Jewel looked at Ethan who now was sitting with his eyes wide and mouth open as he stared at the two little bird fairies.

"What the...? I feel a bit lightheaded," he said. "What in God's name are these...," his voice trailed off to a pause then a whisper, "... what are these creatures?"

Jewel took a big breath. "They were a birthday gift from my uncle."

"Oh? Are they pets?"

Both Mir and Beecher bristled at this comment.

"Oh. No not at all. They're not pets. They're fierce warriors from a clan called *Pulchra avium*. They are my guardians. The tips of their feathers hold an unusual poison that can kill a giant in an instant. They are very well known throughout our land as the most fierce and powerful fairies."

Ethan stifled a laugh.

Jewel went on. "I know. They don't look much like warriors in your world. But believe me it would be unwise to undervalue their abilities."

With that, both Mir and Beecher bowed towards her. She nodded to them and smiled.

"OK," said Ethan, "so you fell through a portal and ended up here in my world. And you are chasing a really bad guy who has stolen the key to the Vault of Souls, Have I gotten this all correct?"

Jewel nodded.

"And now you know who this person is and you are going after the key?"

Again she nodded so he continued: "...and Mir and Beecher are your warrior helpers and once you get the key you are going to go back to the tree and slip back through the portal as the tree talks you through it?" His voice was again taking on a higher pitch.

She nodded.

Ethan looked at Jewel, Mir and Beecher. "I guess I believe you. What choice do I have? I mean, who could make this up?" A moment of silence passed between them, then a subtle realization struck Ethan. He said, "Wait! How does any of this have to do with the fact you and I have the same tattoo?"

Jewel said, "I think you got wings on your sixteenth birthday because you are part fairy."

Ethan burst out laughing. "Are you kidding me? You think my mother is some good fairy who left money under my pillow when I lost a tooth? Then she graduated to a greater fairy?"

Jewel understood how Ethan felt. The information she'd given was a lot to absorb, and she now felt uncomfortable sharing the rest of her tale. She knew, once she told him everything, his life would be forever changed.

"Actually, Ethan, it's not your mother. I believe it is your father who may be the fairy."

"My father?" he roared, "Now you've gone way too far. My father is not," he stammered, "some fairy. Michael is a huge asshole, a dickwad, but a fairy? Come on, that is a stretch."

"Ethan, I know all of this is hard for you, but you just have to believe me. Michael is either part fairy or all fairy and from my world. The tree told me."

"Oh yeah," he said with more sarcasm "That's right, the tree told you all about the guy who stole the key, because of course trees are like policemen patrolling the two worlds."

"No they aren't," said Jewel. She felt that he was making fun of her and she didn't like it one bit. She looked at Mir who then nodded to Beecher and they both climbed into her purse.

She stood up and planted her hands on her hips. Her posture was that of a soldier in a battle, ready to attack.

"Look Ethan, I can't make you believe me. But my story is true. And just so you know…the reason why I am so bloody definite is because your…what was that you said? Dickwad? Asshole? Um… *your father*…Michael was wearing the key to the Vault of Souls around his neck! I saw it today and there is no mistake."

Then Jewel grabbed her purse and stormed out of Ethan's room, down the stairs and out of his house.

Chapter 57

Lost Jewel

As Jewel ran down the street, her long hair lifted in the wind. The sensation made her wish her real wings worked in this world—she wanted to fly! She was feeling angry because she was upset about Ethan not believing her. She was mad at herself because she'd lost her temper and had run from the situation instead of staying to face the issue between them. It was clear that Ethan had no idea who his father was; he didn't know anything about him—except that he hated him.

She slowed her pace on the sidewalk and wondered if she was heading in the right direction back to Sam's house. Jewel remembered that Sam told her to call when she was ready to leave Ethan's house so she could come meet her. To do that now, she'd have to go back to Ethan's house and ask to borrow his phone. She decided against that plan and stopped worrying about getting lost.

"There are a lot of trees in this world," she thought as she walked through the neighborhood. Soon she was lost in thought about all the varieties of plants, bushes and trees on her path. "They know how to get my attention, but they aren't speaking to me. I wonder why things are different with my new powers in this world?"

After she'd been walking for a while, nothing looked familiar. As soon as she realized she had no idea where she was, Mir's voice came into her head.

"Dear Jewel," she said. "Ethan was just overwhelmed with the whole story. It was a lot to absorb. I mean, how would you feel if someone told you that they were from a different world? I think you would, as they say in this world, 'freak out.' So give him some time. He will realize you were telling the truth."

Mir's words gave her some comfort, but Jewel couldn't figure out how she'd gotten so off track on the way back to Sam's house. "Thank you Mir. Now will you and Beecher help me? I'm lost. Do you think you can go and find Sam and bring her here? I can't go on and get more lost. There's a park, over there, with a bench. I'll sit and wait for you to get back. I want to think about how I can get to Ethan's dad and get the key from him. It probably won't be very easy, since it is around his neck."

Beecher said, "I'm hesitant to leave you alone. Maybe one of us should stay with you."

"No! I don't want you two to be separated! And anyway, what's going to happen in the next few minutes? It's a sunny day and I don't mind being alone for a while. I'll be able to think about this situation without any interruptions…not that you two ever feel like an intrusion."

Jewel was flustered.

"We understand," Beecher said. "It shouldn't take us very long to find Sam's house once we fly high enough to see the layout of these neighborhoods. Sit tight and we will meet you back here as soon as we can. Promise not to move?"

"Yes."

As they flew up and away, Jewel walked over and sat on the bench near a large tree. Part of it was shaded; the other part was in the sun. Jewel chose to sit between the two types of light, then leaned back and let bits of sunlight flit across her face. She closed her eyes and breathed in the smell of the woods. Then she opened her mind to see if she could hear the whisperings of the trees. If she could just relax….

"If I could just relax…if I could just relax…," she said to herself, like a mantra.

Now, she heard murmurings from the trees in the woods. She closed out all the other noises and worked to concentrate on their voices. It was like listening to a crowd of people who were whispering with mouths full of food.

"Concentrate, concentrate!" Jewel thought.

The voices got sharper. Jewel could pick up words, and feelings, from the trees. The trees here *did* have souls and could speak to her! It was bizarre and also very magical.

"I am here," she thought, "please…speak to me!"

Once the trees sensed that they were being witnessed by Jewel they paid attention. "Child of the Trees," they were saying, over and over, "Child of the Trees!"

She heard one distinct voice, perhaps a Maple, say, "There is a Child of the Trees amongst us!"

"How is that possible?" a tall Ash asked a taller Pine.

Jewel wanted to explain her situation to them through her thoughts. She projected images from her mind to them—images of her as a fairy, flying among them and whispering that she was of the Fae realm. It was a tiring process to master this communication—it took a lot of her energy.

She wondered if communicating with the trees was made harder because she wasn't in her world. "So many strange things are here that affect my ability to think straight," she thought.

Just then she heard the voice of the Ash say, "Only evil has passed through one of us before you, my child."

As if a strong breeze had sifted through their leaves, all the trees whispered, "Malick...it was Malick...."

And at that, all went silent around her. Jewel felt fear take root in her heart.

"Malick! The evil fairy in the story Grandma Rose told me so long ago? Malick?" She felt shock. The realization that Michael was Malick overwhelmed her. She moved into the sun and slouched down to rest her neck on the back of the rough wood of the park bench. Jewel was trying with every ounce of her energy to sort the information.

Although the warm sunlight felt good, she was exhausted and very anxious. Jewel kept her eyes closed to take some deep breaths and calm down. She let the sunlight spread all over her. It made her a bit feel stronger.

After a few minutes, she felt a shadow cross her face. "Strange," she thought, "there weren't any clouds in the sky." Then she heard a voice...but not from a tree.

"Well, look who is here. And sunbathing! It's Ethan's new little friend."

Jewel opened her eyes and sat up straight. Standing over her, looking down into her face was Ethan's father.

Michael.

Malick!

Jewel felt the hairs on the back of her neck bristle and the tattoo of her wings was heating up. She rolled her shoulders. "Ah...uh... what...do...you...want?"

"I want to get to know you. Any friend of my son is of interest to me."

Jewel was so uncomfortable and nervous that she called out to Mir and Beecher: "Hurry back!"

"That was an odd response."

"I am expecting my friend to meet me here at any moment so I don't really have time to talk with you."

He grabbed her arm, pulled her up and placed something over her nose and mouth. It smelled vile as she struggled against his wiry arms. Within seconds of the struggle, she felt dizzy, and lightheaded. Her mind drifted away, down a long dark tunnel.

Malick smiled. "That was easy," he thought. He lifted her up, carried her to his car, opened the trunk and placed Jewel's limp body inside. As he closed the trunk he said, "Now, we're going to have some fun."

Down the street, two small boys who'd been playing with tree branches as swords stopped and watched the shiny black car pass by. They saw it stop and turn the corner. "Stranger danger!" said the one who was taller.

Chapter 58

Sam Alert

As they neared Sam's house, Mir and Beecher felt Jewel's panic. "Let's go get her! Now!" Mir's voice turned into a screech as they reached Sam's house and landed on the front gate. Sam was standing outside of her front door. She looked up when she heard the sound then ran to where the bird fairies had perched and noticed Beecher's feathers turning bright red.

"Sam, something is wrong!" he said. "Jewel is in trouble! I feel her fear! We must go right now. Mir, you go with Sam and I will meet you at the park. Something is amiss, so hurry!"

Just as his words left his mouth another feeling came to him—a feeling of absence. Jewel was gone. He no longer felt her. He looked at Mir and she shook her head 'no' in response. She no longer felt Jewel's energy either.

"Oh no!" Beecher said, "Something is really wrong now. Neither Mir nor I can feel Jewel. We have never lost connection with her, but now it is gone. Meet me at the park as soon as you can get there. I have to go now." Beecher flapped his wings in a display of nervous energy as he took off high into the sky.

"What's wrong?" Sam asked as she walked with Mir. "How come you can't feel Jewel any longer?"

"We have been bonded to Jewel as much as Jewel has been bonded to the trees. Now I can't feel her, nor can Beecher. Normally we can hear all her thoughts. We don't listen to them unless we have to because we don't want to intrude on her privacy. We are always able to feel her but now her thoughts have vanished from both our minds. It's like a thick curtain has fallen and shut us out, and that is very hard to do unless Jewel has returned to our world or..." she hesitated, "perhaps...she is dead." Mir lowered her voice to a whisper with the last thought.

"Dead? Jewel's not dead! Let's go to her right now—follow Beecher!" said Sam as anxiety overcame her and she quickened her pace.

Now that Mir was flying and Sam was running, they reached the park within minutes. Beecher was sitting on the park bench, distraught and anxious. The two little creatures rushed to each other and started a deep in conversation in low voices.

Sam felt left out. "Hey guys? Remember me? I'm still here—Sam! Jewel's friend! Where is Jewel? Do you know what happened to her?"

Mir and Beecher looked at Sam. Her head was in front of the sun and a golden halo was around her face.

Beecher said, "She's vanished and we believe it was not of her own doing. The only person who could have taken her was Ethan's father. He was wearing the key—and he knew she'd seen it—so he must be the evil one the Great Oak mentioned to Jewel when we passed through it to this world. That tree told us there was an evil fairy in this land and he had stolen the key. Now this evil fairy has stolen Jewel and we know it has to be Ethan's father. We have to find him."

"Wait just a minute. What do you mean, Ethan's father has the key? Do you mean *the* key, like to the Vault of Souls Jewel told me about? How the hell did he get that? I don't understand what you're telling me."

Mir flew to Sam's shoulder and for the next few minutes relayed the events which occurred at Ethan's' house and the interaction with his father. When they were done, Sam sat down on the bench. She was silent.

"We need to find her—but how?" Sam said. "Let's head to Ethan's house just in case she went back there."

Mir and Beecher flew ahead as Sam got up and walked towards Ethan's house. After the first few steps, she broke out into a run.

Chapter 59

Wise Welcome

———————

Still walking toward the castle, the Ancient One saw its doors in the distance. A crowd was milling and he expected a great welcome from the royal family and the villagers. He took several deep breaths before quickening his pace.

The King and Queen walked toward him, and when the two got close enough, they both bowed low to the Ancient One to show respect. Royalty never bows to anyone, so the gesture was a great honor to him. The Ancient One bowed in return.

"Thank you for coming to our aid," said the King. "We are most distressed and at a complete loss. We cannot find any helpful clues to the disappearance of either the key to the Vault of Souls or our daughter, Jewel. I that pray you can help us find both. The sense of doom we are feeling is very unsettling."

The King's face showed the stress of the last few days, and the wizard noticed it. He placed his gnarled hand on the King's shoulder and said, "I am weary from my travels, and hungry. My companions, two *Pulchra avium* are also in need of food and drink. Let us break bread and talk about all that has transpired so I may think upon it and see if I can find some clarity."

With that the Queen took the Ancient One's arm and escorted him into the castle and to the Great Hall. A feast had been made ready and foods of all kinds and preparations were laid on the tables. The Ancient One had not eaten such fine fare in many, many years and savored each bite.

The meal lasted for quite a long time. When he finished eating, he said to the Queen: "I thank you for these wonderful flavors!"

When the plates were being cleared, the King stood and led the wizard, along with Hemson and Pip, to their quarters. "I suggest a good night's rest for we have much to discuss in the morning. We can meet at first light after some breakfast. Please send your assistants with a message to me when you're ready," said the King.

"Yes, Rowland, a good night's rest will suit me well. We will work together to find your most precious daughter in the morn. Be at peace, your majesty, for you know that Jewel was meant for great things. It has been foretold, so do not lose faith. We will find her."

The King was a bit surprised by this statement but let the old fairy go to his bed without further discussion. He closed the door to the guest suite and headed to his own quarters, the whole time thinking about what the Ancient One had just said: "Jewel is destined for great things."

Chapter 60

Between Us?

———————

Ethan sat alone in his bedroom thinking, "What should I do with that story? I've never heard of anything like it...but Jewel is so beautiful...and nice...and we have the same tattoo. Did I make her angry? But that story...it was so...so...strange! What's going to happen between us now?" He let the shock of her story sink in. No one would believe such a tale, but the evidence was interesting.

He wished he could tell someone; he felt it was news that would change the world. It could re-write the history of how the Earth was formed, of mankind's past, not to mention the impact on the world's religions. It was a truth that was so big that Ethan's mind kept coming up with ways in which it would affect mankind's knowledge of the Universe.

Jewel made him swear he would tell no one—even though she said that she'd told Sam, too. But, did she also swear Sam to secrecy? Instinct made him realize he had to maintain this secret. He wondered if Sam would keep the information to herself, too.

He kept thinking how crazy the story was, and the even crazier accusation that his father was a thief from another world—and a fairy. But the appearance of Mir and Beecher —as unbelievable as they were—made the story feel true. No one could create those little fairies, nor make up such a fantastic tale, unless they were truly crazy.

Ethan first thought was that Jewel had returned when he heard the doorbell ring. He raced downstairs to the front door, still feeling upset about how she'd left. He knew Jewel was not crazy. Well, he wanted to believe that she wasn't crazy by the time he'd reached the door and opened it.

"Hey, Ethan." Sam said.

"I thought maybe you were Jewel," Ethan said, bypassing a normal greeting. "We ended our, uh, visit on a bad note. But I guess you know that. I mean, who would believe such a crazy story?"

Sam opened her mouth. No sound came out.

Ethan saw that Sam looked upset. She was pale. "Wait. What's wrong?" he asked.

"Jewel disappeared. Mir and Beecher think something bad has happened because they can't feel her energy or hear her thoughts any more. She got lost after she left your house and she sent Mir and Beecher to come get me. When I got to the park where she was supposed to be waiting, she was gone. The little guys felt her disconnect—I guess by ESP—and they freaked. I think something did happen to her, something bad, and we need your help."

Ethan felt an overwhelming sense of dread rise up and tighten his gut. "What do you mean you can't feel her energy or read her thoughts?"

Mir and Beecher were sitting on Sam's shoulders listening to the conversation. Beecher flew to Ethan and spoke to him while perched on his right shoulder. Then he nodded his head as he looked at Sam.

Sam interrupted. "Guys! I'm here too, you know. It's kind of rude to whisper when someone else is standing right in front of you."

"He's just telling me what happened after she left," Ethan said, "and they think my father had something to do with her disappearance. Just give us a minute, Sam." Ethan listened to Beecher for another minute and said, "Uh, OK. But does it hurt? I mean will I feel anything weird? I kinda hate the pain thing."

Mir flew to Ethan's other shoulder and whispered into his ear. Then she and Beecher took flight at the same time, in a whirr of wings, a puff of something like smoke and a gust of wind. Sam reeled back from the chaos, looked down at her feet and coughed a few times.

"Hey Ethan, did you see that?" she said as she turned to him.

He was gone.

Sam looked back to the sky. She saw Beecher and Mir clamped onto Ethan's ears, one small bird fairy on each side. Each had a feathered arm stuck inside of an ear and they were bringing him back toward her. A look of sheer terror was on Ethan's face.

When they landed in the exact spot where Ethan had been standing, Mir and Beecher were again sitting on his shoulder.

"Did you do it?" Ethan asked.

"Yes, we are all done. Thank you, for we can now trust you. We have examined all of your thoughts and all of your memories. We have been in every corner of your brain. You have no secrets from us now."

Beecher turned to Sam. "Sam, he can be trusted and now we must find Jewel, for we have much fear in our hearts and we must seek relief."

"OK, then. My car or yours Ethan?" Sam asked.

"Yours, because my father won't recognize it and I think that makes it safer." Ethan bounded out of his front door, moved past Sam, turned to her and said, "So... are you coming too?"

Sam ran after him all the way to her house. She pointed to her car that was parked a way down the street. "I have to get my keys," she said as she turned to go towards the front door. "Wait for me...one second."

Beecher said to Ethan, "Go with Sam in the car. We'll follow you in flight."

Before Ethan could reply, Sam came right back out of the house in a flash, swinging her purse. "Uh, I'm embarrassed but the car door on your side is stuck. After Jewel got into it several weeks ago, the handle got stuck and the door no longer opens. You have to get in on my side or go through the window."

"Let me first try the door then I'll think about options two and three if I can't open it," Ethan said. He pulled on the handle for a few seconds then slid through the window on the passenger side.

Sam was nervous about going after Jewel without police back up. She giggled thinking about the word "back up," like from the movies. But this was no movie and they couldn't tell anyone because of course, who would believe her when she told them her friend, a fairy, from another Universe, was missing?

"You have to tell me how to get to your father's house, Ethan."

"Just keep driving straight out of town and I'll tell you when to turn. The little birds are going to fly above us."

There was an ominous tone to Ethan's voice. Despite what Mir and Beecher had said, it made her feel even more nervous.

Chapter 61

Root Cellar

It had been a bumpy ride in the trunk, but Jewel didn't know it. The smell of chloroform had knocked her out. She also didn't feel it when she was taken out of the car, tossed over Malick's shoulder and taken into a room where chains that were anchored to the ceiling were attached to her wrists by cuffs.

It was only when she felt difficulty breathing that Jewel started to see some light. Her eyelids were heavy and felt puffy. Her tongue was thick and she was very thirsty. She realized she was in pain. Her arms were over her head and she felt the weight of the iron chains around her wrists. Was she standing in a thick layer of fog? She wondered how to push it away so she could see. But she just couldn't focus. It was maddening! All she wanted to do was figure out where she was and why everything hurt. She breathed in with effort, gulping the air to see if it would clear her vision.

The room had the scent of a musky burrow, cool and damp, with a sweet aroma of rich earth. That smell calmed her for just the briefest of moments and gave her a new burst of energy. "Focus," she thought. "Clear this fog from your head, Jewel!" And then, again: "I *am* going to clear this fog from my head." She kept saying it over and over like a mantra, willing it to happen.

In dim light, the haze made it seem like natural daylight at dusk. "A cellar room," she thought. "I'm in the basement of a house and the light is coming from small windows above the ground. I have to get out. I wonder if Mir or Beecher can hear my thoughts?" Then she opened her mind to see if she could connect to her guardians. "They must be in such a panic."

Her mind reached out like the long tendrils of a jellyfish seeking a desired target. To her surprise she felt an entanglement of hundreds of new connections wrapped around each other. "Roots! I'm feeling the roots that belong to all of the trees! All of the trees! There must be hundreds of trees surrounding this place. I hear them all!"

A huge sense of calm washed over her. She basked in the knowledge that the trees were aware of her peril. They were going to help her. A sense of hope came in to match her calm and she again closed her eyes and relaxed for a short time—until the darkness went away.

A light from over her head was so bright that she could see it through her eyelids. She felt a shape, a being, walking towards her. Fear replaced calm and crept up her back. Her wing tattoo fluttered under her skin. The leaves on her arms and legs felt like snakes moving over her skin.

She knew who was coming for her: Ethan's father, the evil Malick. She struggled with the chains that bound her.

"My dear, you cannot extricate yourself from these chains. I designed them myself and I made sure these chains will not allow your escape."

Chapter 62

Scribe Sandella

At sunrise in the kingdom of Dorawine, as the King waited for word of his planned meeting with the Ancient One, he stared out of a small window in the royal bedroom. This window, unlike others, was covered with bars. "I am in a prison of worry over Jewel," he said out loud, even though the Queen slept nearby. "I'm going to go to my study now. Perhaps I'll be met with a message on the way."

The Queen rolled over as he created a draft of air while pulling his robes around his shoulders and shut the door in as quiet a way possible.

Click. Click.

The King heard the sounds as soon as he set foot in the hallway.

"Bogart, is that you? I hear you. Where are you?"

Bogart was sitting on a windowsill. With his antennae, he flicked a small scroll to the floor.

The King picked it up and read it. "I see he's waiting. Thank you, Bogart." He walked a ways down the hallway and heard another click. "Yes, Bogart, we do need to find our Jewel."

The Ancient One stared out the window of the study. Sunlight was just starting to creep over the horizon and the view of the village and its landscape was spectacular. He listened as the King told the sequence of events from the death of the guard, to the key being stolen to his daughter's disappearance. Every now and then the old fairy stopped the King to ask a question or get clarification.

As the morning went on, the Ancient One interviewed Aspen and Tomwyn, Thor, Ember, Phan, and all the people who were with Jewel before she disappeared. He also spoke to Thor about how the key could have been stolen; how the manservant had died, the timing of the theft and whether or not Thor had any idea who had stolen the key.

The interviews went on and on until at last the King said it was time for lunch. As they were leaving the King's study the old wizard noticed the tapestry on the wall—the same one Thor had shown the King. He went up to the tapestry and pulled a large round piece of glass out of thin air. The Ancient One used it to magnify the woven details—he too saw a clue.

"Ah," he said, "so there is an image of Lucinda."

He talked to himself in a low voice as he thought back to his time with the blind fairy. "She was born without sight, but the angels blessed her with many special gifts. She was a compassionate and benevolent fairy who lived before my time, and, during my time. She was very old when I was a young man, and taught me certain things, which enhanced my powers. Lucinda was not a royal, but her heart was so pure; the angels gave her much in the way of wisdom. She once told me she could see the angels in her mind even though she had never seen anything with her eyes. I asked her how that was possible. She said that they spoke with her in her thoughts and she could see their beautiful faces. At first they would come when she felt despair from her lack of sight; but in time, as she accepted her situation, they spoke with her much more often—about other people and their lives and situations. Lucinda's life was chronicled in some of the old scrolls."

The Ancient One turned to face the King and said, "Your father, Rowland, had many books and scrolls in his library. He and I visited in that library room in the tower many years ago. Lucinda knew secrets about our world that only she was privy to. She once told me she kept a diary and upon her death would bestow the royals with it as a gift so they too could learn the secrets of the world. Whether she did or not, I have always wondered what her diary contains. She had a *Pulchra avium* who was her scribe. If you give me a moment, I will remember that little creature's name."

There was silence in the hall as the wizard tried to remember.

"Sandella," he said. "Yes, Sandella. She was beautiful, and stayed with Lucinda throughout her life. Like Pip and Hemson—always at my side." A wistful look came over the Ancient One as he stood with blank eyes, his mind traveling back into his memories of Lucinda. "I think we should take a trip to your library. It would be wonderful to find Lucinda's diary and see if there are any answers in her writings."

"Agreed," said the King.

They went back into the King's study and flew out of a large open portal to the library in the high tower. It took just a moment for them to arrive, but when they showed up, the task of finding one small book amongst the thousands and thousands of scrolls and leather bound books seemed quite daunting.

"We may be here quite awhile!" the King said. "The shelves go all the way to the ceiling and I cannot imagine how we will be able to look at every book in here." The King felt deflated and sat down in a chair. "I did find a reference to Lucinda in the *Book of Secrets*," he said, "but I could not make out the riddle accompanying the description of her."

"The *Book of Secrets*! I would certainly like to read that one, but we may not find the answer there. We need to find Lucinda's diary. I am sure some clues will be in her writings. I will conjure a spell to find her book, just give me a moment."

The Ancient One stood in the middle of the circular study. His wings were tucked in close, his old eyes closed tight, as if he were a statue. The King heard some words come out of his mouth. They sounded like riddles.

"Lucinda the pure, I beseech you now to hear my words from the great winds above to the silence below. We need to find the wisdom of your words. Please pass to me the recording of your life as written from your hand. If ever the Fae needed you, they need you now."

The wizard raised his hands. Sparks of energy shot out from them into the room. But nothing happened. No book came forward. The wizard stood in silence for a moment. "Of course. I know I made a mistake," he said, as he seemed to be talking with an invisible person. "I will start anew: Lucinda the pure, I beseech you to hear my words from the great winds above to the silence below. We need to find the wisdom of your words. Please pass to me the wisdom of your life as written by your scribe, Sandella!"

Again the wizard spread his hands out to the room and a tiny spark of light left his fingers. This time, a book pulled away from one of the higher shelves and floated down like a feather into the Ancient One's hands.

Chapter 63

Fairy Father

Sam realized she had too much on her mind. "Ethan, keep an eye on Beecher and Mir! I don't want to lose them and it's getting dark!"

"I still see them, but you're driving faster than they're flying," Ethan yelled. He had turned to poke his head and torso out of the window to look for the fairy birds. "Maybe you should stop so they can ride with us?"

As soon as he made the suggestion, Sam said, "Put your head inside, now!" and slammed on the brakes. "Do you think they'll get it?" she said.

"Uh…well, at least now they're closer." Ethan put his arm out of the window and made a 'come over here' motion.

Within a minute, Beecher and Mir flew into the car and sat on the top rim of the rearview mirror. "Thank you," said Beecher, "we cannot fly as fast when we are trying to communicate!"

Sam looked at Beecher and said, "OK, then, let's go." She eased off the brakes then resumed the high-speed drive towards Ethan's father's house.

The bird fairies were speaking to each other nonstop in their own language and neither Sam nor Ethan had a clue as to what they were saying; nor did they want to interrupt. Finally Beecher spoke in a way they understood. "The trees are speaking with us just as they do with Jewel. They are speaking with her, too and we can hear them. Both Mir and I feel her again, but we cannot seem to reach her mind, something is blocking us. We can be instrumental in this rescue since we can pass through smaller spaces and also we can fly so fast no human eye can trace us."

Sam looked at Ethan. He said nothing, so she said, "I know you guys will be a great help, but we still don't know what we are getting ourselves into. Whatever it is, you are both welcome."

"Thank you for driving, Sam," Beecher said. "We appreciate your help and your friendship to Jewel."

"Well...then...."

"Turn left here!" Ethan interrupted as they sped along the two-lane road out of town. "It looks like a dirt road, but it is actually the start of my father's driveway. When I was sixteen, and I started to drive, I use to come out here and sit and think about going to have a little chat with my dear old dad. But I never did. I figured, why bother? The guy is a jerk."

Sam had made the turn and they drove up that long winding road to the house on the hill. "There's a gate," Ethan said, "but I don't know how we'll get in. We may need to park and walk around. I think if I announce our arrival, he will know we're coming for Jewel. We need to be quiet. This house has a sophisticated alarm system. I remember when I was here before, I saw Michael entering codes on at least two number pads, one on the outside of the door and one inside the door."

As they approached the house, Sam observed the house's modern architecture. It was built of dark metal and glass...she had never seen such a strange looking place. The roof had odd angles; the peaks looked like a pentagram. There was no sound; no movement.

"Park over there" said Ethan, pointing to a level place in the dirt. "If we park here, I think he can't see the car from any window in the house."

Sam parked the car under a large tree with a thick trunk. "Now what?" she said.

"Now we play it by ear and see if my worthless fairy father has my girlfriend," Ethan said.

Sam looked at Ethan. She was surprised by his proclamation that Jewel was his girlfriend and curious how they were going to save her from the wealthiest man in their little town.

Chapter 64

Curiosity Control

Jewel's vision was almost totally clear by the time Malick approached her. She was cold and shivering from the damp air in the basement. She realized her shirt was torn in back—she could feel the cold wall on her skin, and she guessed he had ripped it to see if she had a wing tattoo.

The trees were touching her mind, reassuring her. If not for their attention, she would have been in a panic.

"Time for a little chat," he said. "I think you know what I want to hear. How did you pass through the portal and not turn into a human child?"

Jewel looked at him in surprise. She recalled what the tree told her—that he had been turned into a human baby when he went through the portal. So he'd grown up in the in the human world yet he probably had gotten a wing tattoo when he turned sixteen. Or had he? She kept her thoughts to herself and said nothing to him.

He pulled the fine gold chain out from beneath his collard shirt and said, "I know you recognized this."

And there it was, the sacred golden key to the Vault of Souls.

The surface of the diamond, which adorned the top of the key, sent out a million colors as a recessed light bulb in the ceiling illuminated its facets. In this world, its brilliance was equally as magnificent as it was in the Fae realm. For a moment, time stood still for Jewel. The sight of the key touched off a string of memories that sprang into her head. She saw visions of her family and felt overwhelmed with loss. Her heart constricted, and her stomach formed knots as she looked at Ethan's father.

In her mind she said, "Snap out of it! Do not let him see you cry! Just stare him down. Stare!" As Jewel stared at Malik, she knew he was the coldest of evil beings, whether in this world or hers.

"Is your name truly Jewel? Is that what you wish for me to call you?" The tone of his voice was cold.

When Jewel didn't answer, he continued. "Well no matter, Jewel, let me introduce myself to you correctly. My given name in this god-forsaken world is Michael. You may already know that. However in your world, my name was Malick."

Of course Jewel recognized the name from the stories her grandmother, Rose, had passed on to her. A powerful chill wracked her body and she shivered. Even her teeth were chattering inside her clenched jaw.

"So do you know of my name from your village?" he asked.

Jewel wasn't sure how to respond but as the seconds passed, she couldn't control her curiosity any longer. "Why did you take it? And, and how did you get through the portal?"

"Ah! So you did go through that interesting little worm hole in the tree!" He laughed, but his glee had a bitter edge. "I wasn't well liked in your world. Maybe it was because of those little murders I committed. The Fae, as I know now, are so squeamish about killing unless it is necessary. In this world, these beings kill all the time…and over stupid things, too. I find it so amusing. I have had the privilege of discovering so many ways to kill here in this world that I can't wait to bring them into yours. Of course I will rule your world once I get into the Vault and steal all those old fairy souls." He laughed again.

Another chill went up Jewel's back. So that was his plan, thought Jewel. He did, indeed want to steal the souls. "But…why?" Jewel asked in such a soft voice she could barely hear herself.

"Because I can. And I will. They were horrible to me! All those years of ridicule. Even having to grow into this body with all those memories tainted my human experience. They hate me here, too." With a deep breath and an evil sneer, he continued, "And once I have all this delicious power, your people will bow to me as their new King."

"Never!" she said in the loudest voice she'd ever spoken.

Malick came toward Jewel with such speed it frightened her. He was just inches from her face. It was contorted in anger, then his face changed again. He sniffed the air in front of her and then went calm. "Ah, the scent of a fairy. So delicate and distinct. I didn't remember it until just now." He bushed his face along hers, smelling her skin.

Jewel tried to pull away but the chains kept her in place.

"No wonder my son has a fascination with you. Oh, I am going to have so much fun. How old are you?"

Jewel looked straight into his eyes. She remembered Tomwyn telling her never to back down from a fight or from a bully because that lets them win. "Always show courage," he'd said to her, "even when someone wants to hurt you. Look your attacker in the eye. It shows bravery in a person who is a fighter."

"I'm a royal," she thought, "so now act like one, not some scared little girl." A new courage over came her and she spat out the words "You don't frighten me, Malick."

He seemed surprised by her boldness. He smiled. "Ah, my dear, but you should be frightened—and very much so—because what I am going to do to you will be one of my greatest creations and even though I will enjoy it immensely, you will not."

He licked his lips. "Now, how old are you, and how did you get here?" Malick faced Jewel. His lavender eyes locked onto hers. His hair was black as a moonless night over a pool of crude oil and he'd combed it straight back off his forehead.

"You cannot make me talk with you," she thought. "I won't!"

After a minute, he stepped back and looked down. He seemed to be lost in thought.

"Well, however you got here," he said, "it must have been in a way far easier than mine. You see, I had to start all over again, as an infant in this half-human, half-fairy body. The problem was that I was my fairy age in the body of a baby. I had to endure youth all over again. Funny. In human years, I'm middle-aged man, halfway through his life span; but in the Fae world I am still very young in terms of my life's span. Human beings don't live very long, certainly not as long as we fairies. Why in our world we live more than three times longer!" His tone was one of pride.

"You're a shy one," he said as he stepped in close to her face again; smelling her skin as if she contained the greatest of aromatics. "I may need to keep you."

He hesitated…then spoke to her in their native language, "I will make you an undead."

The undead in the Fae world were uncommon, but they did exist for the purpose of learning a lesson. An undead was a fairy who was under the control of another creature to be in that creature's servitude. It was a willing submission to power that could only be broken by equal and opposite will. Although the situation was part of a contract, it was an unpleasant existence for the fairy, and it was to be endured until they no longer chose to be party to the contract. In choosing to break the contract, the fairy chose freedom...and thus a new responsibility.

Jewel did not want to be the undead for Malick! "Who is he," she thought, "that he thinks I will give my power over to him!"

A strange buzzing noise sounded. "Ah," said Malick, "We have guests. Maybe it's your little girlfriend. She's not a fairy, but no matter; I can have fun with her too."

Malick turned and left the cellar, leaving Jewel where she was. Her heart was thumping so loudly in her chest she could barley hear his footsteps ascend the stairs.

Chapter 65

Artist's Runes

Back in the tower library, the King marveled at the way the diary drifted down from the highest shelf and into the wizard's out-reached hands. The cover looked like a quilt of different colored barks, woven together in a patchwork pattern. Long ribbons drifted out of the seams of the book. A dried flower floated down along with the book and landed on the floor next to the King.

"Let's take a look and see if we can find some answers," said the old wizard.

The King had cleared a space on his desk for the book that allowed them both to see it together. The pages were old and brittle. Runes were written on each side of the parchment pages. Beautiful drawings of Lucinda were sketched in each margin where the story of each day began. Sandella was a great artist. Each image of Lucinda showed a different expression or pose of the beautiful blind fairy.

Some entries were very short and mentioned the weather or someone who'd visited her, but occasionally the men read a message that Lucinda took from the angels and told to Sandella. Some of these messages were about how to make spells, such as one for sleep, or to how to find lost things. Each spell seemed to correlate to something that had happened in the previous weeks when Lucinda asked for help.

They were halfway through the book when the King admitted a secret feeling that this was a fool's errand. Maybe the Ancient One was no longer clear-headed; this was akin to reading a daughter's diary and it held no answers so far. The King's thoughts took him away from the task at hand as his mind drifted to other ideas. He had gotten little sleep since both the key and his daughter went missing and he felt maybe now the exhaustion was affecting him.

The Ancient One kept carefully reading the runes and had not noticed the King's mental absence. Then he said, "Here it is! You see!" he said to the King. "I knew we would find something in this diary!"

The King returned his focus to Lucinda's diary and the old wizard who was pointing to a page on the left side of the book. "Another riddle of sorts, but one which I am sure I can decipher. I will read and translate for you the passage, since these runes are old text," the Ancient One said to the King. In a wise voice, he spoke:

I felt a soft breeze today, even though the winds were still. My sweet angel told me that when I feel such an odd breeze, to not tarry close to the direction of the winds, for there are doors that cannot be seen.

When I pressed for more information as to the danger, she told me the doors only are for those who are able to pass, but none other. How many of these doors exist I cannot tell, but there have been many times as I have wandered the Kingdom when the wind, cool and foreign, did stir when all around the rest of the world was without so much as a stirring, a puff.

The old Great Oak has a portal, and I know this for sure. I placed my hands around its opening, but could do no more than feel and smell the moving air. The Angels said that all will feel this shift if they open up their minds and close the world away. I have asked to journey through the portals, but they are not meant for my kind. These passageways were made by the Creators, the angel said, for only they, and their assigns, can pass without harm.

"This confirms there is some sort of portal in the Great Oak, but if Jewel passed through it, then she may have come to great harm!" the King said.

"I do not believe Jewel was harmed if she did go through this portal. The scrolls do not lie about her accomplishments as they have been foretold, so she is safe."

"What scrolls have foretold my daughter's accomplishments?"

"Sire, I have lived a long time. The sacred scrolls speak of a royal girl born of the trees whose gift of power exceeds all others born to the royal lineage. It was foretold she would have a great power and will thus be responsible for shaping the Universe and saving all of her people from eminent doom.

"The scrolls speak of another royal who was taken too soon to be the chosen one, and another would be born for this task. And it was to be a Child of the Trees. As soon as I heard of Jewel receiving the gift of the trees, I knew she was the one spoken of in the scrolls."

The King was thoughtful but still skeptical about the old wizard's interpretation of the scrolls. "Let us go to the tree now, old man, and see if we can feel the winds!" Then the King flew out the window from the tower, leaving the Ancient One where he stood, still reading Lucinda's diary.

"Ah, wait your majesty! I am coming too," said the Ancient One. But he left with much regret that he had to stop reading, so he closed the book and flew out after the King.

Chapter 66

No Judgment

Ethan wanted to get out of the car. He pushed Sam out of the driver's seat door when she opened it and climbed out after her. They both stood outside the car looking up at the monolithic modern glass and steel castle-like home Ethan's father had built on the tallest hill in town. In the last light of day, it looked even more intimidating. Beecher and Mir stayed inside the car.

"And…now…*what*?" asked Sam.

"Give me a moment to think," said Ethan. "I think there is a back fence with an overhanging tree branch. We can climb the tree and cross over on the branch to the other side, and then we can swing down from there. We'll use my belt." Ethan unbuckled his leather belt.

Sam looked at him like he was telling a big fat joke that she didn't think was so funny. "Are you nuts? There is no way in hell I am going to climb up a tree, balance on some branch then use your belt to lower myself onto the lovely green lawn below? And, it's getting dark!" Now Sam's voice had taken on a strange high pitch.

She stood in front of Ethan, her eyes as big as teacups.

He said, "You look like a deer in the headlights." In his mind, Ethan couldn't believe the badass, tough-looking, don't-mess-with-me Sam was afraid of climbing up and over a tree. He couldn't help it—he had to laugh.

"What? You're *laughing*?" Sam was totally annoyed but after just a few seconds of being angry, she couldn't help herself and she laughed right along with him. "This," said Sam as she took her hand and whirled it in a circle in front of Ethan, "is all theater and makeup and bad ass clothing, but the inside of this," and again she did the outline of a giant circle "is a marshmallowy scaredy cat! I don't like heights and I hate clowns, and cats kind of freak me out not to mention a whole host of other stuff I just really don't like! No judging me, OK?"

Ethan gave her a soft punch to the shoulder, realizing after he did it that it might not have been the right response. At that moment, Mir and Beecher flew out of the car's the window and landed on the top of the car. Beecher said, "We do need to go take a look up there, but Mir had a great idea. She thinks we should set off the alarm."

"Why would you want to do that?" Ethan asked.

Beecher flew to Ethan's shoulder and spoke to him in a hushed voice. "Hmmmm. Good idea. OK."

Sam saw that Ethan was nodding his head in agreement so she said, "We'll wait here until you've accomplished your, ah, task. Good luck and please be careful."

Then the little creatures flew away and disappeared, leaving Ethan and Sam behind.

"You shouldn't have punched me," Sam said.

Chapter 67

Alarm Problem

Jewel didn't like the buzzing—it irritated the insides of her ears. Because her hands were attached to chains she could not use them to muffle the sound. She heard every one Malik's footsteps as he walked around upstairs. The buzzing stopped. It was quiet for a moment and she wondered what would happen next. She got an answer when she heard his footsteps coming back down the stairs. Then the buzzing sound started again. "Damn!" he said as he went back up the stairs.

Jewel could hear him speaking with someone up there. A telephone rang and stopped when she heard him say, "Yes, I'm fine, but this blasted alarm keeps going off. Is there a problem with my system?" His voice was loud and filled with frustration. Jewel also heard Malik say, "Make sure it's not a problem on your end. This has happened before, and I told your manager that the next time this happened I would make sure to replace the services and ruin your reputation!"

Chapter 68

Wind Search

Phan was on guard when the King reached the Great Oak tree. The King landed on the exposed root that held the secret door. "May I help you, your Majesty?' Phan asked.

The King said, "We are just following up on a clue that was written in an ancient book. Have you felt any strange winds coming from the root of this tree, by any chance?"

Before Phan could answer, the Ancient One landed and stood next to the King. Phan's puzzled facial expression did not match the way his confident voice said, "No sir, I have not."

Phan then looked at the wizard, who was running his withered hands along the bark of the root. His eyes were shut and his expression serene. Both the King and Phan looked on while the old fairy slowly made his way around the thick bark of the root.

Quite some time went by before the wizard spoke. Both Hemson and Pip were on his shoulder. At times they would fly off and then return to whisper into his ear, before departing again.

The wizard turned to face the King. "I have felt nothing," he said.

The King bowed his head. He felt his heart sink and the feeling of overwhelming loss enveloped him like a dark shroud.

At that moment, Hemson flew up to the wizard's ear and whispered to the old fairy. "Of course!" said the wizard, "we didn't even consider that! How silly of us! King Rowland," said the Ancient One, "I think we need to step into the earthen room to find the secret portal. Jewel disappeared from within the room, so that is where the portal must lie. I remember the daughter of the guard... what is her name?"

"Ember," said Phan.

"Ah yes! Ember told me when they'd found the room years ago, they discovered old toys left behind by someone else. I believe those toys belonged to Lucinda. She was the one to have discovered this place hundreds of years ago. I found the chapter in her diary where she described this secret place. It was her secret retreat, too. She found comfort in the smell and the solitude the room afforded her. It's where she felt the winds for the first time, and that is how she knew it was something strange because she felt winds where no wind could possibly enter. We must explore the inner walls of the root," he said.

"But we have searched every inch of that room," said the King. "We have been in there a hundred times without success!"

"Then we will make this the hundred and first time we search, but I believe this time we will be lucky!" The old fairy picked up his long robes and entered through the secret door...to the room beyond.

Chapter 69

Party Favors

———————

Mir and Beecher left the inside of Sam's car and flew up and around the house. They wanted to get a view of the whole area to plan their next step of the mission to rescue Jewel. They could feel the trees speaking to her and knew she was in the room below the earth. They flew down to one of the low, grime-covered windows just above the ground, tried to look in but saw only dim light.

Still, they knew Jewel was in there. They sensed her fear.

Beecher wiped away the dirty film on a small portion of the glass so he and Mir could see more of what was in the room. When the glass got clearer, what they saw made their hearts grow cold and anger boil within their little bodies.

Jewel was standing in the middle of a barren room. Her hands were chained above her head. Her clothes were torn and she was bleeding at her wrists.

Mir gasped, and then reached out to Jewel's mind to soothe her.

Jewel felt Mir's thoughts as a comfort. She was thrilled to be back in communication with her *Pulchra avium*! After expressing gratitude, she sent a thought question to Mir: "Where's Beecher?"

Mir whispered their plan. "Beecher has already set off the alarm twice, and the next time the alarm sounds, Malick will give his butler an order to disconnect it. That will give Sam and Ethan a chance to break into the house."

As Mir stayed by the window and communicated by thought with Jewel, Beecher flew around to the other side of the house to the window of a bedroom on the second floor. He used all of his power for the third time to lift the window enough for the alarm to sound again.

Malick assumed that the first time the alarm went off that help was on its way for Jewel. Someone was trying to break into the house. But as he looked out the window to the long driveway, he saw no cars, no movement of any kind. His butler had already made one tour of the grounds and reported nothing amiss.

When the alarm had sounded the second time, Malick again ordered the butler to circle the house. Again the butler reported back that nothing had been disturbed.

"I want you watching the grounds, just in case, so keep circling," Malick said as he walked back towards the cellar stairs.

Back at where the car was parked, Sam and Ethan were sitting as still as statues, waiting for Beecher to give Ethan a signal so he and Sam could move forward. When they heard the alarm sound for the third time, they'd planned to move up towards the house and look for a way in.

The alarm started for the third time just as Malick got to the stairs. "TURN IT OFF!" he screamed towards the hallway. "PULL THE PLUG!"

"Yes, sir!" the butler said. He was in a panic as he rushed to the panel, hit some buttons, and opened a cabinet to disconnect it from its source of power.

"Finally!" Malick said.

Jewel was still scared but also felt confident that Mir, Beecher, Sam and Ethan would rescue her. She looked around the room to see if there were any items she could use, once she was out of the chains, as a weapon. The room was empty except for long metal table with straps on it that was at the other end of the room. It was next to a large sink. She shivered when she looked at it, not wanting to know why it was there or how it was used…but it didn't feel good.

On the floor against the wall were some cardboard boxes. One box had the words "PARTY FAVORS NEW YEAR'S EVE." Several files were marked: "COMPANY FILES 2008-2009." Jewel saw nothing that would help her once she was free.

Malick entered the basement again. He approached Jewel with a smile—one of confidence and pure evil. "Where were we?" he said. "Ah, yes, I think you were going to tell me your story before we were so rudely interrupted by that blasted alarm. Or maybe I was going to persuade you to tell me your story?" He walked past her and headed towards the metal table. "I think we need to move you, so I can begin the real…" he hesitated "…interrogation."

When Mir saw Malick, she flew around the house to meet Beecher. "Let's go!" she said, "in…and to the low room! He's back in there with Jewel!" They both entered the house through the bedroom's open window and navigated their way through the house towards the cellar door.

As all of this was happening, Sam and Ethan were walking towards the house. Sam looked at Ethan. He saw she was scared.

"Don't worry, Sam," he said.

But he wasn't exactly sure that was the truth.

Chapter 70

Pink String

Malick pushed the table with the straps towards where Jewel was hanging. He pulled a small key out of his pocket and placed on the steel bed. "I need my tools," he said as he disappeared into a room under the stairs.

At the point when Jewel's heart was beating so fast she could barely breathe, she saw Mir and Beecher fly down the stairs and come towards her. She reached out to their minds to warn them that Malick was going to be behind them, but the warning came too late.

Malick had picked up a can and was gliding towards Mir and Beecher. They had no time to react. In that split second, Malick sprayed something on them. Jewel had never seen anything like this before. What Malick sprayed on the *Pulchra avium* was a bright pink string that wrapped around their bodies, froze their wings in mid-flight and bound together their two bodies. They struggled in midair then plummeted to a place on the ground where several stones had been set in cement in a strange pattern. In her head, Jewel heard them scream and then heard a thump in her ears as they hit the ground.

All was silent.

Jewel opened her mouth to cry but no sound came out. She was weeping; tears streamed down her face and she couldn't catch a breath. She also couldn't feel Mir or Beecher's thoughts in her head.

Malick laughed. It was a brittle, cold and sinister sound. "It's amazing," he said, "how some of these stupid human inventions can help eliminate a little problem. Who knew this Silly String stuff could put down the bravest and strongest little fairies? Imagine if their enemies in the Fae world had this crap! And now I know you must be very special, Jewel, to have a couple of *Pulchra avium* as your guardians. How did you get them through the tree?"

Jewel was unable to think about anything. Fear, sadness and hatred filled her head. Her anger was now overtaking any of her other emotions and she just wanted to reach out to Malick and hurt him—hurt him with every bit of energy and life force she could muster.

She saw that he now had a bag in his hand. A small leather satchel. He was moving towards her as he reached into the satchel and pulled out a small saw. Jewel knew that saw was meant for her and she screamed.

Jewel's anger was growing into something she had never felt before. It was as if her body gained some sort of strength from this violent emotion and she could feel her blood course through her veins at a different speed. Her skin was glowing and her crown grew hot on her head.

Malick stopped short in his tracks as her skin crackled with light. The floor below her feet erupted and giant tree roots burst through.

Jewel was no longer thinking. Her emotions were leading her, in a new way, brought on by her powers.

The tree roots that were emerging from the ground reached out to Malick. In a stunning moment of realization, Malick saw scenes from his nightmare flash through his head. He turned to run, but the roots were too fast. They grabbed his ankles and wrapped around them. He fell flat. Within seconds the roots were crawling up his body as he screamed, "Help! Help me, my man! Help! Help!" His scream morphed into a roar: "Hhhheeeellllllpppppp!"

Jewel was driving the angry roots to break his body. She was concentrating so hard on the movement of the tree roots that she was suddenly taken by surprise when the chains fell from their anchors in the ceiling. Sam was standing next to her supporting her.

Sam yelled, "Ethan is getting a tool to remove the cuffs! Then we can get out of here!"

Jewel knew by instinct this was her only chance to get the key from around Malick's neck. The roots were all over Malick's body now, squeezing him and progressing up his torso. While dragging the chains that were still attached to her, Jewel ran to where Malick lay face down and in agony. One of his arms was entangled in roots but his other was free.

Jewel saw part of the chain was on the outside of his shirt and she willed a tree root to wrap around it and pull. In the next second, a small root worked its way towards Malick's neck. Its small tendrils sought the chain and pulled it in one quick motion off Malick's neck and over his head.

Jewel grabbed the chain with the key as the root released it to her and ran over to where Mir and Beecher lay entangled in the string. "Sam! Do you have a pocket? Can you take them?"

Sam cried out, "Ethan! Hurry!"

Jewel could see a small rise in each of their chests—Mir and Beecher were still breathing! "We'll get you out of here fast!" she said to them. "Sam, where is Ethan?"

At that moment Ethan came out of the room under the stairs with a cutter. "Put your arms out, Jewel," he said, "let me get these off of you."

Sam tucked the birds-in-string into the hood of her sweatshirt then stood behind Jewel for support while Ethan worked on her. She was feeling very weak from all of the effort she'd just invested in using her powers. When the cuffs were off, Ethan and Sam walked at her sides up the stairs and out of the house. They could still hear Malick screaming and saw the butler running away from the house.

"Faster!" Ethan yelled, "We need to be gone by the time Michael gets out of those roots!"

They shuffled down the hill to Sam's car while Mir and Beecher flew close behind. Ethan opened the back door, picked Jewel up and got her inside. He got in and cuddled her while also demanding that Sam start the car and drive.

Sam took off her sweatshirt with great care and placed it on the passenger seat. While she shaped it into a little nest for Beecher and Mir, Sam replied: "Right, Ethan…don't you think I know what to do? You have Jewel, and I have Beecher and Mir to take care of! Come on!"

From their tangled mess, Beecher's and Mir's eyes were visible. They managed to give Sam a look of sympathy. "Thanks, you two," she said. Sam was shaking so much that it took several seconds for her to get the key in the ignition.

Once the car started, she put it reverse and at a high rate of speed backed down the long driveway to the main road. When she stopped to make the turn, Sam looked back at the house, then at Ethan and Jewel and said, "Now where?"

"To the tree in the parking lot where I met you!" Jewel said with a renewed volume in her voice.

Sam didn't have to ask twice. She could see car lights coming down the driveway behind her so she accelerated on the right turn hit the main road going faster than she had ever driven.

"Wait a minute, Sam," Jewel said, "I want to take care of Beecher and Mir; they need to be untangled. Can you find us a safe place to stop—at least for a minute or two?"

"Fine...I'll just gun it until I can find a place to pull over," Sam said. For a second, she took her eyes off the road to roll them. Sam was feeling like a third wheel in Jewel's adventure by now.

Chapter 71

Pink Skin

While in the human world, a car with three people and two little creatures was parked on the side of a road, the old wizard landed on the earthen floor of the secret room inside the root of the Great Oak in the Fae realm. He dropped into a crouching position and smelled the air with his eyes closed.

The King stood nearby as Phan looked on from the doorway above. "May I help?" he asked.

"No, my lad, no," said the Ancient One as he rose to rest on his hands and knees, "this mission is for old wizards." He circled the room, crawling on the rich earth until he stopped in front of a wall that seemed to be made of solid oaken bark. A gust of wind whipped up and the strands of the wizard's long beard and hair whirled around.

"I have found the portal," he said, "now we need to decide if I go through it or if we figure out a different plan."

"We don't know what will happen to you if you go through," said the King. "As much as I want to save my daughter, I do not want to risk your life. I think we must refer to the scrolls to find out if there is a way for you to pass through without harm."

"Ah yes," said the wizard, "but what happens if our stalling allows disaster to happen?"

The King was very thoughtful for a moment. "Did the scrolls that proclaimed your future speak of this journey?" he asked.

"No they did not."

"Well, then I think we need a different direction, because you are too important to lose in the magic of the portal."

The Ancient One stood up to the wall of bark and laid his hands on it. Then he moved his hands around an invisible line. "It is here for sure, for I can feel and smell the difference in the air from beyond."

The wizard stopped.

His hand moved a bit in one direction, then it disappeared in a flash of light. A loud pop sounded and the wizard was thrown backwards to the ground. "Oh! Oh! Oh!" he said as he held up the hand.

It was burned and black. The skin was peeled back and his skin was smoking. Hemson and Pip flew to his side. They disappeared into the folds of the Ancient One's robe and when they returned they had a thick salve in their hands. They spread the gooey cream on his blackened hand. The blackened, burned skin turned pink and his hand re-formed back to health.

Phan's mouth hung open. He knew he could not say a word about this miracle to anyone, but imagined being able to tell Ember what he'd just seen.

Once the skin was pink and new again the King noticed one of his fingers was missing. The old wizard looked at his hand and let out a guffaw. "It seems I left a finger in the other world! Not an important digit, so no harm!" The stump was perfectly healed. That salve has saved my body parts more than once," he said with a chuckle. "I guess this was a sign not to try and pass through, so we do need to do some more research."

The King stood against the wall furthest from the Ancient One. He slid down into a sitting position on the earth and hung his head. "You realize, old fairy, that we now know that there is a portal to another place or world. This is something, I am quite sure, that will change our lives forever!"

He looked over at the Ancient One and his little protectors.

Silence enveloped the room.

Chapter 72

Reality Returns

After a few minutes on the road at a high rate of speed, Sam slowed down, turned right and pulled to a stop. They were on a side street, underneath a lamp.

"Thank you, Sam," Jewel said. "Please hand me my friends."

Sam picked up the sweatshirt and felt two little dead weights. Now unconscious, Mir and Beecher lay still, breathing in a slow manner. She lifted them out and saw that they were wrapped tight in the pink string. She cradled them in her lap, separated them and untangled the sticky string. They made little movements as they returned to consciousness.

Jewel closed off her mind to other things and concentrated only on them. She nudged their thoughts as a way to revive them.

It worked. Their minds stirred and Beecher struggled to get up on his feet. He nuzzled the still sitting Mir. Jewel looked down at them while love and gratitude flooded her heart.

Ethan moved closer to Jewel and watched as the two creatures came back from danger.

Beecher shook his head as if to clear his mind. He took a step over to Mir, reached down and held her in his arms. The love they had for each other was so obvious and strong it enveloped Jewel's heart as well. Mir spread her wings to embrace Beecher. To Jewel it looked like she was both giving and receiving love in that moment. The sight made Jewel bend her head to the right, toward Ethan's shoulder...the hug they were watching was so tender and so profound. Jewel felt a tear slip down her face.

"What happened to us?" asked Beecher as Sam turned around in the driver's seat to watch what was happening.

Jewel gave her guardians a quick recap of the last moments in the house and their grand escape.

"Do you have the key?" Mir asked.

Jewel nodded a yes. She held the key to the Vault of Souls in her palm. It dawned on her again that she finally had it! Now, she could get back to the tree and to her world. Her mission was complete.

Jewel had the key to the Vault of Souls.

The reality of this truth took another turn when Jewel realized that she had to leave this new world and return to hers without Sam…or Ethan. The lid blew off the place where she kept her emotions.

More tears fell. She was thrilled to have the key but very sad about leaving her friends; happy about returning to her true home yet knowing she'd miss many things of the human world.

She loved Sam, but most of all, Jewel didn't want to leave Ethan.

She turned to him and looked into his crystalline blue eyes.

Sam turned back around in her seat to give them their moment.

Beecher and Mir took the hint and flew out of Jewel's lap and onto the dashboard.

Ethan touched Jewel's face then leaned in for a kiss.

It was the kiss of Jewel's dreams. Ethan's lips were warm and soft; his embrace so genuine and caring. It was as if they had been together their whole existence, but were just now discovering one another.

After a minute, Sam said, "We're back on the road you two." She started the car and was driving so fast that Jewel had to tell her to slow down and be careful. "I can't slow down guys! There's a car behind us! Stop looking at each other. Turn around!"

Jewel and Ethan looked out the back window. Ethan realized that his father was in pursuit. He said, "Jewel you'll have to pass through the tree the moment we get to the park."

"But I don't want to leave you!" Jewel cried.

"You have to...there's no choice," Ethan said. His face showed anguish. "I'll distract my father until you're through so you can return the key to your father. That's more important. I know it's not what either of us wants, but I know if my father has the key, true evil will walk in both worlds and we cannot allow that to happen. I should be kind of selfish about letting the girl I love leave me, but I am smart enough to know that this is—this *thing*—is bigger than us and it is about saving the two worlds. How can I be thinking of myself when so much is at stake?"

"You love me...?" said Jewel in a tiny voice.

He swept her into a closer embrace. They kissed as Sam sped the car into the night. This time it was a long lingering type of kiss that made Jewel's heart beat twice as fast.

"Hey! You two!" Sam called out, "we're almost to the parking lot! Get ready to run for the tree, Jewel. Mir and Beecher need to be on you, somewhere safe, so they can pass with you. I get the impression they would be mad if you left them here. Quick, put on my sweatshirt and let them go into the front pocket!"

"She's right," said Ethan. "You need to run for it!" He released his grip on Jewel, grabbed the sweatshirt and handed it to her. Then he looked back over his shoulder to see his father's car moving fast and coming up even faster behind Sam's old car. He noticed a green sign. The next right hand turn would take them to the park and the tree.

Jewel threw the sweatshirt over her head and opened the front pocket for Mir and Beecher. "Come on you two, get in!"

Sam slowed her car just enough to make the turn without spinning. Her wheels were screeching and dirt got kicked up from the tires as she sped into the vacant parking lot. She headed straight for the Great Oak along the side of the grassy area. "Get ready...!" she said.

"I'll come back to see you, Ethan. I swear I will come back. Please be careful and don't forget me."

"How could I ever forget you? I think you are the love of my life, and I'll wait for you until the end of my days."

Ethan kissed her again.

The car came to an abrupt stop. As Jewel cradled Mir and Beecher inside the pocket of Sam's borrowed sweatshirt she scrambled out of the car and ran.

As Ethan followed after Jewel, his father's car swerved into the park and sped towards Sam's car.

"Run!" Ethan screamed at Jewel as he slowed his pace.

Jewel ran until realizing that she didn't know how to get back through! The first time it happened, in a flash that she wasn't prepared for, she'd fallen through the portal into the human world. Now she didn't know how to find it.

She'd stopped running out of sheer panic and turned to look back at Ethan. "What do I do? I don't know how to get back!" she wailed.

Malick ran up to Ethan from behind and grabbed his son in a bear hug then put one arm around his neck. Malick screamed at Jewel: "Give me the key or I will snap his neck and he will be dead in seconds!"

Jewel was a few feet away from the tree, frozen in her tracks.

Now out of the car, Sam was also frozen in her tracks off to the side of Malick and Ethan. She was looking from Ethan to Malick to Jewel.

Ethan struggled against his father's hold as he yelled, "Run Jewel! Just go! Get out of here! Remember what I said. Get to your world and save the key from this asshole!"

Jewel backed up towards the Great Oak. She turned to it, placed her hand on the tree and looked back at the struggle of Malick and Ethan, father and son. Ethan was now halfway out of his father's grip. Ethan was punching the body areas of his father that he could reach. Ethan's strength and age gave him an advantage and Jewel could see he had a chance of overcoming the man behind him.

Jewel felt her hand tingle and looked to see it disappear into the bark. She looked back at Ethan and Sam and yelled to them, "I love you both and I'll return as soon as I can!" Then the tree sucked in her life force and pulled her through the portal.

She felt herself spinning. Then darkness enveloped her. She felt nothing.

Chapter 73

Buzz, Click

From the place he was standing guard, Phan saw the King and the Ancient One move towards the portal.

"Come," said the Ancient One to the King.

"Ow!" said Phan as he felt a sharp pull on his leg. He looked down to see some claws and recognized Bogart. The beetle wanted Phan's attention. He was agitated and made a lot of clicking noises.

Phan said to the King, "Jewel's pet beetle Bogart is here and he's making a horrid racket and pulling on my leg. He appears to be very upset." Bogart's wings buzzed and lifted him up into the air so he was now eye level with Phan. "I think he wants to get into the room with you. I've never seen a beetle act this way. Something's wrong and…"

A loud explosion erupted from the interior of the tree. There was an intense light that left all three of the men blind. It took several seconds for their vision to clear and once it did they discovered Jewel was lying in the dirt on the floor.

Her hand was clamped shut.

A golden chain was hanging between her fingers.

Chapter 74

Sealed Portal

The King rushed to Jewel. He swept her up into his arms. "Jewel! Wake up my girl, wake up!"

Jewel opened her eyes. "Hi," she said in a weak voice. She looked down at her hand and opened her fingers to reveal the key to the Vault of Souls. Her father gasped at the sight of the key and pulled her into an even tighter embrace.

The Ancient One began a chant, but both the King and Jewel were oblivious to his voice. The chant got louder and louder until the King looked over at the Ancient One who was standing in front of the portal. His hands were moving in the air, his eyes closed. Then he stopped the chanting and a bright glow outlined the portal door, which then glowed bright red before it faded to black and disappeared.

"The portal is no more," he said. "I have sealed it forever."

As Jewel became more aware of her surroundings and realized what he'd done, she screamed "NOOOOOOOOOOOOOOOOO!"

She pushed away her father's arms and rushed to the site of the portal. "You can't seal it! I need to go back! You don't understand! I left someone there and I have to get back!"

She was beating on the bark with her hands. Tears were streaming down her face. "Ethan! I need you! Oh my God, please let me go back there."

The language she was using was foreign to her father and the Ancient One. The King looked stunned as the old man walked towards her. "Calm yourself, my child. I had to do it. It was written. I knew when the time came I was chosen to close this portal. I am so sorry for what you left behind, but it was not meant to be."

Jewel crumbled to the earthen floor and blacked out.

When Jewel awoke, she was in her own bedroom. She could feel her wings now — they were tucked into the folds of gown as she lay on her back. "Home," she thought. She saw the anxious faces of her mother, father and siblings standing over her. Even Ember was in the room, sitting on her bed holding her hand. She heard Bogart clicking from behind this crowd. Even Mir and Beecher were seated on her pillow by her head, waiting for her to lead the telling of the adventure. The Queen looked older since Jewel last saw her, and she felt her heart constrict that the worry she'd caused was so obvious on her mother's face.

"Hello, everyone. I'm fine, thank you," she said. "I found the key." She looked up at her father and saw the gold chain with the key to the Vault of Souls hanging around his neck.

Her mother leaned over and kissed her. "I think you have quite a story to tell," she said. We are awaiting the tale. Your disappearance had us worried for days, my dear."

"DAYS? I was only gone for days? I was in the other world for many weeks. How is it that I was only gone from this world for days?"

Queen Cordelia's eyes widened. "Other world? Now we must hear what happened and how you came to find the key. Who had the key and how did they pass through the tree? I imagine you have the answers to all of these questions…is that right?"

"Yes," said Jewel, "but I fear the story will change our world and our people forever."

There was a moment of silence, then the King spoke: "Jewel, whatever it is, we will face the truth together as a family and as a community of beings that inhabit our world. The truth is always better than myth, so let us hear what has only been told through our ancient scrolls. It seems you have experienced something that was foretold, but now is new."

Jewel hesitated for a moment, sat up in her bed, then told entire the story of passing through the tree and the discovery of the person who had taken the sacred key to another, parallel world. It took a long time to tell the story to the anxious group around her bed. They asked a lot of questions, and she was patient while supplying the details.

While telling the story, Jewel decided the one detail she would not include in her story were the feelings she'd developed for Ethan. That information she would only share with Em, but no one else.

Her heart was broken. She didn't know if she would ever see Ethan. Or Sam. She wondered if Ethan had managed to get away, and what had happened to Malick. She knew that the portal in the tree was closed and there would never be a way to find out what had happened. Would Ethan be worried about her on the other side? She had promised him she would return.

That hope was gone with the permanent closure of the portal by the Ancient One.

When she spoke about her last moments with Sam and Ethan, tears were streaming down her face.

Her mother took her in her arms. "Dear Jewel! You are safe again and home with us. Nothing more can happen. The portal is sealed."

"I know, mother, I know."

But Jewel was crying about the one thing she couldn't tell her mother. She was crying for the loss she now felt—the loss of Ethan. Jewel had never experienced such a loss and her grief gripped her heart like an iron fist.

There was a short interruption when food was brought to her room for all to share. Eating a snack helped Jewel stop crying, so she continued telling more about her time in the human world.

When her story was completed, and the food eaten, most of the group left Jewel's room. The King asked that she be left to rest, but Ember asked to stay with Jewel and the Queen gave permission for Ember to stay the night.

The two friends stayed awake most of the night talking about the experience. Jewel told Em about Ethan as they lay in her bed as the candlelight grew dim. Fat tears rolled down Jewel's face as she expressed her love for this half fairy.

Ember felt her sadness and knew that the best way to comfort her friend was to just listen.

Then Jewel finally asked Ember to tell her what had happened while she'd been gone. Now it was Ember's turn to tell Jewel that she had also met a boy who was in the process of stealing her heart. She told Jewel about Phan and how he had tried to help find her.

———————————

It wasn't until the light of morning came in through the windows that the girls drifted off to sleep. And, they awoke when most of that day was already gone. Jewel felt refreshed and comforted to find Ember still with her.

Bogart was sitting on the end of the bed. He'd been clicking at her. She got up and scratched his head until he rolled over so she could do the same to his belly. Ember woke up and stretched. "It all seems like a weird dream," Jewel said, "but I hope Ethan and Sam are OK!"

Jewel went to the window and looked out over the kingdom. She closed her eyes and reached her arms out to the Great Oak in the center of her village. She heard the tree stir and whisper to her. Again tears rolled down her face as she thanked the tree for allowing her to pass back through unscathed and she said that she was sorry that the portal was sealed forever. The tree whispered back reassuring words, but it had another message for Jewel. "My portal is closed, dear young princess, but there are many more in the kingdom! They just need to be found."

Jewel sucked in her breath and turned to Ember. "Not all is lost, Ember! There are other portals that must be found! I can go back—I will go back!"

Ember stared at her. "Really? It sounds like a risk, Jewel."

Jewel didn't know what to say. She thought for a moment and said, "The Kingdom of Dorawine is such a large place. How will we ever find the portals?"

"We?"

Jewel shook her head yes...and then she heard the tree's voice in her head.

"There are ways, my princess, for you are the Child of the Trees and we are many, and soon even that secret will be yours."

The End...

...for now.